# The Worst Daughter Ever

**Aarti V Raman** aka #WriterGal is the author of over ten novels, most of which have hit the Amazon India and US bestseller lists in various categories. These novels include the indie-published contemporary romance 'Geeks of Caltech' series, the action-romance 'Royals of Stellangård' trilogy as well as standalone romances—*Kingdom Come, More Than You Want* and *The Perfect Fake*.

Aarti has also traditionally published novels with prestigious houses, namely *White Knight, Kingdom Come*, and *With You I Dance* in the mid-2010s. *The Worst Daughter Ever* is her first attempt at desi chick lit. Appearing as a panellist at various literature festivals across India since 2014 and as a motivational speaker during college fests, she also conducts writing workshops and dabbles in poetry in her spare time.

Before turning to writing romances full-time as a successful indie-published author, Mumbai-based Aarti spent over a decade being a commercial editor and business journalist for prominent media houses in India and Southeast Asia.

To learn more about Aarti's writing journey, follow her on Instagram and Facebook (as aartivraman) where she eagerly interacts with avid reader-friends.

# The Worst Daughter Ever

## AARTI V RAMAN

RUPA

Published by
Rupa Publications India Pvt. Ltd 2019
7/16, Ansari Road, Daryaganj
New Delhi 110002

*Sales centres:*
Allahabad Bengaluru Chennai
Hyderabad Jaipur Kathmandu
Kolkata Mumbai

ISBN: 978-93-5333-633-2

First impression 2019

10 9 8 7 6 5 4 3 2 1

The moral right of the author has been asserted.

This Book Is Dedicated To

*C.V. Raman, Thatha, without whom the Chakrapani clan wouldn't exist.*

*My family, the Viswanathans and the Iyers.
All my uncles and aunts, and my Thathu and Paats—
the people who raised me.*

*My parents who are (thankfully) almost nothing like LJ's parents.*

*My cousins, Karths, Pooj, Sang, Anu, Anju, Venkat and Sharanu, all of whom are a lot like LJ's cousins—in the best way possible. You guys put the fun in 'dysfunctional' and I couldn't be more grateful for it.*

*Balaambaal Chakrapani, a grand dame of a woman, my grandmother, whom I have partially based LJ's grandmother on, and whom I only remember in my fondest memories because she was taken from us so early.*

*Susila Viswanathan, the most evolved, sage woman I know. My other grandma, my dearest Paati—the woman who, after eighty-plus years, still manages to surprise us all with how cool she is.*

*All my readers who've loved me all these years.*

*And Max, the one who will always be.*

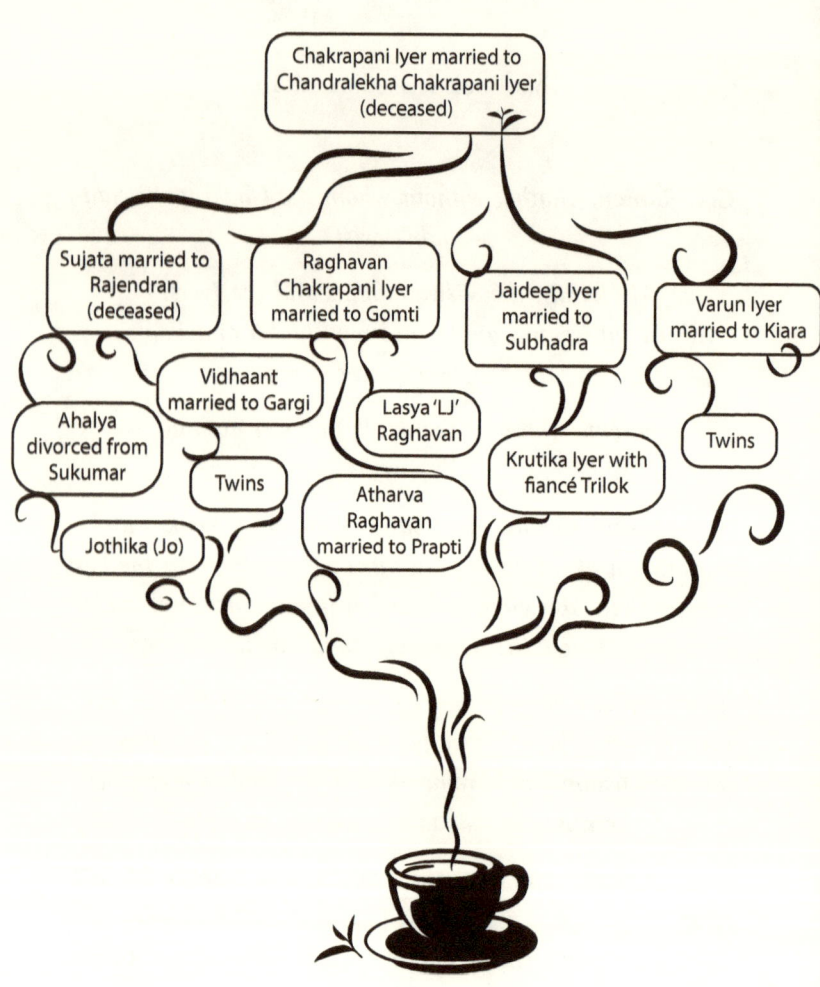

# Prologue

25 December
Christmas Day
Mumbai

### LJ Raghavan's Six-Point New Year Plan

1. *Lose weight. Seriously. No, really seriously. Lose some fucking weight so I don't resemble a beached whale and get eaten up by stray dogs.*
2. ~~*Have a conversation with Dad that doesn't end in anger or tears.*~~

   *Have a conversation with Dad. Period.*
3. *Find a better job. Pronto.*
4. *Re-upload the online dating profile. Two years is long enough in sexual Siberia.*
5. *Stop thinking about the spectacular melancholy of living.*
6. *Sell the house and become financially solvent like other people my age.*

# Chapter One

'Grandma's dead,' Mom sobbed on the phone. Okay, that is a slight exaggeration. My mother never sobbed. She cried quietly, in a dignified manner. Mom was dignity personified, even when crying. I, on the other hand, was the queen of screw-ups.

'What?' I was still groggy. And I wasn't sure I heard right. Grandma couldn't be dead. My mom's mom, my grandma, had already passed away when I was a toddler.

I squinted to see the time on my moon-shaped alarm clock. 11 a.m. I was late to begin my day by about five hours, screwing up my plan for the New Year.

New Year began two days ago and I spent them curled up in my bed underneath the comforter, ordering cheesy pizza and watching sitcom reruns.

If my mother knew what I was up to, she would be appalled and ashamed. She'd give me this look: *Oh, LJ. Why can't you wake up on time and live up to your potential?*

And I'd feel like shit. No, thank you.

'You heard me, Lasya.' Mom's exasperation came through loud and clear. 'Grandma…your paati.' She swallowed audibly and I heard the faintest break in her voice.

The words computed. Barely.

I put a shaking hand to my forehead.

'I don't understand,' I whispered. 'How did this happen?'

'She didn't eat yesterday. Complained of chest pain at 2 a.m. We called the doctor but she was sleeping by then. At least, your

1

appa[1] thought she was. The doctor came and...' Mom trailed off.

'Mom, I'm so sorry.' My head pounded, my vision went blurry. It could be a byproduct of eating too much junk instead of real food.

'Take a hair bath now. Then get the first flight out. Come to Munnar today. We're holding the body till Varun gets here.'

I sat up straight. The comforter fell off and dislodged stray pieces of crusts and string cheese from my chest. Yeah, my mother would die of shame and disappointment if she saw the slob I'd become. 'I don't know if I can,' I said carefully.

It is true. Kind of. I actually had deadlines that I was determined to meet.

'What do you mean you don't know if you can?' Mom was sharp. Intentionally so. My dear grandmother has died not twelve hours ago and my mom's second-favourite offspring was behaving like her typical self. Underneath the sharpness I could hear that— the resignation of having to fight yet another battle with me.

'I mean...' I dug out a hardened cheese piece from the comforter; it reeked of onions and tomato sauce. Yuck. 'I have work, you know. I can't just drop everything and come to the mountaintops in Kerala.'

'LJ.' Mom gritted her teeth. 'This is a very difficult time for everyone. Please, don't make it any harder than it already is. Book a damn flight and come *now*.' Unspoken were the words: *That's a fucking order.*

I ran a hand through my messy bedhead. Looked at myself in the mirror propped on the opposite wall. A frightening vision confronted me. God, I was going to have to get a makeover before I caught the first flight. *Oh, LJ. Why can't you take care of yourself?*

I swallowed. 'Okay, Mom. I'll come as soon as I can.' The call ended without any more words.

---

[1]Father

Other families would say, 'I'm so sorry. I love you. I will always be there for you.' And sure, sometimes, maybe once a year, my family does this too. But, not today. Not on a regular basis.

Recriminations and regret formed the bedrock of communication in the Chakrapani clan.

A second later, my phone buzzed again. I checked the caller ID. *Gotta answer this.* I flipped the screen to video mode and my twin brother's handsome face filled the 5-inch display.

When the family genes were being distributed, my brother got tall, fair and handsome, like the fairness cream ads, while I got dumpy with unmanageable hair and a single dimple as consolation.

His perfectly groomed hair glistened with water. Of course, he had already taken the hair bath.

'You heard?' he asked without any preamble.

'Yeah.' I nodded.

'Well, at least, she went peacefully. Unlike Madhav uncle who had that aneurysm thing, remember?'

I nodded again. Death was uncomfortable. Real. Discussing it casually like this made no sense to me. It's a little disrespectful in my opinion. 'Why did you call?'

'Dad asked me to check on you.' He frowned, rubbing a hand over his stubble. 'You look like shit.' My brother was as subtle as a battering ram. 'What happened to you?' He peered closer to the screen. 'Is that cheese in your hair?'

I frantically combed through my hair and sure enough, there it was. More evidence of the bacchanalia I'd conducted with my lonesome self to bring in the New Year.

'Atharva, stop harassing LJ. She's going through a tough time,' Prapti, Atharva's wife, said gently in the background. Atharva rolled his eyes at me. 'She needs a fucking reality check is what,' my brother muttered helpfully.

'*She* need not be referred to in the third person,' I grumped out, shaking the comforter one-handedly, while my feet found terra firma for the first time in twenty hours. That's exactly how long ago I'd gotten up to use the bathroom and drag two 12-inch pepperoni and cheese pizzas with extra jalapeños and onions back to the comfort of my bed.

Looks-wise, Atharva might resemble my father, all tall and lean, with athletic grace, while I got stuck with the family genetic lottery of looking like how you'd expect a typical South Indian woman to look—dark skin, frizzy hair and boobs. Lots of boob. Even sideboob.

But that was where Atharva's paternal resemblance ended. He was all mom in his snooty judgement. Along with his determination to uphold the family honour at the cost of personal happiness and fulfilment. In other words, the perfect son to the often-rebellious, eccentric daughter.

He shook his head at my continued shame spiral.

'You need to stop behaving like this. That bed cannot be your home.' His words, meant kindly, brought unexpected tears to my eyes.

It was the only common feature we both shared. We had brown eyes that turned golden in certain shades of light.

'It's not.' I made my voice brisk and my face as stoic as I could under the circumstances. 'I am fine, Atharva. You can tell Appa I am alright. Mom already called me and read me the riot act. Is everyone else coming? All the kids?'

Atharva hesitated. 'Yeah. Vidhaant is coming but the kids and Gargi aren't.'

'Oh.' If Vidhaant was coming then that meant...

'Is Ahalya coming?'

'Yeah, she's coming and bringing Jo.' Atharva waited a second. Then, as expected, 'I want you to be nice to her.'

'Hey!' I paused, untangling the cheese and other detritus from my hair. 'I am not the one who has issues.'

'She's had a difficult two years, LJ.' *No thanks to you*, the subtext was clear. 'Just don't start anything with her.'

'God! And Mom wanted to know why I didn't want to come,' I gritted out.

Atharva was patient as a long-suffering saint with me. Or as only an older twin could be. 'If you text me your flight details, Praaps and I'll figure ours out and we can all go together.'

'You don't have to do that.' I folded the comforter back. I looked at the pink cotton bedspread that had stains in various places and my favourite pillow, which looked permanently smushed with a dent the exact shape of my head.

I was going to have to buy new sheets at this rate.

I placed one knee on the edge of the bed and, I kid you not, the whole thing kind of sagged towards me, while the takeout boxes and laptop slid to a stop in the middle of a crater that looked like the shape of my butt.

GOD! I was going to have to buy a new bedroom.

I closed my eyes as tears threatened again.

'I am not asking, sweetie,' Atharva said grimly.

'Maybe I am not coming.' Speaking to my brother immediately made me regress to a needlessly defiant fifteen-year-old. Old habits. 'Maybe I have plans and a life and I don't want to come and be a part of the Chakrapani family drama.'

'Lasya,' Prapti—she of the perfect cheekbones and a warm smile for just about everyone—appeared on the screen. In a gesture that slayed me where I stood, my brother kissed her softly on her temple while she gave me her patented warm smile.

'Honey, it's our grandma. We have to go. You can't not go.'

Note her usage of the pronoun 'our.'

Yeah, on the list of things perfect son Atharva did right, marrying Prapti in the time-honoured tradition was number one. Prapti homogenized so well into our family, sometimes I felt like the unwanted, surly daughter-in-law, while she was the cosseted, favourite daughter.

I would hate her if I could. But Prapti was actually fucking decent. I was a monster for thinking unkind thoughts about her and hating the lovely relationship she shared with my own brother.

'Hey, Praaps.' I mustered up a smile for her. The inside of my mouth felt rotten. Physically rotten. Talking was making noxious fumes rise from the cavern of my mouth. I was pathetic. 'How's it going?'

'Its fine, babe. You need to steep two teabags in water for five minutes, then keep it in the fridge for ten and then apply it to your eyes. It will take care of those eye bags.'

Great. I now had bags under my eyes on top of stinky breath and cheesehead hair. 'Thanks for the protip. But to complete this beauty ritual, I am going to need teabags.' I grinned. 'I ran out of them in November.'

'Anyway, did the agent come by with any new buyers?'

I shook my head. 'No. Apparently, it's not a seller's market during the New Year. He said we'll have better luck in the coming weeks.' I was just the right amount of cheerful and offhand to throw her off the scent.

'That's awesome, LJ. Should we come pick you up once you book the flight?'

'Mom just told me five minutes ago, Prapti. I need time to figure everything out. I can't just drop everything and rush back home.'

Prapti's face fell and Atharva shot me the evil eye. I sighed. 'Sorry, I didn't mean it like that. I am just...trying to assimilate what's happened.' I sniffed for added effect. And my sister-in-law bought it.

'Oh, sweetie. I am so sorry. I know you were close to Paati. You take all the time you need to figure things out. Let me know if I can help in any way. I'll just go pack now, okay?' She blew me a kiss and I must have made some appropriate response because she handed the tablet to my brother and exited stage right.

'Anyone ever tell you, you should have been on the stage instead of writing for it?' Atharva asked me conversationally while he lounged on the recliner I'd gifted him for our thirtieth birthday last year. The thing looked immaculate. Even the leather dared not squeak when he moved.

Back then, I'd been flush with running my own theatre production company and believing in such things as 'art maketh man'. Now, of course, I knew better.

'Anyone ever tell you, you were adopted?' I asked sweetly.

He grinned and the fucking dimple appeared in his cheek too. 'I popped out of mom first. You came second. So, that's a lie.'

'Can we not discuss our messy birth at this time of bereavement?' I plumped the pillow as best I could, one-handed.

'Oh, now you're the bereaved granddaughter? What happened to "I got shit to do"?'

'Your wife convinced me to do my familial duty. What's it to you?'

Atharva sighed. 'I love you, brat. Text me your flight details.'

I shrugged. 'I still think I don't need escorts to take me back home.'

'Of course, not.' His conciliatory murmur was worse than any insult he could have made.

'I mean it,' I insisted, sitting on the edge of the bed. The boxes tottered and fell on my laptop's keyboard, further spreading the cheesy mess. I was such a *slob*, they'd probably rename the sin, 'LJ

Raghavan'. 'I am doing fine. So, the play I wrote tanked horribly and I am now writing the arts and culture section for a viral website called Toilet Humour and my editor is an oversexed, unintelligent child with a chequebook. Doesn't mean my life is so bad.'

'Actually, I was referring to the fact that our entire family collectively hates you with a passion they only reserve for Wasim Akram and the 1992 Pakistani World Cup team.' Atharva winked at me and I stuck my tongue out at him. 'You know. For the thing you did.'

'Shut up, Atharva. And stop trying to be helpful.'

'Text me…'

'The flight details. Yes.' I nodded emphatically. 'I will. Varun's supposed to fly down from Tacoma. He'll probably get here tomorrow. We have time.' Varun was the youngest Chakrapani sibling and my favourite uncle, my chitta.

Atharva shook his head. 'Dude, he's left already. He'll be there by nightfall. So has Vidhaant, who is coming from Dubai.' Atharva carefully avoided any mention of Vidhaant's sister Ahalya, my nemesis. 'Dad said he will text us the exact cremation time. We need to make it before that. So, come on. Take a fucking shower, become semi-human, and book a flight to Kochi already.'

'Oh.' My grand plan of avoiding my family for a day longer deflated like weak soufflé. 'Shit.'

'Also, in case it's slipped your mind and I am sure it has, Kiki is losing her shit.'

My eyes rounded. 'Oh. Dammit! It did slip my mind.'

I was such a bad cousin. I'd forgotten my beloved soul sister's wedding. Due to take place next week. The one for which I had actually booked my flights and everything.

Atharva nodded soberly. 'Yeah, I am sure she is driving Trilok crazy with her drama. I am surprised she hasn't called you yet. Or like, everyone.'

'It's Kiki. She is the sensible one,' I argued. 'She is not losing her shit or anything. Knowing her, she has a plan and it's going to be executed with military efficiency.'

I bit the bullet and started clearing the bed. From the vantage point of actually standing up and seeing the monumental mess I'd created for two days straight, even I cringed. I wasn't the most domesticated of creatures and my mom was not far wrong when she despaired of me displaying traits such as cleanliness and orderliness, but I had surpassed my own admittedly low expectations of good housekeeping.

'You're right, I guess. I have to go help Prapti pack. You get everything done, alright?'

I nodded. My brother paused in the act of getting up from the chair and regarded me with unusually serious eyes. 'I mean it, LJ. You have to come. It's Paati. And, like it or not, you have to show your face. So, don't be a brat like you always are and do the right thing for once.'

His matter-of-fact words left me breathless with hurt, anger and a thousand other sick emotions that churned along with two-day-old cheese and pepperoni. 'Fuck you too, brother.'

Then I ended the call before I compounded the image of the family drama queen by bursting into sudden and uncontrollable tears.

# Chapter Two

*M*y flight was at 3 p.m., which gave me about forty-five minutes to get my shit together and pack for my grandmother's funeral. It was a one-, maybe two-day trip at the most. The cremation would be tonight or tomorrow early morning, and then we'd have the reading of the will in the evening—Grandma was loaded as fuck, after all—we would all break bread tomorrow night and disperse by the next day.

All my salwar kameezes were for a slimmer me from six months ago, so I pulled my two most comfortable tunics, and two pairs of washed jeans (did not know I had those!) and chucked them in a bag, while I frantically brushed my teeth. The laptop, adapter and mobile charger went next. My toiletries and lingerie were packed in cute drawstring bags Prapti got me from a work trip in Venezuela.

Prapti was a fabric buyer for a large textile company and travelled a lot for her work. She'd also done her PhD in textile and fabric design. My sister-in-law was hella brainy too, on top of being nice and curved in all the right places. No wonder my parents wanted to adopt her and make her the de facto daughter.

Next, I dragged the sheets and comforter and threw them in the largest bucket in the bathroom. While they soaked in detergent-y goodness, I made one of two important calls. The first was to my maid, Malti bai, to explain the situation to her.

'I won't be there for two days,' I told her in perfect Marathi. 'My grandma—dadi—passed away so I have to go home to Munnar. You can come in today and wash the clothes and vessels.'

'*Arre deva!*'[2] she exclaimed. She spoke in shuddh[3] Marathi for the next two minutes, half of which slipped through my brain. I interrupted her firmly with, 'Malti tai[4]! Did you understand what I told you?' hoping she knew that the clothes and utensils had to be washed. '*Kapda aani bartan kara.* Please.'

'*Ho,*' she said. '*Tumhi kaalji naka kara.*'[5]

Right. Like that was even an option.

The second call was to the office, the ambitiously titled ToiletHumour.com. Exactly what you think it was. A website that produced such gems as '13 Thoughts Your Boyfriend Has When You Enjoy Period Sex' or 'Why Iron Man Is the Least Sexist Character in the Marvel Universe.' Or, and I was ashamed of this: 'Why Men Look Better in Sneakers than Women.' (I wrote the Marvel one, and yes, I was unmercifully sober when I did so.) The office was located in a shady part of Mumbai's industrial complex, Marol, like most of these small, privately funded ventures.

Our audience was that coveted 18–25 demographic with surgically attached smartphones. A hotbed of culture and class it was not. We catered to the least common denominator and we did it well enough that brands paid us top money to collaborate.

The work was mostly demeaning and made zero sense of my Master of Fine Arts with a specialization in Creative Writing. Searching for the perfect fart GIF was only borderline humiliating on a bad day.

Although, to be fair, I enjoyed attending movie premieres and going to a few of the Bollywood-related events we covered semi-seriously.

I couldn't complain, because it paid the bills: my online

---

[2]Oh God!

[3]Pure

[4]Elder sister; also a way to address older women respectfully in Marathi.

[5]Okay. You don't worry about a thing.

streaming bills, my mobile bills, my groceries, my utilities and my mortgage. I cared about that.

Failed playwrights with a modestly successful novelist career, before they took on too much and squandered it all away, could not be choosers. They couldn't even be beggars.

My boss and editor-in-chief, one of four editorial employees at ToiletHumour.com, answered at the first ring.

'Puru Kayastha,' he said.

Puru Kayastha was not my boss's real name. But he'd christened himself so during his first and only St. Xavier's spoken word poetry competition seven years ago and the name had stuck when he won. And because of this vigour and scope of his idea for Toilet Humour, just when native advertising and desi viral content was taking off in 2012, it meant that he'd managed to garner some funding. The content was OTT and ridiculous; nothing I could be proud of.

'Hey, Puru,' I said cautiously.

'Hey, Lasya.' Puru drawled my name out, like the buttermilk concoction—Lassi-yaa. It was actually 'Luh-sya'. 'What's up? How's that French film festival?'

I winced because I remembered the reason I'd given Puru for not coming in to work since before New Year's Eve. A four-day French Retrospective was playing at the Roxy Opera House in town, showcasing the films of Jean Luc Goddard and Alain Resnais. They'd even thrown in a small exhibition of postmodern prints by the famous Austrian artist Gustave Klimt to sweeten the deal. It was very elite, very snooty.

I had not so much as shown my head through the doors of the Roxy.

I was supposed to 'deconstruct' the French Film Retrospective for the 18–25 crowd, using words such as 'cool', 'slaying', 'fleek' and—my personal favourite—'on point'.

'It's fine,' I lied through my teeth, zipping the bag shut. Money had to be withdrawn from the ATM at the airport, I reminded myself. 'I'll file the story soon. I was actually calling you because I have a family emergency, Puru.'

'What happened, bro?'

'My grandma died. I need to go to Kerala for a couple days. I'll file the French Retrospective piece from there. Chanchal can pick up the Op-Ed piece this once.' It was a scathing rebuttal of Trump revoking the ivory trade ban in Africa that made me cry when I YouTubed cute elephant videos 'to add juxtaposition' to the story. I was happy to delegate it.

'Your grandma died?' Puru was instantly suspicious.

'Yes, Puru. Would you like the time of death and the death certificate too? It's legit. I am not making this up. I'll attend the funeral. And be back as soon as I can. Okay?'

'Okay. Sure.' He paused for an awkward second. 'I'm sorry for your loss, Lasya.' He had the good sense to say my name right. 'Come back soon. And do turn in that piece. And I'll email you the stories I have edited for next week's anniversary edition. Tweak them before I send them to Chanchal, the idiot.'

He was doing 'the idiot' on the down-low even though they tried so hard to keep the affair a secret. I mean, really! How many times did the printer cartridge need to be refilled?

'Sure. Tomorrow evening would be best. We don't know what time's the funeral.'

He made more sympathetic awkward noises and then I hung up.

With the call-making and sorting out such practicalities as work and the domestic help, I was left with about thirty minutes before Mumbai's traffic swallowed me up and I missed my flight.

The hot water was on the fritz, so I ended up taking a super cold shower and shivered my way through shampoo and conditioning. I had no time to dry my hair so I tied it up in a messy bun that dripped steadily down the back of my favourite black alphabet tee and the waistband of my former size-30 jeans.

I was going home for a funeral so I didn't bother beyond moisturizing, a light brush of eyeliner and gloss. As I was locking up, the phone buzzed a number of times. I clenched it between my teeth as I placed the lock in the exact position and turned the key in. After that, I checked my messages.

It was Krutika Iyer, fondly called Kiki. My soul sister and the bride of the hour. With six voice notes, each over five-minutes long.

Clearly, Kiki had either lost her shit or just sent me everything I needed to do in order to execute her Wedding Plan B.

'*ANSWER ME NOW, LJ.*'

Okay, she *had* lost her shit.

I rubbed my aching head once again. It wasn't like I expected the New Year to be some harbinger of change and adventure. I just didn't think I'd be caught in the middle of family drama and my grandma's departure for the heavenly abode.

The cab arrived and I lugged my cutesy faux leather backpack and suitcase down three flights of stairs.

My phone buzzed once more. The name displayed was Gordhan Vithaldas Real Estate Agent. I let it ring as I chucked the phone in my backpack's front zipper and located the driver of the White Honda.

'Good morning, madam,' the helpful driver said, stowing my luggage away in the trunk.

'Morning.' I wore my shades and got inside the car, suppressing the urge to flee back upstairs, hide under the comforter and never emerge. It seemed like the safer alternative than facing the extended Chakrapani clan, who collectively hated my guts.

'Where to?'

'International airport. T2.'

'Vacation, madam?' The driver smiled in the rearview mirror as he smoothly reversed from my little cul-de-sac in the heart of Mumbai's suburbs.

'No. Jet Airways flight.'

'Going home, then?'

I nodded and lay my head on the leather headrest. Tears pricked at my eyes again and this time they did roll down.

'Yes,' I murmured, wiping them away. 'I'm going home.'

# Chapter Three

By 2020, the city of Mumbai, run by the Brihanmumbai Municipal Corporation, has promised the moon and the Metro to us. The Metro system is an elevated train transport network that should, when done, span the length of the majority of the 40-km island stretch and make commuting in the most crowded city in India less of a pain. It would comprise central, south and northern Mumbai but not Navi. At least, I don't think so.

Right now, however, what this meant was that traffic snarls abounded every 10 feet on all major roadways, especially the Western Express Highway. So, the thirty-minute commute from my two-bedroom apartment in Kandivali, to the airport, takes thrice as long as it should. The driver, bless his heart, didn't talk and I was grateful for that.

On the other hand, Kiki needed immediate and urgent attention, so…I braced myself, plugged in my headphones to the mobile and pressed play on a random voice note.

'And he said, what's the big deal? So I threw the shoe at him and told him to go fuck himself and that I wouldn't marry him if he was the last man on earth.'

Kiki was usually mellifluous, even-keeled. She never behaved like a blithering idiot. Usually.

I sat up straight and paused the note. If Kiki was having a meltdown, it was serious business.

I scrolled to the very first note and started listening. I also texted Kiki that I was listening to her notes and to hang tight. With lots of Xs and Os. Kiki loved herself some XOs.

The next thirty minutes passed in listening and unravelling the rambles of my loveable cousin sister, who, in the real world, wasn't such a drama queen. She was actually a respected doctor who had just finished her Masters and now practised oncology at AIIMS, one of the premier hospitals in the country. Her fiancé, Trilok, was also her boyfriend for the last fourteen years. They had hooked up on the first day of junior college in one of the army bases my Colonel uncle was stationed in.

Lightning had struck, period.

Of course, the path of true love never did run easy and so it had taken Kiki the better part of the next ten years to convince my very traditional and patriotic uncle and aunt that Trilok Gujral—no major, captain, or any other rank of import—was as much a true-blue Indian as the parade of sexy jawans they had lined up for her. Colonel Jaideep Iyer had definite ideas about how things should be done. The marriage of his only daughter to a nerdy VP in a multinational corporation in Gurugram did not figure in those plans.

The gist of Kiki's long and incoherent ramble was this. The venue and caterers were all booked, Trilok's parents were here, Trilok and she wouldn't get a holiday this long again. And Grandma had been about to hit ninety so it's not like she would mind. Kiki wanted a big wedding. She wanted the wedding of her dreams. And she was not going to let anything, *anything*, stand in the way of it.

Trilok, in a fit of common sense, had suggested they could downscale the wedding and proceed as planned. At which point, Kiki had dramatically broken off the engagement.

Of course, Trilok was not a dummy and he knew she didn't mean it. But apparently, it had turned into a thing on their social media, a fact I was unaware of, having uninstalled all the posting, hearting apps on my phone six months ago.

I claimed it was because I wanted to be on a digital cleanse. In truth, all my writer friends were doing so much better than me all the fucking time that I couldn't stomach seeing their statuses. The rest of my classmates and ex-workmates or whoever-mates were settling down—going on cute trips with their significant others, popping kids with alarming regularity, celebrating promotions and buying houses and cars. I couldn't take it. I was envious of the filtered, picture-perfect lives shared by these strangers.

I debated calling versus texting Kiki. The airport was still fifteen minutes away so I gave into the inevitable and dialled her number.

She answered midway through the first ring. 'What the fuck, woman?'

'Hello to you too,' I said cheerfully. I might not have seen Kiki in two years, even though we lived in the same country, but the bonds of girlhood were unbreakable. The bro code had nothing on us. 'Are you done throwing your tantrum?'

'Dammit, LJ. Not you too.' But she spoke without rancour, so I assumed that her righteous anger had dissipated in the last one hour. 'Trilok insisted on returning the ring to me. The ring I got him with my very first salary. What a dick, na?'

'Total dick,' I agreed quickly. 'Now, what's the problem, Kiki? Or is it all sorted?'

'Nothing is sorted. But I can't really be up here anymore, although the attic is the only place on this godforsaken place where we get network. Your mom is already giving me the evil eye from the lawn.'

'Crap. Sorry, babe. Just hold tight for a few hours more. I'll be there soon.'

Kiki paused and huffed out a breath. 'I...'

And I heard something in her voice with my super-sister radar. 'Is everything okay, Kiki?'

Kiki's breath hitched on a sob. 'You know, I was here till yesterday afternoon. I should have checked on her once before I left. But Trilok and I wanted to check out the Taj property where we're putting up most of his family and I was distracted.'

Of all of Chandralekha Chakrapani's grandchildren, the guilt was strongest with Kiki. Probably the byproduct of all that military upbringing.

'There's nothing you could have done, sweetie.' I could be kind, on occasion. This was an occasion. 'You know that. You're the doctor. She's lived a long, happy, fulfilled life and, God knows, she drove our mothers batshit, didn't she?' Kiki's mom was the second daughter-in-law of the house. My mom was the first and eldest.

Kiki gave a weepy chuckle. 'That she did. Even yesterday, she yelled at Gomti perimma[6] for bringing her weak tea. The woman had a set of lungs on her for such a bitty thing.'

'I bet.' The moment of family sentiment passed. Briskly. 'Is Trilok with you?'

'No. He's downstairs. Talking to Dad and making a sleeping chart.' It was sickening how in love she sounded.

'He's doing what now?'

'About twenty-five of you guys are coming in the next few hours. We need to figure out who sleeps where. The house is big but it can't handle a battalion, can it?'

'Right.' Practical, helpful Trilok. I still couldn't believe Deep uncle and Subhadra aunty had taken the last seven years to see what a wonderful gem their would-be son-in-law was. Stubborn Trilok got props for sticking it out this long. 'Makes sense.'

'He is handy in a crisis like that.'

'Of course, he is.'

There was a small, telling lag in the conversation. Then I said, 'So, I'm nearly at the airport. I'll see you in a bit. Okay?'

'Cool. Atharva texted and said you guys are coming together.'

---

[6]Father's elder brother's wife

'Yes. We are. You know how he gets.'

'Perfect Prapti is coming too?'

I didn't even bother answering. 'You know what time they're holding the cremation?'

'Not till Varun gets here. Vidhaant's flight just landed.' She too didn't mention Ahalya by design. Kiki had my back like that. 'But Dad and Perippa[7]'—aka my dad—'have called the vaadhyar[8] at 4 tomorrow morning.'

'FOUR? A.M.?'

'Just get here soon, LJ. I am losing my mind. I need you.'

Kiki was younger than me by about eight months, but we'd been best friends in the way that only cousins are, when they are forced to spend their summer vacations together since they are five years old. At first, we tried to kill each other. When that didn't work and our parents insisted on throwing us together, we stuck to each other for sheer self-preservation.

Now, I can't imagine life without Kiki. Even if we are in our thirties now and don't actually talk to each other much at all.

'I'll just request the pilot to fly the plane faster because my sister's having a meltdown.'

Her expletive was the end of our call. And I realized that, whether I wanted to or not, I was going home.

Kochi, a major port during colonial times, carries much of its British lineage on its rather graceful shoulders even now: in its architecture, layout and the cosmopolitan air of the citizens. The airport, both domestic and international, operated out of the same

---

[7]Father's elder brother
[8]Priest

small space. Disembarking was an exercise in patience and space management.

People stand way too close to each other in airplanes after landing, like in Mumbai's local trains, and I can never figure out why. It's not like the aircraft is going to leave you at Andheri station when you really need to get off at Santa Cruz. But, there you go. People jostled, with their elbows, bags and backpacks hitting each other, while they waited impatiently for the crew to open the doors.

I was still comfortably ensconced in my window seat, watching the rest of them jockey for pole position like this was a race that needed winning.

At last, the line started moving forward and pretty soon I was breathing the smoggy, tangy air of Kochi, while I checked for messages. Predictably, there were two from my mother and one from Atharva, directing me to come to a specific location where they were waiting for me at the terminal.

After collecting my baggage at long last, I made my way to the exit and to the Saravana Bhavan where Atharva and Prapti were pigging out. I knew this because my brother had the annoying habit of foodstagramming everything that went into his stomach. There were things you did for family. Liking their social media posts was one of those things. But because I was off social media, he'd been gracious enough to send me a plated picture of his dish.

'Hey.' Atharva greeted me with a one-armed hug as soon as I spotted the two of them. He was busy consuming his nai roast at a standee table. Atharva toured the country and he stayed in Pune, but he still loved idlis, dosais and nai roasts. Unlike me, who had given up anything that vaguely smelled of South Indian food as soon as I stepped into my hostel in Mumbai for my Bachelor's.

'Hey.' I took a sip from his cup. It was delicious filter kaapi. The one thing I was fiercely attached to. I took a larger sip, and felt the caffeine hit my system like a really good toke would. 'Yum.'

'That's not mine,' Atharva said mildly.

Prapti gave me a wide smile and we did the over-the-table hug thing. A not-real hug. Which suited me just fine.

'Prapti doesn't mind if I have her coffee, does she?' I asked her.

'It's not mine either.' She was chagrined. And I was confused. If it wasn't Atharva's or Prapti's, whose was it? 'Hey, LJ. You look great.'

I knew I looked like shit but she was decent to make the effort. Brownie points to her. 'Thanks, Praaps. You look amazing.'

And she did. All svelte curves and poreless skin. She even had on an appropriately demure parrot green Patiala suit with a tinge of sindoor on her forehead. God. The woman *did not* give up.

Atharva cocked his head and made no comment as he took in my appearance. He wiped his hand on the tissues provided. 'We should leave as soon as we're done. You want anything for the road? We aren't stopping till we reach the Illam.'

Chakrapani Illam was the sprawling 70-acre tea estate my grandmother had managed until old age finally defeated her just ten years ago. My parents, as the eldest son and daughter-in-law, then moved to the movie-perfect climes of Munnar and took over the management of the estate and my grandma. As my mother used to say, the estate was easier to manage.

'Nah. I'll just have this coffee and I'm good.'

'Of course, you're good, LJ. Why won't you be? It's not like it's your coffee, is it?' My hand froze where it was, halfway to my mouth.

That voice, and the female that went with it, belonged to my oldest cousin sister, Ahalya. The last time Ahalya and I had been within ten feet of each other, she'd tried to yank out my hair by the roots. I still had the smallest bald patch where she had been successful.

I immediately touched my hair.

'Hey, Ahalya.' I kept the Styrofoam cup down nice and easy; out of reach of the woman who'd almost caused me to go bald. 'I didn't know you were here.'

'Hello, Lasya.' Ahalya, 5 feet 7 inches, with the first strands of grey in her hair, glared at me with all the fury of an avenging angel. Ahalya was older than the rest of the cousins by five years. Her younger brother Vidhaant was closer to us in age and temperament. And, as kids, when we had gathered at the Illam, she'd lorded her 'older sister' status over us.

I felt a stab of pity as I took in the pinched look in her eyes (also like mine) and the wrinkled state of her casual pants and linen kurti[9]. Once upon a time, before life had beaten the shit out of her, Ahalya had been stunningly beautiful. Now she just looked exhausted. It probably had something to do with the energetic kid ploughing through strangers to get to us. I picked up the little girl. She weighed next to nothing, and clung to me like a little monkey.

'Hey, Jo baby,' I cooed to her.

'Atha![10]' Jo screamed and smacked her lips against my nose. 'I have grown 5 inches. Do you know?'

'You're so big, my baby.'

I allowed Jo to scramble off of me and she kicked me only once in the sternum for my effort as she clambered down. Wrapping her arms around her mother's thighs, Jo grinned through gapped teeth at the three of us. Prapti's eyes glimmered suspiciously but I figured it was just the lights of the airport.

It was nearing seven and night descended in January with sudden and total darkness.

'We'll get you some coffee,' Atharva said quickly before any of the women could say a word. He propelled me away before I, particularly, could say anything and ruin the touching reunion.

'Let go of me.' I jerked my elbow out of his hold and glared

---

[9]A short tunic
[10]Aunty!

up at him while we stood in line to pay up. All around us, people spoke in varying volumes in Malayalam. I only understood a third of what they were saying.

'Don't mess with that woman,' Atharva was all serious eyes and grim tone.

It annoyed me on a good day that Atharva was a full head taller than I was, so I always felt like a little midget when we stood together for family photos or movie lines. Today, it was enough to make me stomp on his toes.

He howled and shot me a dirty look. 'What was that for?'

'Don't mess with *this* woman,' I shot back.

He didn't respond but gave me a look of injured dignity. Then, by unspoken agreement, we wrapped our arms around each other's waists as the line inched up. It wasn't much but it passed for affection and tight love in our family.

'I should have come to see you,' he murmured. 'I'm sorry I didn't. Work has been insane the last few months.'

'Don't be an idiot. Of course you had to work.' I shot him a sidelong glance. 'And then there is the hot wife you need to service on a nightly basis.'

He dug his elbow in my stomach hard and now I howled.

'DUDE! That hurt.'

'Stop making references to my sex life, then. For the next fifty years.'

We moved apart and finally it was our turn at the counter. I dug out my wallet and paid up. He chatted with the cashier in a familiar manner in broken Malayalam. Atharva could do that; make friends out of thin air. I took time. I was warier. I believed in the bottomless cesspool that was humanity. And I was proven right time and again.

The last time had nearly broken me.

We finally emerged with small, steaming cups of coffee (I had very low resistance when it came to coffee) and I blew on it to keep it from singeing my fingertips.

Prapti and Ahalya were standing next to a black SUV at the restaurant entrance.

Our luggage was already loaded on top of the thing. Ahalya got into the driver's seat and I raised my brows. Atharva shrugged.

'We don't have to pay someone return fare. Renting's cheaper,' Ahalya said.

But we both knew the real reason. Ahalya didn't want to split the return fare because she couldn't really afford it on her single-mom salary, even though she worked for the family business. And she was too proud to allow Atharva and me to pay her share.

I trudged around to the driver's side and handed the coffee to my cousin. Ahalya raised one brow in a gesture of contempt. The Rock had nothing on Ahalya Sukumar when it came to eyebrow game.

'For you. For the coffee I borrowed.'

'I don't want it.'

'Just take the coffee, Ahalya. It's a long drive and you're going to need the sustenance. I haven't poisoned it, if you're worried about that.'

Jo, settled next to Prapti, said, 'We are reading about poisoned apples in *Snow White and the Seven Dwarves*, Atha. How cool is that?'

'Very.' I kept holding the little Styrofoam cup and stared Ahalya down.

'Thanks,' she said finally and accepted the coffee. Ungraciously. She wasn't grateful for anything. And of course, she wouldn't be. I'd ruined her life as she knew it and it hadn't been pretty. She blamed me for it, even if it wasn't really my fault. (It was how I justified what happened to myself.)

I stuck my earbuds in before climbing in next to Prapti. Atharva and Ahalya were in the front, with Atharva playing navigation guide. Jo immediately crawled over to me and laid her bony little head on my chest. She fiddled with the wires of the earphones and I finally relented and stuck one in her ear.

She wrinkled her cute little nose. 'I don't like this music. There aren't any words in it.' I had Bach on.

'Then what kind of music do you want to listen to, baby?' I brushed my hand over her cheek.

She gave the question due consideration. 'How about Ed Sheeran?'

My jaw dropped open and I gave Ahalya a shocked glance in the rear-view mirror. 'She knows Ed Sheeran?'

Ahalya's smile was rueful. 'She even dances to him.'

I scrolled to the one song I figured she might love and, sure enough, the second the bass beats came on for the number one blockbuster, her little body started jiving on the seat. She started singing along with the goofy, talented redhead.

'She's grown so much,' I whispered, sharing a wondrous, adult smile with Prapti. She smiled back, although there was a tentative quality to it.

'Yeah,' Prapti said. 'She's grown so much.'

The song played to its conclusion with Jo singing along badly (a combination of mumbling and actual words). When it was over, she threw her arms around my neck and squeezed me tight. 'Thank you, Atha. Let's listen to it again.'

I swallowed a lump, put my arms around her, and put the song on repeat. While the rest of them might consider me persona non grata, starting with the driver of the SUV, at least this little human still considered me worthy of her hugs.

I'd take the win.

# Chapter Four

*M*unnar, the hill station, was the home of most Mollywood and Bollywood dream song sequences of the 70s and 80s, before Yash Chopra discovered Switzerland. It is a good three hours by road from Kochi Airport and doubly dangerous for night driving. The hairpin bends and winding roads up the hills are accident central waiting to happen.

To my utter non-surprise, Ahalya was an excellent driver, cautious and great at manoeuvring over other vehicles, so we kept at a steady clip. She was also a great mother because she had all sorts of healthy snacks, carrots, celery sticks and a juice box for her daughter when the kid started making 'I'm hungry' noises, tired of listening to Ed Sheeran for the first 100 kilometres.

Kerala after 8 p.m. was like most of India, with the exception of Mumbai and other metros. Everything shut down and no one stirred out unless they couldn't help it. This applied even more during the coldest week of the year on a hilltop national highway. The rest of us huddled with grumbling stomachs and I regretted my decision to not share Atharva's nai roast.

Clearly, these guys planned ahead, unlike me.

Finally, the gates of Chakrapani Illam came into view after we climbed the nth mountainside. The SUV's headlights picked out the 3-feet-by-3-feet sign proclaiming our family's heritage in English, Tamil and Malayalam.

My family had stayed on the good side of the Britishers by brewing the best tea in three states, or so my grandfather liked to joke. The estate had been a sweet 20 acres passed down from father to son in the nineteenth and twentieth centuries. My grandfather turned it into the thriving tea estate it was now, with the help of his intrepid wife, Chandralekha.

He also built the sprawling ten-room house that hugged the side of a mountain, defiantly named it Chakrapani Illam, announcing our lineage and nouveau riche money for all and sundry. As a teenager who considered herself too cool, I was horrified to discover my family made a lot of its money by scoring tenders with the colonials stationed in the Madras Presidency. It was a point of personal shame for me and a fact I had milked in my previous career as a novelist and playwright.

Now, of course, I understood how business worked. What made money, made money. What didn't was discarded like yesterday's newspaper.

It was completely dark by the time Ahalya turned the SUV into the little lane that led directly to the house instead of the plantation. I rolled down the window and breathed deep of the foggy air. The sharp, bitter taste of tea lingered in the air along with the earthy scent of plants watered regularly.

It was the precious scent of my childhood.

Jo, who'd fallen asleep blissfully, turned and hit me square in the face with her little clenched fist. My trip down memory lane ended abruptly and painfully.

'Fuck,' I hissed out.

'Don't cuss,' Ahalya snapped out, braking to a stop in front of the house. 'There's a kid present.'

'She's sleeping,' I pointed out.

'We're sorry, Ahalya. It won't happen again,' Prapti, ever the peacemaker, said. Then, as if she had done this a hundred times, Prapti hopped out and gathered the sleeping kid in her arms and carried her competently. I couldn't even sit comfortably while Jo snuggled with me during the ride.

Atharva got out the passenger side and stretched out his stiff neck. I looked at Prapti's long legs going up the half-a-kilometre walk, the child bouncing with each step.

'What's up with Perfect Prapti?'

Atharva twisted my thumb back until I let out a little yelp. 'Sorry,' I muttered. 'That came out wrong.'

'Everything's fine,' he said shortly.

I knew. It wasn't. But this wasn't the time to court a broken thumb, so I helped with the luggage while Ahalya juggled with carrying all the mom-kid stuff. Atharva and Prapti had an enormous suitcase and we placed his laptop case on top of it. My bag and backpack went on my shoulders. Ahalya carried a giant roll-on bag, and I didn't even bother asking her if she needed help.

Atharva asked and she gladly relinquished control of her bag and hurried ahead to catch up with her sleeping daughter. I trudged up the gravelled path, wheeling a giant suitcase that scrunched on every single stone there was.

I blinked as floodlights came on in a few seconds and a squeal was heard. A woman with waist-length curls came flying down the front steps of the enormous castle-like structure that rose in the hills in the moonlight. She tackled me with full force and I staggered a few steps back, taking the bag with me.

'LJ!' Kiki said, breathless. She grabbed my waist and the bag on my shoulder, banging it against my chest. 'I am so glad you're here. Mom is losing her mind and Dad won't listen to anything I have to say. Trilok's being Trilok, you know how he gets.' She hugged me once, hard, and my chin banged against her shoulder. My eyes watered but I held on, more out of fear than any real affection.

Okay, that was only half a lie.

I hugged her back tight and then we separated. Atharva wrapped Kiki up in a bear hug and lifted her off her feet. She held on and smacked her lips against Atharva's cheek much like

Jo had done with me.

'Hey, bear,' she said, with great affection.

He gave her waist a quick squeeze and set her down on her feet. I should note here that I have never been greeted with such exuberance by my flesh and blood. Kiki and Atharva were always tight-knit. They even had their own secret handshake that even I wasn't privy to.

'Hey, star,' he said. 'I heard you're throwing a tantrum and cementing your reputation as a Bridezilla.'

'I heard that they call you the tree now,' she retorted, referring to his tall and athletic physique, which was nowhere tree-like.

I cleared my throat and rolled my eyes till they finished their Rahul-Anjali reunion scene. 'I am starving,' I said helpfully.

'There's only curd rice and sambhar. We can't cook anything today,' Kiki said apologetically. I frowned and some of my hunger abated. I wasn't a huge fan of the curd rice that is such a staple in most coastal regions of India.

'How are things?' Atharva asked as we resumed walking. Kiki walked between us, as per usual. 'I texted Dad a couple hours ago telling him our ETA, but he never responded.'

'Mom had a small breakdown, so Perippa and Dad had to get the physician. Gomti perimma is handling things now.'

Also as per usual. Subhadra would have one of her spells when the going got tough and my mom held it together. Too bad, the holding-it-together genes had skipped the next-generation women. Atharva and I shared a look of perfect understanding over Kiki's head and finally we were at the house.

The ten-foot-tall teak doors were open and Mom stood silhouetted against the floodlights. She wore a crisp lemon yellow cotton salwar kameez covered with a shawl in deference to the weather. Her glasses dangled by the earpiece around her torso.

Atharva, ever the nalla pullai[11], immediately bent down to touch her feet and she brushed a trembling hand over his hair. 'Bacha[12]', she said softly as Atharva bent in half to hug her just as softly.

Then her eyes met mine and my spine straightened. My chin jutted out an extra inch and the light of unholy battle entered my eyes.

'Lasya', she said shortly.

I gave a short nod. 'Mother.'

I was wonderfully, ridiculously British in that moment.

Kiki sailed past with my bag, while my mother considered welcoming me with open arms. In the end, Atharva pushed me ahead and I sort of stumbled into my mother's arms. Tears spurted out of my eyes just as her arms closed around me and she hugged me tight. As if holding me together. I hugged her back just as tight, feeling the way her waist caved into her stomach and the way her shoulder blades stuck out under the shawl.

'Ponne', she whispered. Girl. My girl.

'Amma', I whispered back. I willed the tears back. The moment passed as my mother stepped back with a brisk pat on my back.

'You've put on too much, LJ. Are you eating the flaxseed powder I sent you? It has to be had first thing in the morning. Provided you wake up in the morning, of course.'

Atharva snickered and I shot him an evil glare. Then Mom looped her arms around both her offspring and ushered us inside.

'You're in the attic. All the rooms are occupied.' Mom served us

---

[11]Good, obedient son
[12]Kiddo

curd rice in little earthenware bowls. A jar of lime pickle with the Chandralekha Chakrapani brand logo lay open on the dining table. I scooped a generous portion over my rice and dug in with gusto, if not actual relish.

'Okay,' I said.

'Atharva, you and Prapti have the ground floor guest room. It doesn't have an en-suite bathroom.' I heard the apology in there and Atharva squeezed Mom's waist in silent reassurance. 'Kiki has a room to herself because she has all her bridal stuff with her. Ahalya and Jo are on the first floor. Vidhaant is bunking next to them. Varun and Kiara are in the room with the en-suite bathroom. I don't want her thinking we are peasants. The kids didn't come because they are both working for Habitat for Humanity in Puerto Rico, I think.'

Kiara was my Uncle Varun's Scottish wife. They'd recently celebrated their silver wedding anniversary, but to the Chakrapani siblings, she would always be the white chick who stole their NRI brother. Kiara had produced a son and a daughter, one of whom was studying to be a geneticist in Princeton University and the other picketed for migrant workers' rights in Washington while studying pre-law in Georgetown University. They were pretty driven, very brilliant, and very American. They were also years younger than the other cousins. Needless to say, we did not have much in common with them.

'They're all already sleeping, so let's be quiet when we go upstairs.'

Prapti had declined dinner and was already setting up their room. All the while looking like a bahu from an Ekta Kapoor soap, makeup and dupatta pleats intact.

'If Atharva gets a room, I want one too,' I insisted, while my brother demolished one bowl of the rice and started on the second without breaking a sweat. 'Or I'll sleep with Kiki. She won't mind.'

'Subhadra is resting in Kiki's room. You're not going there.'

'But—'

'Paati's suite can't be used, so three rooms are out for us. We have to make the best of things. Don't be difficult, LJ.' My mother looked and sounded exhausted.

I put an arm around her waist, where she stood, waiting for us to finish the food, just like she had when we were kids. She absently brushed my hair back and the gesture hit me like a blow. I couldn't remember the last time my mother had touched me with casual affection. Had it really been that long?

'Appa and Deep uncle?' Atharva asked. 'Where are they?'

Mom swallowed. 'They're filling out the paperwork for the death certificate.'

'You guys.' Kiki came into the room, dressed like a cute bunny rabbit in flannel pyjamas and a purple sweater, with her hair done up in braids. 'Get done soon. Trilok's half asleep and he wants to say hi.'

'Is he also sleeping in the attic?' I couldn't help asking.

'What? No. He's in the first-floor guest suite along with Naresh uncle and Anvesha aunty.' She made a clicking sound. 'I mean, Pa and Ma.'

I barely resisted rolling my eyes at the officious titles. As if just marrying someone made someone else's parents yours. As if anyone could just instantly assume pride of place as the number one and two people in your life, for better or worse. But, after having learnt my lesson on making my family understand that homosexuality was not an actual sin and, in turn, being interrogated over whether *I* was a lesbian, I bit my tongue and kept some of my thoughts to myself.

'Cool,' I said.

Atharva rose and washed his bowl and mine, and my mother gave me a look. *Why can't you wash your own bowl, LJ?*

I shrugged and walked out with Kiki. If my brother wanted to wash up after us, who was I to stop him?

Trilok was actually half asleep as he met us in the little drawing room that is part of the first-floor suite. The house had four suites, a fancy way of saying, 'with inbuilt toilet and bathroom and a small anteroom that passed for a drawing room'. Mom and Dad shared one on the ground floor. Deep and Subhadra were in another, on the first floor, while Trilok's folks got the nicer one as the newest in-laws to be welcomed into the family. Paati's suite was also on the ground floor but it was at the end of the corridor and we could avoid it by taking the Palladian staircase that wound to the top of the house. I was glad I didn't have to see it. Close to midnight was not the best way to see the place where my grandmother took to her heavenly abode. Trilok and I did the 'hey man' hugs and he gave me an extra squeeze; we've always gotten along well for an engineer nerd and an artist. Then he mumbled something about waking up at three in the morning.

Atharva's phone buzzed and I shamelessly peeked at the screen. It was his father-in-law, Prapti's father. 'They're planning to come in the afternoon. They won't be able to make it to the funeral. I have to tell Mom,' he murmured.

'I'll have to redo the sleeping chart,' Trilok said.

'They'll stay at the Vivanta,' Kiki said firmly. 'We'll figure it out.'

We all trooped out the way we came in and split in different directions to crash for the night. None of us had any talk left in us anymore. For the moment.

Trilok's dire words proved true indeed when my mother woke me up in exactly 180 minutes and rushed me to the ground-floor bathroom for a quick shower. I shivered and froze my way through the two-minute hair bath, emerging colder than before.

'That attic needs central heating,' I complained, even though my bed was supremely comfortable and I had buried myself under two huge fur quilts.

'Tea is ready in the kitchen. Your coffee too.'

For a family that made its money with making tea the number one beverage in the Southern belt, the younger kids loved coffee more. It was an affront my grandmother never understood.

'The vaadhyar is coming in ten minutes. Please wear a dupatta.' Mom looked at the plunging apple neckline of my neon pink tunic and the rolled-up jeans. 'You have a dupatta, don't you?' Then, without waiting for my answer, she said, 'I'll ask Prapti to lend you one.'

Mom looked elegant and gracious in her soft cotton sari, which was not ideal for the chilly January morning. But if I knew my mother, she'd tell me that the cotton was easier to wash and they needed the clothes to dry quickly with so many guests staying at the Illam. I didn't bother answering. I had forgotten to pack a dupatta and that was pretty much the truth.

Anyway, it didn't matter. A day, two at the most, and I would be out of here. We all would be. Even Kiki couldn't possibly believe she was getting married in the middle of the funeral.

'Ahalya looks tired, doesn't she?'

I made a grunting kind of sound, both to avoid talking and also because I did need the coffee. I was not a chipper morning person. Neither was my brother—the only common (terrible) personality trait we shared. Atharva was already in the kitchen, guzzling down coffee from the smaller thermos that held it, while he blinked the sleep out of his eyes.

Prapti was nowhere to be seen. Weird.

'Yo,' I said, cheerfully. It always put me in a good mood to see my brother flail about.

'Shut up.' But he poured me a steaming mug of filter kaapi so I reached over and gave him a kiss on the cheek.

'I love you, bear,' I said.

'You need to brace yourself,' he said quietly.

I sipped on the coffee: fragrant, bitter and filled with gooey sugar. It was perfect, life-saving. My neurons started firing. 'Why?'

'I spoke to Dad. Apparently, the lawyer said the will is not going to be read today. It's going to be read on the day of the devasam[13].'

'But that's thirteen days away.'

Atharva nodded, his eyes bleary. 'Exactly.'

'We can't...nobody can wait that long. That's thirteen days, Atharva.'

'I don't know. It's what Dad said. I could have heard wrong.' Atharva was not loquacious first thing in the morning. One of the more human things about him.

I finished the rest of the coffee in bitter silence.

Prapti, dressed in a tasteful cream Patiala suit (how many did she own?!) and muted maroon dupatta, came in with a garish pink dupatta that was nothing like my tasteful cute tunic. She wore soft makeup, just a touch of kajal that accented the little bit of sindoor she sported on her forehead. Her hair was demurely braided up.

Honestly, did she not sleep at all? No one woke up looking like this. No one.

'Thanks.' I draped the thing around my neck, even though I immediately felt strangled. Easier to do what my mother wanted me to instead of getting into another argument.

Prapti smiled briefly, while she squeezed her husband's hand. 'It suits you. I'm sorry it isn't more matchy.' But her eyes were shadowed.

---

[13]The final day of the thirteen-day ritual when the offspring finish the last of the last rites for the departed soul.

I wondered again, what was going on with the two of them? But we had far more pressing problems than matching the dupatta colour to my tunic.

'Why would Gopal uncle agree to something like this?' I demanded of my brother. 'Thirteen days of being cooped up here will drive us all to mass murder-suicide.'

He shrugged, the seams of his cream kurta stretching with the action. 'Apparently, it's not Gopal uncle who's handling Paati's will.'

I frowned. Poured Prapti a cup of coffee, but she shook her head. I took it as an omen to have another one myself. 'He's the family's lawyer, isn't he? And he is legal counsel for the estate. Of course, he *is* the lawyer.'

'No,' Atharva said. 'He isn't.'

Ahalya trooped in, freshly showered and dressed exactly like my mother, in a cotton sari and fitted blouse. She carried a sleeping Jo, who wasn't showered and dressed. She still wore her 'My Little Pony' jammies.

Deep uncle and Subhadra aunty came in next, followed by Varun, Kiara and Appa. Subhadra aunty gave me a hug and Deep uncle nodded at me but we didn't talk. Varun winked at me. My father avoided looking at me. It was par for the course. And if I felt any hurt at the fact that my father even refused to acknowledge my presence, I put it down to waking up at an ungodly hour in the morning…

…for my grandmother's funeral—a reality I hadn't fully grasped yet.

They all gathered around the dining table and clamoured for tea and coffee. My mother, the general of household planning, had had the foresight of arranging for a huge thermos of tea, which was now being put to generous use.

'Then who the fuck is handling Paati's estate?' My question, which had been posed in a low murmur to my brother, who stood right next to me, was heard by everybody in the overly silent kitchen.

Everyone froze in place around the dining table. Varun chitta, the one man who encouraged my crazy flights of fancy as a kid and even bought me my first Cross Fountain Pen to sign one million copies of my book with, winked at me again. He didn't take any offence at what I said. He was cool like that. We'd catch up later, Varun and I.

Deep uncle and Subhadra aunty wrinkled their noses in distaste, while my father looked through me. Atharva, Prapti and Ahalya shook their heads in dismay while my mother gave me a look: *Why can't you keep your mouth shut for once, LJ?*

'That would be me,' a voice said pleasantly. A tall, spare man, in a kurta-pyjama much like Atharva's, moved into the kitchen with fluid grace and picked up a stainless steel tumbler.

'Hmmm. Estate-grown tea.' He sniffed appreciatively while I stared in mortified fascination at him.

He wasn't as tall as Atharva, topping just below six feet. But he had a tree-like quality, exuding a quiet, compact kind of strength. This was absurd and my caffeine-deprived brain talking, of course. No one exuded anything in 2019.

The man came to a stop right next to me and I got a look at his eyes first, because he met my gaze fearlessly. They were brown, like mine and held polite sympathy. And something deeper, I couldn't exactly place my finger on. He had decent cheekbones if you went for that kind of thing and his nose was long and kind of flaring at the base. He had curly hair that looked like it had been hacked at the collar by a butcher. I logged all these details before I could tell my brain to stop. He also smelled of soap and cologne. My nose tingled in appreciation.

I hated my nose.

'You must be Lasya, the family's black sheep,' he said conversationally.

'I am Lasya,' I said, cradling my coffee tumbler. 'But I am not the family's black sheep.'

'No,' Ahalya said snidely. 'For that, you have to be part of the family and LJ disowned us all years ago.'

I gasped in silent indignation at the full-on attack.

The Shylock lawyer's shockingly full lips quirked in a smile, under the faintest beard. 'That's great then. One of you can take her share of the inheritance, right?'

Kiki sniggered. 'Get in line, bro. Ahalya probably wants all her share anyway.' She chuckled and looked straight at a shocked Ahalya. 'Lord knows she needs it.'

Much as I loved my soul sister, I could have cheerfully begun the predicted mass murder-suicide with hers right then. As the Shylock lawyer continued looking at me with laughing eyes and a serious countenance, and I felt the slightest flare of heat in my belly, I added him to the list of potential murder victims too.

And judging by the fulminating glare Ahalya was shooting the three of us, I was number one on her hit list.

I didn't blame her one bit for it.

## Chapter Five

*I* haven't attended any funerals. This would come as a shock for anyone who's lived past thirty like I have (and that is all I am going to say about my age) but it is one of those mysteries of life that I never really questioned. Grandpa Chakrapani died before we grew up and Paati only had death scares and near-misses like clockwork for the last decade or so.

Other than that, the only major death in my family was Vidhaant and Ahalya's mom, Sujata. She died of a sudden heart attack about eighteen months ago. I was banned from attending that particular funeral so, yeah, this was my first formal gig of bereavement.

And, let me tell you straight up, it was uncomfortable.

For one, there is an elaborate praying ritual to lay the body at state among us Iyers. For another, I couldn't comprehend that I was seeing my paati, my grandmother, the doyenne of Chakrapani Illam, lying so still and quiet on a small mattress, dressed in the cotton nightgown she'd preferred in the last five years. Her hands were mottled, with blue veins sticking out in sharp relief. Her skin was still unlined, a miracle at eighty-nine, and she still had the diamond nose ring she'd worn at her wedding. Her face was peaceful; it looked like she was sleeping.

She was small as a bird, so shrunken that my eyes bugged out when I saw her.

Beside me, Prapti gave a small gasp and laid her head on Atharva's shoulder. He gripped her tight and gave me a stunned look. I shook my head and slipped to the back of the small crowd gathered in Paati's room. My head was spinning. I couldn't breathe.

'Hey,' the lawyer said quietly as he brushed his shoulder against mine. Intentionally, I am sure. 'You're okay? You look like you're going to puke.'

I opened my mouth but words wouldn't come out. Somewhere ahead, the vaadhyar and his deputies started mouthing the prayers to begin the dressing ritual. I shook my head again and still my air passages felt clogged up. Someone, Subhadra aunty probably, started weeping quietly. Even Varun chitta, lackadaisical in the face of most tragedies, was white-faced.

I knew how he felt. Until now, until right this moment, this wasn't real. None of it. We'd all just gathered back home for something that had happened to someone else. We weren't pleased to be under one roof, but even so.

Grandma wasn't dead. She couldn't be.

No one would yell at me now for wearing men's boxer shorts and enticing the help, when I went on my morning walks on the estate. No one would berate me for being single and childless at my age. No one would patiently listen to me read *Pride and Prejudice* for the fortieth time and marvel at Darcy and Elizabeth's chemistry or proudly proclaim that I, LJ Raghavan, was a better writer than even Austen.

The coffee came up in a rush, along with acidic bile.

'Hey, Lasya,' the lawyer whispered, leaning down.

I simply shook my head and backtracked quickly. The vaadhyar droned on and Subhadra aunty let out a wail. I whirled, ran for the nearest bathroom and my feet hit the concrete door stop where I'd skinned my toes more times than I could count as a child.

I threw up, loud and disgusting; my breaths heaving out in a symphony of tears and vomit. The curd rice, the coffee, even some of the pizza I'd consumed a day before, all came out. I knelt on the infernally cold tiled floor, the chill biting into my knees as I hugged the ceramic commode and retched my stomach lining out. When I was done, I sagged against the toilet and wiped at the tears.

More came. I wiped them too. There was a knock on the door.

'Lasya, you okay?' It was the lawyer again. Couldn't he take a hint?

I closed my eyes and more tears poured out. I wanted to think it was grief, but honestly, it was just exhaustion and embarrassment. I was at my lowest point here. Physically. Emotionally.

'Go away,' I whispered.

He tried the door knob and found it unlocked. Dammit! I scrambled back in alarm as he stepped in. He raised his hands in a gesture of peace or surrender, and looked down at me.

I gave up. This was happening. I couldn't escape this. This man was seeing me like this. With vomit dotting my sister-in-law's dupatta and dribbling down my chin. With tears staining my chubby cheeks. I probably reeked too. And I was so tired. I couldn't muster the strength to stand up and shoo him out. Or even raise my hand and flip him the bird. GOD!

'Please,' I whispered. I rapped my head against the white, functional tiles.

The man sighed, a sound that echoed in the bathroom. With one long hand, he flushed the toilet. Then he knelt in front of me and took my cold, cold hands. His hands were warm. Like really warm. Like he'd kept his hands in front of a fire right before stepping inside the bathroom.

'Come on,' he said. 'Let's get you cleaned up.'

He pulled me up with a grunt and I landed against him, transferring some of the chin vomit on him. I closed my eyes. My humiliation was complete.

He brushed the curd rice-bile fleck off casually and led me to the washstand. Then he stepped back and waited, patiently, with his eyes trained on mine in the mirror.

I bent down and splashed freezing water on my face, hair and the front of my kurti. The water stung my skin. I blinked and did it again.

'I used to love nachos,' he said.

I blinked at him too. For the smallest second there, I'd forgotten he was there. Okay, that was inaccurate. My skin was pretty aware that he was there. It sort of hummed? But, in my head, I had disappeared into a deserted island.

'What?' I asked. My mouth was disgusting. Worse than 1 January, when I'd added a can of whipped cream and stale beer to the pizza and gobbled the whole thing down. I immediately swished water in and gargled.

'I used to love nachos. Can't stand them now. They are crispy and crunchy and the salsa dip, when it's good, it is the perfect combination of tomatoes, salt and chilies.'

'Okay.' It seemed like an appropriate response to his nacho love.

'But, then, one night. It was a special night? My long-time American girlfriend, we'd moved in together when I was in grad school and were planning to come back home and get married and raise a bunch of mixed-race babies. This night, we were driving back from a movie, I'd like to claim it wasn't *Legally Blonde*.' His smile was goofy, self-deprecating.

I blinked a third time. I wondered why he was telling me such an intensely personal story, in the first place.

'Anyway, I'd had a bag of nachos. It's my favourite theatre food,' he continued. 'And I think they were a bad batch, because I was talking to Michaela about the movie —driving the car—and I actually projectile vomited on her.'

I shuddered. That sounded gross. And unhealthy. 'Oh my God. You're joking.'

'True story. I don't joke about vomit.' He shrugged, folded his arms under his chest, crossed his legs at the ankle while he leaned against the bathroom tiles, just like a desi male model advertising bathroom tiles would. This man, with his damned golden-brown eyes and a hint of sexy beard and those shoulders; this man would not projectile vomit or even regular vomit. It just didn't seem probable.

'I'm almost afraid to ask.' I gargled again and almost gagged at the sour vomit taste in the back of my throat. I spit the water out. 'But what happened next?'

'Well, I ended up in the hospital with an epic bout of food poisoning. And when I came back home two days later, Michaela had moved out.' He smiled again, but this time I saw his eyes. They were watchful, quiet. It was freaky.

And kind of hot.

'She sounds awful.'

'To be fair to her, it was an awful lot of vomit. An *awful* lot. Her leather jacket was ruined. Forever.'

'I guess vomit's a deal-breaker when it comes to true love.' I bent back to the basin and considered the simple wisdom of his words.

'It is, indeed.'

The lawyer rummaged in the shower caddy tacked on the wall next to the mirror and washstand. I continued washing my mouth thoroughly, desperate to feel halfway normal again. He handed me a tube of toothpaste. It was a herbal one with neem leaves and salt.

'There's no brush here. But you can just use your finger, right?'

He was so matter-of-fact, I actually didn't protest his handling of the entire situation. I just took the tube, squeezed some of it out and mechanically rubbed the paste against my teeth. It felt minty and leafy but did the trick. By the next gargle, my breath felt almost fresh.

When I was done, he helpfully offered me a faded washcloth and I wiped my face and hands with it.

'Better?'

I nodded. I actually was. I gave my reflection one last look in the cracked mirror. A lost, frightening creature stared back. I clearly wasn't winning any beauty contests today. I regretfully removed Prapti's dupatta, now forever flecked with my vomit, and took a deep breath.

A button popped off my kurti. Pinged off the man's shoulder.

I looked down at the plunging neckline, now showing a lot of boob. Revealing my lacy bra with the frayed edge. I raised horrified eyes to the lawyer who was manfully struggling to not stare at my displayed chest.

'I...'

'Don't worry about it,' he said quickly and stepped out of the bathroom in one quick, agile lunge. It wasn't very agile though, because he went flying back after hitting his elbow against the door.

So I lunged forward and tried to balance him. It worked. Sort of.

But I couldn't let it go. 'This is all water weight. I used to be a size M, medium. And then I took up this new job and everyone over there is under the age of twenty-seven, everyone! Like the chai-wala[14] guy is twenty-two and is interning with us. And we all eat a lot of junk food.' The words kept pouring out of my mouth, like I had verbal diarrhoea, and the more I talked, the more my chest heaved.

And the kurti tear became wider. He glanced at my chest once, quickly, and I caught him looking and everything went sort of quiet.

'It's all just water weight,' I offered weakly, in conclusion.

'I bet.' He sounded so odd. Breathless even. Could guys lose their breath, like the heroines in romance novels?

'I am not such a big mess usually. But my paati just died and I am trying to be brave about it all. Be adult, you know?'

'It's okay,' he said, gently. 'You can cry. Or not. You can do

---

[14]One who prepares and serves tea.

whatever you want that helps.'

Those words were so kind. He was so kind. I wanted to hug him and never let him go.

'Thank you,' I said, following him.

He stepped further back and banged his hip against a side table. He placed his hand on the table and pierced it on the edge of a sharp lamp.

My eyes widened in distress and concern. 'Oh my God, are you okay?'

The curse that followed turned the air blue.

'I'm so sorry. Do you want a Band-Aid?' I wanted to check his hand out but I was afraid of what would happen if we touched.

He sucked on his bleeding thumb.

'Thank you,' I said again. 'And I'm sorry.'

'Don't worry about it,' he repeated. Then he gave me a short nod and disappeared back into Paati's room.

I wrung the dupatta in my nerveless hands and contemplated the sad, pitiful state of my life. Not only had I vomited my innards, I was now the prize owner of a projectile vomit story starring a thoroughly decent man I just tried to maim.

The house filled up pretty rapidly as news of my grandmother's demise spread all over the small town. By the time she had been laid in state, garlanded and wrapped in her cremation shroud, the living room and yard was SRO—standing room only. The crowd, mostly men, workers and managers from the nearby estates as well as all the A-list crowd (local MLA, Chamber of Commerce head, hotel and shop owners) were largely respectful and quiet as they watched the proceedings sombrely.

Dad, stoic as always, was front and centre, right next to my paati. He complied with all the mantrams[15] the vaadhyar made him repeat. He wore the traditional panchakacham—the dhoti as worn by Mahatma Gandhi. His body lean from the 10 kilometres he walked daily. But his hair was whiter than it had been two years ago and his jowls had wrinkles. As Dad performed the rituals, pouring ghee over the homam[16] fire, I saw that he had the exact same hands as Paati, long and lean, like a pianist's. And they were becoming mottled like hers had been.

My father, nearing sixty-five, was growing old too.

My head started swimming, so I squeezed Kiki's waist tightly. Her nails dug into my waist. She had come downstairs with her fiancé and his parents while I was in the bathroom. The Gujrals, who didn't understand a word of the Sanskrit shlokas[17], were valiantly on their feet for the last four hours while the vaadhyar did his thing. To be fair, none of us did, either. We all were the primary circle of mourners. My mother was right next to Dad, dressed in the traditional nine-yard sari, as befit her status as eldest daughter-in-law. Deep and Subhadra were next to them. Varun and Kiara stood behind them, followed by us kids in the second circle. Vidhaant, Ahalya, Atharva, Kiki and me. Prapti and Trilok rounded out the group. Jo clung unashamedly to her mother's knees, her eyes huge.

I didn't blame her. I wanted to cling to someone solid who had all the answers too. I was just happy Varun's back was broad enough so I didn't have to see any of it happening directly.

Surprisingly, the lawyer had melted into the crowd by the time I fixed myself and showed up in a different kurti than the torn one. Prapti's dupatta was in the hamper and I was not looking forward to telling her about the vomit situation. Mom had raised her brows

---

[15]Sanskrit chants
[16]Sacred or holy fire prepared with dried cow patty and ghee/butter/oil.
[17]Verses

when she saw the pale mauve kurti with a matching stole I had wrapped around my neck like a dupatta. But she'd not been able to do more than that since we were in the middle of the ritual.

'I heard that you had a scene with Ben,' Kiki muttered in a low voice, when there was a pause in the chanting. 'Right before the vaadhyar came.'

'I had a scene with whom?'

'Ben? Banjeet? The lawyer? You had a scene with him, right?'

So, the lawyer's name was Ben. Catchy. And unimaginative. 'I didn't have a scene with him. I was just asking Atharva why Paati…,' my voice broke at the word, 'changed lawyers in the end.'

'I don't know too much about it. But Ben's a great lawyer. He used to work in Chennai in one of those named law firms. Now he has his own consulting gig. He apparently went to Yale to do his Master's.'

'Of course he did,' I murmured, remembering his story about the American girlfriend. Then I aimed an enquiring look at my cousin. 'How do you know so much about him?'

She shot me an almost apologetic look. 'Ben is Trilok's Ben. Ben Dewar. The best man.'

Aka Trilok's mysterious best friend.

I shook my head and removed my hand from Kiki's 28-inch waist. 'No way. Not *that* guy. Trilok said his best friend was an asshole with a Ferrari.' I'd heard the stories about Trilok and Ben's escapades when they were in their twenties.

Kiki shrugged. 'He changed. What can I say?'

'What's the story there?'

'His dad left his mom on their fortieth anniversary to shack up with a thirty-year-old gynaecologist. It messed him up or something. I don't know. Anyway, he sold the Ferrari, which, by the way, was a BMW and not a Ferrari. And became a responsible adult citizen.' She gave me a half-smile. 'Atharva 2.0, we call him.'

'God, not another one. I haven't recovered from Atharva the First.'

Varun turned and glared at the two of us and we were duly silenced. For the time being, I was distracted from the terrible proceedings. Anything was better than thinking about what was happening ten feet away from me. Where they were readying my grandmother, the strongest, most opinionated woman I knew, for her cremation.

*Ben Dewar.* I mulled the name, mouthing it silently. He was handsome in an off-kilter way, and he had the kindest eyes. He was also good in a crisis and was not put off by crying, puking women. Plus, he was gainfully employed.

'Appa said he'd be a good match for Ahalya, because they're the same age. Thirty-six,' Kiki whispered quickly.

I blinked, as all my mental speculation ground to a halt. 'Ahalya?' I whispered back.

She nodded even as Trilok and Atharva gave us identical bland stares. Prapti sobbed softly into her handkerchief. It was probably a terrible thing that the granddaughter-in-law was able to produce tears on cue, while the real thing discussed dudes.

'Yeah. He saw her picture on the matrimonial site, the one your mom forcibly made her put up, and he liked it. He's even on board with adoption. It says so on his profile.'

The man was damn near a saint. And, God knew, Ahalya needed the break. Life had been rotten to her for the last few years.

'Good for him.' I caught Ahalya's eye on Mom's other side and nodded. She looked through me. 'She's welcome to have him.'

'We need to discuss the wedding at some point,' Kiki continued. 'It's next week and Dad says we can still have it on a really low scale but Mom is adamant about postponing it. Trilok's like let's go on our honeymoon in the Bahamas and get married there. And I don't know what to do.'

She sounded close to tears and I had to wonder at the single-minded absorption of someone who wanted to discuss their wedding at a funeral. Then again, she was Chandralekha's granddaughter. Selfishness abounded in us like tea sludge.

I squeezed her waist and she leaned her head against my shoulder. 'We'll figure it out. Later. Let's just not talk for a bit?'

'Okay.'

The vaadhyar pronounced the ritual complete and the circle parted for my father, who walked to the head of the body. Placed two flowers on each of her eyes. Tears dripped down his nose and he wiped them off angrily. Subhadra wailed again and the crowd murmured uneasily.

'Paati's gone,' Kiki whispered forlornly. 'She's really gone.'

Yeah, she really was. And she was never coming back.

As is customary in most Hindu homes, the men took the body to the burial grounds; in this case, to the next town where there was a cremation ground. The rest of the day's rituals would be performed at the ground itself and take a few more hours. They weren't going to burn the body in the traditional manner, preferring the incinerator. Apparently, it was in Grandmother's will. The one drawn by Ben Dewar, saviour of vomiting women everywhere.

They had also debated keeping the body for a few hours more in order for everyone to come and pay their last respects, but decided against it. She was already dead for more than twenty-four hours.

So the procession, followed by a large crowd (seriously, they numbered in the hundreds!) followed the ambulance that held the body. Dad, his two brothers and Atharva, who looked distinctly hollow-eyed at the prospect of traveling with the body, were also in the ambulance. Trilok, Ben and Vidhaant followed in the SUV.

Trilok's dad elected to stay back and manage the crowd gathered at Chakrapani Illam and I was so incredibly proud of the family Kiki had chosen to marry into. They might not be second-generation Indian Army, but they were amazingly decent people. She could do worse. And Subhadra aunty wanted to stop the damn wedding even now.

The women stayed in the courtyard and held on to each other. My mom supported a weeping daughter-in-law on one shoulder and a wailing sister-in-law on the other. She was remarkably, admirably, dry-eyed. Kiki, fanning herself with her black phulkari dupatta (she wore a grey chikan anarkali[18]) made an exasperated sound next to me, sort of between a sniffle and a grunt.

'I know Mom means well and she was really close to Paati, but her wailing is getting on my nerves,' she muttered.

Kiara, who was edging closer to us, paused in her momentum. I gave her an apologetic shrug, which she returned with a blank, polite smile. I patted Kiki's shoulder a little harder than required. Kiara was a fish out of water on the best of days. She knew that hanging out with the noisy, inappropriate kids was not good for her image. She inched closer to Mom, the epicentre of calm and propriety.

'Let's use our inside voice,' I told Kiki quietly.

We trooped inside, followed by the womenfolk who had come to offer condolences to the bereaved.

The house, built of marble, stone and wood, threw off intense chill even though the sun was out. In the cold light of day, I could see that the living room décor had changed drastically from the last time I had seen it. The huge sectional sofas in the two seating spaces were now brown leather and not black. The floor was veined gold marble edged in black and not the massive 3-feet-by-3-feet

---

[18]A flared tunic with pleats, called kalis, usually paired with narrow pants.

cream tiles they'd been. The coffee table stand was in the shape of a dolphin instead of a horse. Knick-knacks stood in all corners of the room, in little stands and side tables.

The stone tiles on the wall next to the huge TV held black and white prints from a spread that a national lifestyle magazine had done on the estate and Paati a few years ago. A wind chime tinkled against the bay windows that opened out into a vista of the Munnar hills. The estate gleamed in the pale morning sun—lush and verdant. Alive in a way my grandmother wasn't.

'We'll all have coffee and breakfast,' Mom said, ever the practical, take-charge kind. 'Subhadra, you need to make the chutney. I can never quite get the tamarind-to-coconut proportion right.'

Subhadra nodded, wiping her wet cheeks. Usually, she wasn't such a watering pot but these were extenuating circumstances. Then again, making a tasty coconut chutney trumped even crying. Mom did know how to handle these things like a pro.

'Then we all have things to do,' Mom continued, as she unwrapped her shawl and placed it on a chair near the twenty-seater dining table. The dining set was new too. 'Guests are here. They need to be taken care of. We have to find a good picture of Amma and have it blown up for the rest of the ceremonies, before the men get back. Lunch has to be—' Mom shook her head, as if overwhelmed and Prapti hugged her hard.

'I'll help with the food,' she announced.

'Me too,' Kiara offered awkwardly, along with her.

'LJ and I'll get on the picture,' Kiki said before I could stop her. 'We'll also begin taking care of the guests. LJ can make Tang while I serve them water.'

'No,' Ahalya said. 'I'll make the Tang and you and the brat can serve them.'

Oops. For a second there, I had actually forgotten that Ahalya had stayed back too.

'I can make the juice,' I insisted, for form's sake.

Ahalya took in my bedraggled and frankly street urchin-like appearance and her bow-shaped lips curled in contempt. 'You'll probably mix in salt instead of sugar. I'll take care of it, Lasya.'

Kiki placed a warning hand on my shoulder. I smiled and let it go. 'Sure, Ahalya. You know best. I defer to your superior opinion.'

Our group split in different directions, the older women to the kitchen along with Prapti and Ahalya.

'I can't wait for the lawyer to marry her and take her far away from here.' I arranged my stole around my neck for the third time.

Kiki shuddered. 'The horror.'

We both took one look at each other and burst into a fit of giggles that only subsided when we realized we were in the living room and about fifty women had come to pay their respects to our grieving family for our loss. We might have grown apart in the last decade or so when life and work and sheer adulting had gotten in the way of us being connected but, as always, I could still count on my soul sister to crack me up at inappropriate times. The living room décor might have changed, and I was not as pretty and put together or thin as I had been the last time we hung out, but some things did remain the same.

I was absurdly glad for it.

*Chapter Six*

4 p.m.

> *Madamji. Urgent hai.*[19] *Please call.*

I ignored the text from Gordhan Vithaldas Real Estate Agent because I was in no mood to have him tell me once more why I should consider lowering the asking price. I wanted to; I really did. But I also wanted to pay off the loan I'd taken for the house I'd bought with so much optimism.

Recklessness, my father termed it when we were still on talking terms.

By the way? Do *not* buy real estate and start a brand new business that requires significant capital at the same time. You won't be able to plough the money back into the business and you won't be able to pay your monthly mortgage. You'll be neck-deep in debt and your self-esteem will be in the nearest gutter.

Especially, after you're forced to declare bankruptcy on the brand new business when capital runs out and you have no more money to keep it afloat.

'Check this one out,' Kiki said. She held up an old, coloured still of Chandralekha that we'd dug out from her suite. Her rooms smelled medicinal, like Dettol and phenyl mixed together. Probably one of the help who'd stayed back had done the needful. Someone had also helpfully chucked all her clothes—saris, blouses, petticoats, worn cotton panties with holes in them—inside a massive suitcase that was now placed in her almirah.

---

[19]Madam. It's urgent.

The almirah, a massive wooden affair with ornate golden handles and peeling corners, had two shelves at the top, with thick ledgers. Household accounts kept meticulously by my grandmother till Mom took over and everything went digital. The albums were kept on a lower shelf in the cupboard, stacked end on end with cracked plastic covers, all of which contained so many of my childhood memories.

From the surreptitious sniffles Kiki was trying hard to cover up, I guessed the photos contained a lot of her memories too. She was an only child, so I suppose, in a way, all the pressure was on her. To be perfect, to not be a disappointment, to be loved regardless of how much you screw up...

I gave the photo a critical once-over. Paati was looking off-camera in this one and her hair was iron grey, put up in the bun I'd never seen her without. I could make out the border colour of her silk sari, red and gold with a midnight blue pallu. Her nose was formidably sharp and the mookutthi—diamond nose ring—glinted off the page. Her cheekbones, which she had only passed onto Ahalya and Vidhaant, were also sharp.

But her eyes shone with intelligence and ambition. All her kids, all four of them, had her eyes. Not for nothing did she manage to stay married to my grandfather for close to fifty years before he'd croaked. All the while running a prosperous multi-crore business.

'Pretty,' I said. 'But too young, don't you think?'

I paused as I saw the thick orange spine of a book sticking out from the shorter, stouter albums. The title: *The Spectacular Melancholy of Living*. The author of the book was I.J Raghavan.

I pulled the book out with trembling hands. Opened it to the dedication page, which read,

> *To my paati, Chandralekha Chakrapani. A dragon of a grandmother. My fiercest critic. My staunchest supporter.*

The endorsement on the cover, written by a prominent literary personality in India, read 'LJ manages to capture the melancholy and morbid fun of belonging to a dysfunctional family with unerring accuracy.' Tears blinded my eyes as I closed the book. I stepped back from the almirah and perched on the edge of the bed.

Memories rushed at me. Random and chaotic. Tumbling over one another.

Paati braiding my oiled hair while I wore a grey pinafore and sang a popular Madhuri Dixit song—badly... Paati handing me an empty notebook and pen and telling me to write down everything I saw over the course of the summer... Paati expertly chopping up raw mangoes for pickling in the monsoon season... Paati and Mom, walking on the edge of the property, their heads bent close together as they argued about one thing or the other. Two small, slight women, who ruled their world with an iron fist. Who had *built* this fucking world with nothing more than polite smiles and spines of steel.

How was I their progeny? How did I even think I belonged here, when I had screwed everything up so cataclysmically I had to write shitty articles in order to make rent?

Without a word, Kiki handed me another picture. It was Paati with a miniature version of herself, Ahalya's mom, Sujata. Sujata looked about twenty-two and she sported a thick yellow thread and gold pendant, the thaali[20], which signified a newly-wed bride. Paati was looking at the camera this time, unsmiling and sombre in her Kanchipuram.[21]

'Jesus,' I whispered. 'They were so young. So beautiful.'

'This was such a bad idea.' Kiki slammed the albums shut with

---

[20] A yellow thread that is knotted thrice around the bride's neck, to signify her married status.

[21] Woven silk sari from the town of Kanchipuram.

a bang. She looked miserable. 'I don't want to go through all these pictures and know that Paati won't...' She worried the threads on the coir mattress we were sitting on. The bedspread and sheets were already discarded, as was custom.

'She won't ever not smile for the camera again.' Kiki wiped one stray tear from her cheek.

I took the album instead. 'We need to figure this out now. Or Ahalya will hold it over my head as yet another thing I am not good at. Can you look online for the nearest photo printing shop?'

'Trilok said we can go to the Vivanta's business centre and scan and print it there.' Kiki got up from the bed and touched the closed window. The panes were old and spider-webbed from not having been used for years. Paati was not into looking at scenic views in the last few months. 'They also have some sort of art gallery inside, so those guys will be able to blow it up.'

I went back to the picture Kiki handed me. The one in which Paati was looking off camera, her profile in regal display. It must have been taken when she was younger, much younger. Maybe in her seventies. The woman carried on my dad, uncles' and brother's shoulders did not resemble the woman in the picture as much as she did a dried-up husk.

'This one,' I decided. 'It's classy and formidable with a touch of sexy. This one.'

'How are we going to justify this to the elders without using the word sexy?' Kiki could be wry when the mood came upon her.

'Look at her.' I held the photo up at chest level and pointed at it. 'This is Paati. We won't have to justify using it as long as you agree with my choice.'

'I do. I picked it out, remember?'

'Alright. Do we have a car to go to Vivanta, or are we walking?' I gave her a worried look. 'Are we even allowed to leave the house?'

'Our menfolk just went to the burial grounds, didn't they?' The logic in the rhetorical question was sound. 'Of course, we can leave. It's official funeral work. I'll get us a car. You get photo approval.'

In a house of grief, the primary driver is always food. And even though we had plenty of staff to do all the chores around the house, archaic tradition dictated that the women of the house cook for the most part. The regular cook, a rotund woman by the name of Bhartimma, was in charge of refreshments. Her two helpers were on serving duty.

Mom, Subhadra, Ahalya, Prapti and Kiara were all cooking. Well, Prapti and Kiara were chopping massive mounds of okra and potatoes. I could spy a huge vat of rice and another of sambhar, along with some kind of dal without any spices. The kitchen, a huge space, was suddenly super crowded. So, it didn't take me all that much time to slip in, show the picture to the distracted women who were busy stirring and adding things to various pots and pans and slip out before they could say more than 'Huh.'

I slipped out through the back door, wanting to avoid the living room throng. The thin winter air was crisp and smelled of burnt tea. On this side of the mountain, the slopes gave way to rows and rows of tea plants, bound by wire and kept in place using stalks. Growing tea was much the same as growing grapes for wine. The air needed to be clear and less oxygenated and stalks were used for binding.

I considered taking a short walk through the personal tea garden Paati had tended to herself, but my phone buzzed. It was a work email. I swiped right on it immediately. It buzzed again. This time it was a text from Kiki: *Found transpo. Come to driveway.*

I went, not knowing what I was letting myself in for.

'When you said transpo, I thought it meant a car. Four wheels. Safe to drive. Not this death trap,' I yelled and held on for dear life to Kiki's waist, while she took yet another turn on the Royal Enfield Classic recklessly. Kiki had bribed one of the estate labourers with a ₹500 note and come away with the death machine. To be fair, she wasn't a bad driver—she owned an Activa back in Delhi—but I was terrified of motorcycles.

'We'll be fine,' she yelled back. 'Just relax.'

The Vivanta was a couple of hills away and took about fifteen minutes since we didn't have to battle incoming traffic in a bigger vehicle. I was shaking by the time she braked to a stop inside the portico of the huge sprawling five-star resort. Set amidst the stunning and lush greenery of Munnar's tea estates and mountains, the resort was the perfect getaway for urbane hipsters, the clients of choice for such an upscale establishment.

As luck would have it, I spotted Prapti's parents, a trendy-looking couple who were sophisticated and nice, just like their daughter, checking in at the reception. Beside them stood Giridhar uncle, the man in charge of figuring out logistics during the next few days. He had his ear glued to a phone and was gesticulating as he talked in shuddh Malayalam.

'Prapti's folks,' I said through the corner of my mouth. 'We should exit, pronto.'

But Giridhar uncle spotted me and waved eagerly. Kiki and I were made. I clutched the little sling bag that contained Paati's photo a little closer to my chest. I did not want to meet these people right now, when I was still feeling physically vulnerable from that death ride and emotionally raw from spending time in Paati's suite. But Kiki had already pasted a mellow smile on her face and went forward, dragging me in her wake.

'Hello, Uncle, Aunty,' I said. Kiki echoed my hello and immediately bent down and touched their feet and I followed. I rolled my eyes at her but the elderly couple touched our shoulders briefly before hugging us.

'LJ, beta[22],' Suresh Krishnan said, as he pecked the side of my temple. 'I am so sorry about everything.'

'It's okay, Uncle.' I hugged Aunty too, who patted my cheek in a manner I defensively found condescending. But that could have been my chafing emotions, which were all over the place at the moment.

Jalaja and Suresh Krishnan were a tall, slim couple in their sixties. Uncle wore a tasteful kurta, jeans and open-toed sandals with socks in deference to the weather. Jalaja aunty was like a glamourized, iron-haired version of Prapti. Her cheekbones were still sharp and the skin on her neck was still taut and firm, no doubt a product of monthly facials. She wore a cotton sari (did all these women shop together at the same store?!) and what looked like a pashmina shawl.

Her jewellery consisted of diamonds dripping from her neck and ears and a diamond-studded watch strapped on her wrist. I frowned internally and tried to remember if either Prapti or I wore any jewellery on our necks, ears or hands. I had even removed my weed-shaped earrings on 31 December, as a gesture of depressed defiance.

It was a measure of how rattled my mom was, because she hadn't reprimanded me or her daughter-in-law for going without jewellery on such an important family occasion.

'Lasya, you look lovely,' Jalaja said graciously. She tucked my wayward hair behind my ear and tapped my bare earlobe. 'Wear something, no?'

Yep, there it was. The female demand.

'Can we not do a style makeover right now, Jalaja?' Suresh gave

---

[22]Kiddo

Kiki a sideways hug and she stuck her tongue out at me over the two of them. 'The poor girl is devastated. Can't you see?'

Actually, I didn't feel devastated so much as…ended. As if there was a version of me that had walked these paths in Munnar two years ago and that woman had disappeared under the monumentally bad choices I'd made since then. The new year combined with the loss of my grandmother just brought home sharply and anew of how completely ruined I was. Of course, Suresh uncle didn't know this. Mostly. Everyone only knew the PG-13 version of what had happened.

'I am just trying to be helpful.' Jalaja's eyes flashed, indicating this was an ongoing argument between them.

'Excuse me, sir,' the receptionist interrupted the conversation before it derailed any further. 'Here's your Aadhaar card and madam's. Welcome to the Taj Vivanta. The bellboy will take your bags to your room.' Suresh collected everything and Giridhar uncle supervised the luggage logistics.

'You should rest,' Kiki said. 'You guys have been travelling non-stop. We will send the car for you by 7? For dinner? Everyone will be back by then too, I think.'

He hesitated, his eyes shadowed in a strange way. 'Atharva has gone to the burial ground?'

I nodded. 'Yeah. He looked freaked out. I don't blame him.' Then, I added lamely, 'Prapti will be happy to see you. If I'd known you guys were coming now, I'd have brought her along.'

Jalaja shook her head immediately. 'She needs rest. We spoke to her before checking in. She's helping with the cooking. Why aren't you two doing the same?'

'We are getting the portrait done for Paati,' I said softly.

She nodded sombrely. 'Okay.' Then she hesitated before asking, 'Prapti? She isn't stressed, is she? By all this?'

I reached up and gave her a tight hug. 'Of course not, Aunty.

Your daughter is a rock. My mother wants to adopt her for good reason. You have nothing to worry about.'

We made our escape then while Kiki commented, 'That was weird. You'd think Perfect Prapti was a china doll princess who'd never seen death before.'

'You are a doctor. You've seen death, woman. The rest of us haven't.'

'You remember this time, last year? How Mom almost faked a heart attack in order to avoid the engagement? And I told you, I'd die if I didn't get to spend the rest of my life with Trilok.' Kiki's gamine features were soft, as she remembered epic battle number 671 she'd had to fight.

'Yeah. I was right there. Next to you.' I was gently wry. 'Trying to not roll my eyes at all the melodrama.'

'I never thanked you then, I never felt the need to, but what you did with your book? What you wrote about that family and the Hindu-Muslim intercommunal marriage almost tearing them all apart and bringing them together in the end? It made a difference. You standing there next to me, while I told my parents to show up for my engagement and behave like adults, it made a difference.' Her voice trembled and she gave me a side hug.

I was taken aback. Did she really remember all that? I had been *that* person for her?

'Atharva was supposed to fly down but he chickened out at the last minute. But you didn't, Lasya,' she said softly. 'You showed up. And you stood by me. Remember what Dad told you?'

I grinned. 'That my openly defiant and decidedly feminist views were the reason why Shaadi.com auto-deleted my profile.'

'And you said that it didn't matter. You were my sister first. And my happiness came first for you. I loved you so much for that. For doing that. No one stood up for me like that. And you got Gomti perimma to talk some sense into my mom and we had the best time ever.'

'Kiki,' I said quietly, while regret and colossal love filled me. 'I love you. And you'll always come first with me.' *Even when I hadn't come first with you.* I didn't add that part. She had enough to deal with, at the moment.

Kiki suggested, 'Let's give the picture to the business centre guys. I want to show you something.'

Twenty minutes later, I found myself climbing a mini hillock on the Vivanta property in open-toed sandals that pinched.

When we reached the top, Kiki pointed at the flat expanse of perfect lawn spread out before us. Currently, a few lawn chairs and shaded umbrellas dotted the area and hotel guests milled about aimlessly, taking selfies and sipping fruity drinks. Exhausted souls enjoying the first week of the year before the other fifty-one weeks sucked the life out of them.

Their grandmother obviously hadn't died.

'That's my reception venue,' she said mournfully. 'We were going to put up pink satin tents and the chairs would be all white and the four-course menu would be a mix of North Indian and South Indian being catered by the Vivanta chef herself. Our wedding cake was strawberry cheesecake with sugar paste shaped like a stethoscope and a laptop screen. My dream wedding. Which is in seven days, by the way, in case you forgot.'

'I haven't forgotten, Krutika.' Kiki knew I was serious because I said her actual name. I *never* say her name. Not unless it's Armageddon. 'We are going to talk to your parents tomorrow. I'll rope Mom in. She'll convince them. We've done it once before, right?'

'Trilok's parents are being so amazing about this. Especially after everything we've been through. I can't believe this is happening to us.'

My heart went out to her. It hadn't been easy, studying for ten years straight while battling her Army-obsessed parents and maintaining a relationship with a workaholic, non-verbal geek like Trilok.

'Maybe you should do what Trilok suggested. Elope to the Bahamas and have a beach wedding,' I suggested lightly.

'I swear to all the gods, LJ, I will take all the bends at 90 kilometres if you suggest that to anyone.' She even shot me a determined scowl to go with her threat.

'Hey, I am kidding, I'm kidding. What do you want?' I sat down on the edge of the jutting hilltop and dangled my legs over. Kiki carefully positioned herself behind me. She had a thing about heights. I rested my hand on her knee. 'You want the fancy party? The cake and butter chicken and rasam rice and the satin ribbons?'

She sighed and briskly tied her hair back into a casual bun.

My ponytail was already half-undone and I despaired of my hair unfrizzing itself without the help of my stylist.

'I don't know what I want.' She gave a whimsical smile. 'I want to turn the clock back day before yesterday and stay back, so I could admit Paati in the hospital. And then the doctor would have had to put her on ventilator.'

'So you could get married?' I wasn't exactly censuring her.

Kiki pinched me on my arm. 'You're fucking insensitive, behena[23].' She used the childhood nickname we always used for each other. 'No. Not because I don't want to postpone my wedding.' She paused and admitted in a small voice. 'Okay only about 10 per cent for that. But mostly because I became a doctor because Paati spoke to Dad and convinced him to let me go and not enrol in

---

[23]Sister

the fucking organization.' The 'organization' is code for 'Army' for Army brats. 'And, in the end, I let her down. I wasn't there for her.'

She sniffed loudly and two large tears rolled down her cheeks.

'Your mascara is not equipped to handle waterworks,' I warned but held on to her.

I knew that guilt. Familial guilt was insidious, like a precisely calibrated piece of shrapnel lodged under your gut designed to *hurt* when squeezed. I used the edge of my stole to wipe her tears away and touched my forehead to hers.

'You're getting married to Trilok next week. I promise. I'll talk to Mom and get it done.' I sighed. 'I'll even talk to Dad if I have to.'

Now she squeezed my knee. 'You guys have spoken any?'

I shook my head. 'He told Atharva to wish me a happy new year. The feud still continues.'

I smiled crookedly, while the guilt shrapnel twisted and inched closer to my heart. Of all the people who'd been affected by everything I'd done, my father was the worst. And most vocal. He'd never been in my corner; never understood why I needed to write. Much less write thick books that no one read.

Except, people *actually* read what I wrote and all hell broke loose.

Now, we had less of a relationship than what we'd had through my teens. And I had been your quintessential troubled rebellious child, with obvious daddy issues.

'You have to talk to your father, LJ.'

'I have to get back to the Illam in one piece, so I can campaign for your dream wedding. That's what I have to do,' I informed her. 'Everything else is up for grabs.'

Kiki's phone buzzed. 'That'd be Trilok. Checking up on us.'

I sighed. 'Can I just clone him and marry that guy? It would save me all this hassle of having to actually find a man to tolerate me for more than five minutes.'

'You may think he's perfect, behena. I know the truth,' she shot back. But she had the tiniest smile playing on her lips. 'He snores like a fucking pressure cooker and he leaves his phone everywhere. I have to be on constant phone patrol with him.'

'Shut up and don't make me hate you anymore, behena.'

For once, Kiki took my suggestion seriously and shut up. And my shrapnel dissipated the tiniest bit because at least this, sharing secrets and hopes and dreams with Kiki, remained constant. And I had so few of them right now.

# Chapter Seven

The menfolk were ensconced at the dining room table, picking at cold sambhar and curd rice by the time we came back.

They had all showered again, Ben included.

I felt a small jolt at seeing him next to my brother, with Trilok on the other side, heads bent in discussion. They all wore singlets and track pants, hair wet and curling at the nape, Ben's especially. He had a dusting of hair on his not-too-beefy arms. But, more than the matching outfits and same dark hair, Ben had this air around him. Like he was comfortable in his own skin. Like he had to make no apology for himself. He looked like he belonged.

Something I immediately resented him for.

Ahalya moved towards Ben, pouring sambhar over his rice and bending low to talk to him. Whatever he said made her smile and tuck her hair back, and my resentment grew a notch higher. Which made no sense whatsoever, of course.

'You two need to take a shower pronto. I'll take that,' Prapti said as soon as she spotted us. She took the enlarged portrait from us. It weighed a ton and I was glad to pass it off to someone else.

'We just had a shower in the morning,' Kiki protested. Prapti gave her a 'Don't argue with me' look that would have made my mother proud. 'Fine.'

'I don't have anything to wear,' I hissed at the two of them. 'The other kurti tore in the morning. Ben got an eyeful of my boobs. And I don't think the elders will appreciate me wearing track pants and a T-shirt.'

'I could lend you something,' Prapti said bravely.

Kiki rolled her eyes. 'Dude, you know she won't fit into your clothes on a regular day. Now she has all that water weight she is carting.' Kiki eyed my chest appraisingly. 'I have a couple blouses that will fit you. You can wear a sari tonight.'

'What? No way. No way, Kiki.' My mouth dropped open in a very unattractive manner.

As if on cue, Ben looked in our direction. He gave us a tiny wave; I saw that he'd stuck on a pink Band-Aid on his thumb. He nodded at me formally, that same short okay nod he'd given me before. Probably checking to see if I was having another mini-meltdown.

'It's either the sari or the track pants. One of which will get you a lecture on dressing appropriately for the occasion from your mother, an angry look from your father, and Ahalya will have more fodder to torment you with. Choose fast.' Kiki was a pragmatic woman who was not above blackmailing me when it suited her.

Prapti gave me a soft, conciliatory smile, but she didn't have a solution other than the one at hand either.

'Fuck.' Yeah, the word pretty much summed my feelings on my choice.

'I didn't figure you for a sari girl,' Ben commented an hour later.

I descended-slash-carefully navigated the Palladian staircase without tripping over my two feet, the pleats of the sari and the pallu. I was the opposite of all clichés, an Indian woman uncomfortable as fuck in a sari, the height of feminine fashion in a feminine fashion-obsessed country.

He carried his laptop casually in one hand, a slim silver machine I had briefly considered buying, back when I had the means to do so.

'Hello Ben, how's the butt?' I asked. Then I bit my tongue.

Firstly, I wasn't supposed to know his name since we hadn't formally introduced ourselves so far and bathroom encounters don't count. Secondly, he'd made a perfectly innocent comment about my outfit and I immediately and defensively sexualized the whole thing. I sighed.

'I'm sorry,' I grunted.

He grinned and my stomach fluttered the slightest bit. He belonged with Ahalya, I reminded myself. She'd earned this man. 'The butt's fine, thank you for asking. The thumb, not so much. And hello, Lasya. You have nothing to be sorry about.' His grin widened. 'Much.'

This man had only ever seen me being rude and inappropriate or sick. It was time to change things up a bit. So I held my hand out, the one that wasn't holding the sari pleats and pallu.

'Hello,' I spoke as formally as I would for an interview. 'I'm LJ Raghavan. Very nice to meet you.'

Ben shook my hand, the grin simmering down to an amused smile. He stood far too close for someone who was apparently interested in my older, *much* older, cousin sister. But, then again, that could just be me. 'Hello, LJ. Very nice to meet you. I'm Ben Dewar. The asshole handling your grandmother's will and estate.'

'I gathered as much.'

We proceeded to walk down the stairs.

'So,' Ben said abruptly, like before. 'I hear you are a writer? Trilok can't shut up about how amazing you are.'

'Trilok exaggerates.' I placed my heel carefully on the step and watched each step as I went. 'I am not at all amazing.'

That much, at least, is true. Failed playwrights are the farthest from amazing, unless you count amazingly bad. Which, one reviewer in *Time Out* magazine had actually called me when he wrote a review of the play I had written and produced. *Amazingly bad*.

'I'm sure you're being way too modest.'

I threw him a surprised, sideways glance mid-step. He was in actual earnest. He meant what he said. *Oh man.* I stumbled the slightest bit and lost my death grip on the sari.

'Fuck,' I mumbled and felt my stomach drop the way it does when you miss a step and gravity pulls at you inevitably. Luckily, my feet found purchase.

Ben touched my elbow to steady me. I liked his touch. Maybe a bit too much. I re-gripped the sari and pallu and took a steadying breath.

'Are you okay?'

I nodded. 'I just need to concentrate on not tripping and negotiating stairs in the sari. So, let's talk once we are on firm ground, okay?'

'Sure.'

We went down three steps. Four. Five. He walked two steps below me so we were the same height, even though he was a full head taller than me. It felt nice when it shouldn't have. Companionable. (I was obviously losing my mind.)

Then he asked, 'If you aren't comfortable in the sari, why are you wearing it?'

I risked another glance, this time keeping both feet on the same step. He was still in earnest. The question was innocent. No undertones here.

'You wouldn't believe me if I told you.'

'Oh, I think I would.' And his deep, essentially masculine voice was rich with laughter. He even leaned in a bit closer so it felt like we were sharing something intimate, a secret. And maybe it was the moment, or the way he smelled, all soap and detergent or the fact that he had seen me at my lowest ebb and shared a deeply disgusting personal incident, but I told him the truth.

'I don't have anything to wear. I only brought two kurtis and jeans and you know what happened to one of them.'

He gazed quickly at my chest, which was right now swaddled under layers of pallu and blouse. The sari was a cumbersome pale grey georgette and the blouse was a soft velvety material in a darker grey, and I couldn't believe that I found all this hot—him looking at my rack. *Get a grip, LJ!*

'Right,' he murmured. 'Of course.'

'I have clothes,' I said to cover up the suddenly thick silence. 'At home. In Mumbai. In my apartment. I just didn't think I'd need more than two pairs since I'm going back tomorrow. We all are.'

That raised his gaze from my boobs to my face. I flushed, hot and fierce, at the frank appreciation he couldn't hide before he registered my words. The appreciation faded instantly and I was a bit sad. It had been nice to have someone admire me, even if it was just my 36B breasts. I was such a loser.

'Is that what you thought?'

I nodded. He opened his mouth but then thought better of it.

'What?' I asked him.

This was odd. Us standing on the steps, nearly at eye level, him in another kurta-pyjama and me in a sari that was slithery and made me feel more naked than actually being naked. I mean, air rushed in from everywhere. If this happened in a book I wrote, I'd add an accidental hug and a passionate make out session to end the scene.

But this was real life and he had a profile on Shaadi.com, approved by Ahalya, who I had already screwed over enough to last me two lifetimes. That's the only thing I had to remember.

'What did I say?' I asked.

He shifted the laptop to his other hand. 'Let's get downstairs?

I would hate to have you blame me for a Draupadi vastraharan[24] if you trip and fall.'

I laughed. It was a small sound, a tiny burst of genuine mirth and happiness. He smiled back in kinship.

'You're not as funny as you think,' I told him, as I carefully picked my way down the last few stairs.

'Oh, I know I am not.' He sketched a short bow as we reached firm ground and I could finally let go of the dratted pallu. 'I'm funnier.'

And I laughed again. Even though it wasn't that funny.

Either by accident or design, the living room was empty when Ben and I made our way to the dining table where all the family was gathered. Kiki and Trilok were having a whispered conversation, while his parents and Prapti's parents had tactfully disappeared to another part of the house to have coffee and 'catch up'.

Ahalya was talking to her younger brother, Vidhaant, and I caught the tail end of their conversation.

'...I just don't want it to seem like I can't run my life. Because I can.'

Vidhaant shook his head. 'Ahalya, you've been running both your life and mine successfully since we were babies. In fact, I worry sometimes that I married Gargi because she's so not—Hey LJ.' His eyes brightened as he caught sight of me.

I nodded back while Ahalya moved to the other side of the table. Like I was contagious or something.

---

[24]In the epic Mahabharata, the Pandava Queen Draupadi is disrobed publicly by Prince Dushasana as a mark of disrespect to her husbands. This incident is called Draupadi Vastraharan.

I got a sideways, compensating hug from Vidhaant. Kiki's eyes widened as she took in my ladylike appearance. With Ben by my side.

The next second, Ahalya waved Ben over and he took his place next to her, as if they were already a couple. A unit. Even Jo, that little traitor, tugged at his hand and smiled widely at him when he tousled her head.

Why the hell had he ogled at my breasts not five minutes ago? *Because*, my common sense pointed out, *I had made a reference to my breasts and he had just looked. Because they were there.*

'Hey,' Vidhaant said, as he squeezed in beside me. 'You look like you've swallowed a teabag. Everything alright?'

Vidhaant was only three years older than me, the middle cousin who did what everyone else wanted to do. For instance, when the younger kids like Kiki, Atharva and I wanted to do dumb things like pig out on jackfruit fries and climb trees in the back of the house during summer vacations and his older sister Ahalya wanted more grown-up pursuits like weekly kirtan sessions.

'Everything's fine.' I hugged him fiercely. He was stockier than the other men, but he had nice broad shoulders and his hugs were always bearlike. Plus, I always had a soft spot for him. It was not easy growing up with Ahalya as your nagging, perfectionist, general whip of a sister.

Probably.

Even if everything Vidhaant had said was true and she had practically raised Vidhaant when they were younger and their dad succumbed to prostate cancer.

'How are Gargi and the kids?'

Gargi was a Punjabi girl with a loud laugh and the best taste in shoes in all of our families. She'd produced a pair of twins—the next in the generation—within two years of marriage and was now a happy homemaker. It also helped that Vidhaant was a hands-on dad, changing diapers and singing lullabies and learning to make idli batter in his spare time.

'They're great. Vansh is down with fever, so we decided they shouldn't come.' He gave me a quick up-and-down appraisal. 'What's up with the "Bhartiya nari"[25] outfit? Who are you trying to impress? Perippa?' As the eldest son in the family—Sujata was the oldest daughter, but she was a daughter so it apparently didn't count—my dad was Perippa, Big Daddy to everyone.

'Shut up, Vidhaant. Go die.'

He tousled my already frizzy hair like Ben had Jo's. 'I missed you, kiddo. How are you doing? How's that awful job of yours?'

'It's...awful.' I tugged the slithering pallu back up my shoulder. How did women manage the pallu and travel in local trains back in Mumbai? Every second I was upright in the outfit, afraid that a single strategic tug and the whole thing would unravel right there, in front of everyone. 'And I am doing fine.'

'Really?' He tugged at the end of my shoulder-length hair and I glowered at him. But his expression was the slightest bit shadowed. 'I know Ahalya and you are having a thing...'

'It's been two years, you know,' I pointed out. '*Things* don't last this long. Feuds do.'

'Like I was saying, I know Ahalya and you are having a thing, and Perippa's taken a maun vrath[26] where you're concerned and you just told me your job is awful, so I am concerned. So is Gargi. She misses your monthly video calls. You didn't even respond to our "Happy New Year" message, babe.'

I couldn't un-hear the gentle reprimand in his statement.

This. This was what family love was all about. This passive aggressive way of digging around in your business under the guise of concern. And I know, okay? I know that Vidhaant and Gargi

---

[25]Traditional Indian woman
[26]Vow of silence

were genuinely worried about me, but it sucked that they were. It sucked that I still hadn't got my act together. And it double-sucked that they knew it.

'Everything's fine, Vidhaant. You need to stop being such a bleeding heart. And, Gargi doesn't have energy from running after the Twin Terrors. She doesn't have time to miss me.'

Vidhaant squeezed my hand. 'Trust me,' he said. 'She misses you.'

The guilt shrapnel dug in once more in my heart, piercing through the shaky walls I had to build every day. The walls came down again and a sickening mix of guilt, anger, regret, terror and absolute grief flooded through me, paralyzing me with their force.

I gripped the back of the chair I was holding on to very tightly. 'Let's not talk about it, please.'

'But, LJ—'

'Vidhaant.' I looked him straight in the eye so he could see me. Really see me. See the terrible version of me I had become. 'Let's not talk about it, please.'

He nodded slowly, his eyes still shadowed with concern. But that wasn't my problem. I needed to repair the walls once again, brick by brick.

By the time I was done, all the various conversations around the table had also ground to a halt and we all looked expectantly at Dad, the de facto decision-maker, seated next to Ben, who had Jo playing on his lap with a tablet and she was, no surprise there, humming Ed Sheeran again.

That one scene was enough to remind me this man was ready for such commitments as fatherhood and marriage. To my lovely, deserving cousin.

GOD!

# Chapter Eight

*D*ad cleared his throat and I focused on the matter at hand. He leaned back in his chair exposing the faintest line of sweat around his armpits. The grey T-shirt he wore was old. I remembered it from my early twenties and it had, at one point, been navy blue in colour. Dad believed in 'waste not, want not', a thing that drove my clothes horse mom crazy. I wished I was close enough to my dad to tell him something as casual as to throw the T-shirt away. But I wasn't and that was that.

'Banjeet, why don't you do the needful?' Dad invited.

Ben nodded, sitting up straighter. Ahalya scooped Jo from his lap in a practised move. I felt a tiny pang right inside my chest.

Ben opened his laptop and moved the touchpad around till the proper document opened up. 'I'd like to begin by saying how very sorry I am for your loss. Chandralekha Chakrapani was a tough, formidable businesswoman, who strongly believed in the core that was her family.'

He paused and lowered the screen a bit so he could address each of us gathered around the table, making eye contact with everyone. He had on a lawyer face—a face I knew from watching too many episodes of *Boston Legal*. It was a distantly concerned but polite look and began and ended in the eyes. Ben was very good at it.

'I know this is a very, *very* unusual way of doing this and I'd have been fired from my previous place of employment by conducting a will-reading in such informal circumstances.' He smiled, as if to lighten the moment. No one smiled back.

'Luckily, Chandralekha took a chance on me when my solo practice was just getting started three years ago and I am grateful to her. So, here we are.'

Silence.

'Tough crowd,' he murmured almost to himself. 'Okay, then. Let's get down to it. There are bequests for everyone in the family, including those not present here, beginning with a check of one lakh for all the family members. Including the new granddaughters-and grandson-in-law.'

The crowd murmured. A faint murmur.

'Does it include great-grandkids?' Ahalya asked.

Ben nodded. 'Yes. Including the great-grandkids. But first let's tackle the business, shall we?'

He read out a bunch of formal-sounding terms, which basically boiled down to Dad, Deep and Varun—the three sons—inheriting all of Paati's assets in the company, something already executed four years ago, at her eighty-fifth birthday. This was expected. The proceeds of the house in Chennai and Bengaluru, both company properties, which had been sold off six months ago, were equally divided between the three daughters-in-law. This was a surprise move that I hadn't expected.

All other corporate estate matters such as bank account transfers and credit lines were tabled for later. Ben was apparently very thorough at his job.

I was impressed.

But, then again, he'd studied law at Yale, where he'd been dumped by a woman named Michaela. He'd have to be thorough to get through a fancy Ivy League school and run his own business.

'The business side of things is still being handled by Gopal Shankar of Sharma, Shankar and Associates. I just gave a thumbnail version,' he said. 'Now, we come to the matter of Chandralekha's actual last will and testament. Her personal effects, jewellery, her personal checking and savings account, and…this house, Chakrapani Illam.'

'And the bequests,' Ahalya added.

I wanted to ask her to hush. Yes, I knew she was working twelve-hour days for CP Tea, the family business. And yes, I knew that having your mother die and divorcing your philandering husband on the grounds of mental cruelty, all within months of each other, meant that you turned into a grasping shrew, but jeez, she needed to calm down. Talking about money was so uncouth.

'And the bequests,' Ben agreed.

He read out the list of jewellery Paati had, a lot of which went to the three daughters-in-law, equally.

'The diamond nose ring, part of Chandralekha's wedding trousseau, she bequeaths it to Gomti Raghavan.' Mom blinked rapidly and clutched Dad's shoulder. *Good for you, Mom.*

Ahalya and Kiki also got smaller diamond studs, which they had always admired, while Gargi and Prapti, the granddaughters-in-law received sturdy gold chains. Ben moved on to the bank accounts, while I felt myself grow hot under the neck. *Where was my jewellery? Why didn't I get anything? What was this?*

Unfortunately, Subhadra interrupted the reading. 'You forgot to share what jewellery Lasya gets, Banjeet.' He paused and gave me a quick look. I adopted an unconcerned expression. He checked the document on screen and gave a small shake of his head. 'Sorry. She doesn't get any jewellery.'

The expression froze on my face. My neck flamed. I clenched the chair tighter, while my gut churned.

'She can have my chain,' Prapti, ever the generous soul, offered immediately.

'Don't be silly,' I said casually. 'I hate jewellery. Everyone knows that. Paati knew it too.' I waved a cold hand at Ben. 'Please continue.'

Mercifully, he took my cue and continued. The bequests were

again mentioned, each of us receiving a cool six figures for nothing other than being related to Paati. The rest of the money in her checking and savings account was to be given away to a charitable organization of our choice. It was a hefty sum, amounting to eight figures, so we tabled that discussion for a later date.

'Finally, we come to the house, Chakrapani Illam, and the surrounding 1 acre of personal property and lawn, solely owned by Chandralekha after her husband's demise. As you all know, Chakrapani Iyer bought the land in 1935 and had the house built after Independence. The original value of this estate was around ₹3000. Now, it's worth a thousand times more, at our most recent estimation.'

I did the math. That was like 30 crore. Some *serious* money. Legit money.

'The house and all its contents is willed to Vidhaant and Gargi Rajendran, Ahalya Sukumar, Krutika Iyer and her husband-to-be Trilok Gujral, Atharva and Prapti Raghavan, Vivek Varun Iyer, Maya Varun Iyer and Lasya Raghavan. With the sole condition that they don't sell it for the next year.'

'But—' Deep was blank as he tried to find words. The rest of us were too shocked to make any sound.

'The bequest checks will appear in your bank accounts as soon as the devasam concludes on the twelfth day and the paperwork for the deed transfer is already underway. There is a single clause though, that I have to mention here.'

'What clause?' Varun asked heavily. 'What now?'

Ben was faintly apologetic, especially towards my dad. 'Everyone in the family, including the great grandkids present, have to live together in Chakrapani Illam for the duration of the twelve-day rites. Without leaving the house for any reason whatsoever.'

For a second, we could hear a pin drop.

Then Varun asked calmly, 'What?'

'Are you nuts?' This was Kiki.

'This is fucked up,' Vidhaant muttered.

'I'm sorry, but those were her express wishes. And it's all signed and documented in the proper manner. If any of the inheritors leaves before the stipulated days are over, the whole will is null and void and all the money, the house, excepting the business, which is handled by Gopal Shankar—all of it, will go to the Munnar Tea Estate Labourers' Association.'

'I don't understand,' Kiki said slowly.

'What's to understand?'

'It's just ten more days,' Mom said bracingly. 'Yesterday and today are already over, we count it from the day of death, not cremation. So that leaves us ten more days. Right?'

She looked to Subhadra for confirmation, who did some mental math and nodded quickly.

'But I am getting married in seven days,' Kiki insisted. 'Dad said I could get married. It would be a low-key wedding, but that we could still go to the venue and everything. We've booked a tent. We've booked a *caterer*.' Her voice rose at the very end.

We all looked as one at Ben. He shook his head, some of his hair falling on his forehead. 'Can't leave the house. For any reason whatsoever.'

Kiki shook her head desperately. 'But Paati knew I was getting married. She knew how much this meant to me. She wouldn't do this to me.'

'Can we put the house on the market when we are done living here for twelve days? Sell it next year?' Ahalya asked.

Deep sucked in a shocked breath. 'What are you talking about, Ahalya? This is our home. This is our family's home. No one is selling anything.'

'No offence, Chitta, but that decision belongs to me, I think.'

God, she could be such an avaricious woman sometimes.

'And us,' Atharva added quietly. 'We own the house too. All of us… And I can't stay. I have a job to get back to. All of us do. Vidhaant's kid is sick. Gargi can't make it. Prapti has…a work thing she has to get back to, on Monday. We can't be under house arrest for the next ten days. It's barbaric.'

'It's just ten days, guys,' I said equably, trying to be the peacemaker for once. 'It doesn't mean much in the larger scheme of things. And, of course, we aren't selling the house. It's our home.'

Ahalya whirled on me with all the fury of a banshee. 'You! Nothing means anything to you in the larger scheme of things. Not this family and not this home. And it's all alright for you, isn't it? You can take ten days off, it's not like you have a real job that requires you to punch in a time card. Or school lunches to plan. You have a fancy house in Mumbai and all that blood money you profited from our misery. YOU DON'T NEED ANYTHING, DO YOU?'

# Chapter Nine

*I* stared, stricken at my cousin sister in utter and deafening silence. The venom that dripped from her words, the corrosive bitterness she carried under her impressive chest and the hostile accusation in her eyes, I felt like a worm. I felt lower than a worm. I was worm fodder.

'I didn't mean it like that,' I spoke in a small voice.

My dad's contemptuous glance withered what little self-respect I had left. Clearly, he believed everything Ahalya said. And, even worse, he was right. They were all right. Dad held up a hand when everyone else started talking at once, in a combination of rapid-fire Tamil and English. 'The elders need to discuss this,' he said in Tamil. That shut everyone up. Then, he continued in English, 'Ben, have you emailed me a copy of this document?'

Ben nodded. 'I did yesterday before flying down. I wanted to check and see if everything was alright. I could stay and go over it point by point, if you have any doubts.'

'Thank you, but I think we need to talk about things ourselves, right now.' Dad sounded like the ruthless businessman he was. When Ben acquiesced wordlessly, he continued, 'Alright, then. We'll discuss this and let you all know what we come up with. Ahalya, Jo's really sleepy. You should take her to bed. The rest of you also. You must be tired.'

'But, Mama[27]—' Vidhaant began.

'Bed. Now. All of you.' Dad was terrifying when he set his mind to it.

---

[27]Mother's brother

So, the youngsters, meaning all the grandkids and their respective spouses, dispersed in various directions. Jo was actually sleepy, so Ahalya went to her room to put her to bed. Atharva, Prapti, Kiki and Trilok ditched me to hang out with their respective parents, which left Ben and me alone again, at the bottom of the stairs.

'Ahalya probably needs help with Jo. Jo likes to read stories before sleeping.' I pulled the sari up and tucked more of it under my waist. It created a huge tire-like bulge but I didn't really care about that anymore. I cared about nothing much actually. The charged encounter with Ahalya and my dad had drained me.

'That's alright.' Ben walked cautiously up the stairs beside me. His laptop brushed against my side. 'I think your cousin would like some alone time to cool down.'

'Yeah, like all she needs is some time.' I couldn't keep the bitterness out of my voice.

'This whole day has been a bit of a shock for everyone, you know,' he said quietly. 'Including you.'

'Did you even try and talk Paati out of her crazy requests? Or did you just type everything up for her like a dutiful little drone?'

His eyes widened, registered shock and hurt and I bit my lip. That watchful thing also came and went in his eyes. I wanted to believe it was interest in me, sexual interest, but who was I kidding? I was no one's idea of sexy at the moment.

Also, I was lashing out at a perfectly decent guy for no reason than that he was here. 'I am not going to apologize to you once more. I physically can't do it.'

'I didn't ask you to apologize.'

'Even if I was being a dick?'

His lips quirked up, under the beard. 'Even so. You get a free pass today.'

My stomach fell, just like it had when I'd missed the step.

Timing had never been my strong suit. Neither was picking an appropriate man to be attracted to. So, it was a combination of desolation and defensiveness that made me open my mouth.

'I shouldn't get a free pass after what I did. To Ahalya. You know, she hates me because I ruined her marriage and my aunt died of the shock and shame, and I can't ever make it up to her. I can't make it up to anyone. And I can't apologize for that because apologies won't bring my athai[28] back or make my ex-brother-in-law a decent human being. And I don't have a fancy home anymore. I put it up in the market but it won't sell. It won't sell,' I whispered.

He made a gesture, lifting his hand like he wanted to touch me, but I flinched. I kept my wounded eyes on him. I knew they were wounded because my soul was. Every part of me was.

'Everyone feels sorry for her and they should. She's had rotten luck with men and marriage. The last two years have been unkind to her.' I touched his shoulder. He tensed and I dropped my hand. 'Please make her happy, okay? Please change her luck. She needs it more than I ever will.'

Then I picked up the trailing pallu of my sari and climbed the stairs awkwardly. Ben stood where he was and I didn't really expect him to follow me.

Tears poured down my face by the time I reached the second-floor attic. I stumbled inside, the sari coming undone and trailing alongside me. I made a beeline for the bed, which was just three mattresses piled one on top of another, tucked with a cotton sheet, and sank down into it while I sobbed. Loudly. Unendingly. Like my heart was breaking.

---

[28] Aunt

And it was. For the grandmother who did not think me worthy of passing on her family heirlooms, for the father who would not even speak to me anymore because I'd brought shame and dishonour on his family name, and for the cousin sister who hated my living guts. I was weeping my heart out, burying my face in my hands, my hair hanging over my head.

Subhadra aunty would have been proud of me.

I didn't even know when Ben entered the room and crossed over to the bed. But, I did feel the mattress sink under his weight. Then I felt his arm come around my shoulder and he tucked me against him, a warm and solid presence I could rest against.

He didn't say a word, while I cried like the world was ending.

A long while later, I raised my aching, cotton-heavy head and sniffled. There was a huge wet patch on his chest where I'd done some serious water damage.

'You're a glutton for punishment.'

His arm fell off as I put a sedate 2 inches of distance between us. I'd left exactly one small bulb on as illumination and I'd be damned if the bulblight did not flatter Ben Dewar, just like the bathroom tiles had.

'I am a lawyer,' he said easily. 'Gluttony and punishment are two of our favourite things.'

I sniffled again and inelegantly used the edge of the quilt to wipe at my hopelessly blotchy face. 'That's twice you've seen me with tomato nose.'

'Yuck. I hate tomato noses. I like bulge-y ones. They show character.' He tapped his own.

I mock-glared at him. 'You're being very insensitive, you know? What happened to me getting a free pass for the day?'

'I changed my mind.'

'I beg your pardon?'

Ben shrugged negligently. 'It's not just women who get to

change their minds. This is a new world. Equal opportunity and everything.'

I grimaced in answer.

His slight smile faded and his expression changed. 'Ahalya was out of line back there. She shouldn't have said those things with everyone present. I'm sorry about that.'

He placed his laptop on the other side and stroked it. He didn't have perfect fingers. They were a bit hairy and ended in square, stubby tips. But they were long. I wondered how they would feel against my waist, which was about 3 inches from his left hand.

'The Chakrapani clan is used to public showdowns.' I smiled a bit. 'And public executions.'

'I am guessing you've seen a few in your time?'

I worried the quilt and dabbed at my gritty eyes again. 'There was one. When my grandpa found out that an employee had been embezzling from the company. It was summer vacation so we were all there, Atharva, Kiki, Vidhaant, Ahalya and me. I must have been about eight. The man was called home for lunch. Paati had the cook make a four-course meal, with elevan, morkootan, avial and pappadam. The dining table was different back then, smaller. So we kids ate in the kitchen. But we came out when the yelling started.' I smiled, remembering the hijinks and drama of that long ago day.

'It was a very vivid scene. Thatha, my grandpa, was gesturing wildly and the man was yelling back, "You can't do this to me," in Tamil and with a lot of curses in between. Then, Thatha threw a white packet at the man's feet and a bunch of ₹100 notes spilled out. And the man shut up.'

'Whoa! Dramatic.'

'So dramatic,' I agreed. 'The man picked up the money, spit at my grandfather's feet and left. At the time, it was such a grand scene. We enacted it for days in this attic. All of us wanted to be the guy who spit at Thatha.'

'That must have been…fun.'

'It was only after I grew up that I realized how fucked up the whole thing was,' I said softly. 'My grandpa acting like some sort of colonial feudal lord and the employee spitting on him.'

'Well.' He leaned back, palms on the mattress and looking up at the wooden rafters that supported the stone columns. 'All's fair in the tea-growing business.'

I gave a watery chuckle. My voice was dull from the crying and my nose was clogged up. Impulsively, I reached over and squeezed his hand. He stilled instantly and gave me a wary look.

'I'm sorry, Ben. You're not an asshole. Not in any way. So, I was epically wrong about that. And I am glad Paati chose you to execute her last wishes. Even if you had to bear witness to all that family drama just now.'

'My entire profession might die out if we didn't have family drama to sustain us.'

To my eternal surprise, he left his hand underneath mine. He didn't twine our fingers together like the hero does to the heroine in the movies but he didn't seem to be totally repelled by me.

'That is a gross exaggeration, I am sure.'

'Then it must be true.'

Somehow, our heads were close. Closer than they had been seconds before. Our eyes and mouths perfectly aligned. And he smelled of crisp linen and hope and whatever it was that he felt for me, it was back in his golden eyes. We were still holding hands.

'I can't stop thinking about the projectile vomit,' I said. I could not believe I'd said it out loud.

He slid his hand out from under mine. Tilted his head back. 'Projectile vomit. The most effective mood killer, ever.' Then, he gathered his laptop and balanced it on one knee.

I drew my knees up and balanced my chin on it. I spoke to

the ground. 'My last relationship...if it could be called that...it ended disastrously.'

'Most of them do, LJ.' He stood up. 'That's why they end at all.'

'It wasn't projectile-vomit bad, of course. Nothing can be. But it was bad enough that I spent New Year's Eve pigging out on pepperoni pizza and whipped cream and crying while watching *Sacred Games*.'

'Okay,' he said cautiously.

Now the moment was well and truly ruined. And the mood was murdered beyond repair.

'I'm just saying, I am a piping hot mess. I know it and I am not going to...inflict myself on anyone right now.'

Something about him, that tree-like quality maybe, made me open my normally filtered mouth and spill everything.

'Sure.'

'And besides,' I gave him an indignant glare, as I realized how unfair this whole thing was. 'You're into Ahalya, right? You guys even matched on Shaadi.com and what not. You shouldn't even be here in the first place.'

'Are we in high school or something?'

My indignation turned into fury, because he sounded more amused than upset by my accusation, which sounded perfectly logical in my head.

'What does that mean?'

'It means that I know when I am not wanted and I make a graceful exit. You take care of yourself, Lasya Raghavan.'

Then he did the nod thing which I was beginning to hate, and that was ridiculous, but there you go. And then he left.

I told myself Ben leaving was a good thing. He was way too put together and decent for me. I'd probably just destroy what was left of him. That argument worked for all of three minutes, then common sense reasserted itself and I rushed up to go after him.

Of course, I'd forgotten what I was wearing, so I spent precious seconds untangling myself from the sari, dumping it on the bed, and tugging on a T-shirt over the petticoat so I was somewhat decent before I rushed downstairs.

I skidded to a stop on the landing of the first floor, because the first door on the left was ajar and I could see Ben inside. He was talking to my father, of all people. I didn't move. I couldn't.

Ben ran a hand through his hair. 'Look, Mr. Raghavan, I know the situation and I still think the best thing for you to do is—'

'Ben, you don't know the situation as well as you think you do,' Dad interrupted him quietly.

'I spent the last fifteen minutes consoling your weeping daughter. I know the situation,' Ben shot back.

My eyes widened; my breath froze. They were talking about *me?* Whatever for?

'So, then you know why I am not going to do it.'

'Mr Raghavan.' Ben put a hand on Dad's shoulder, somehow dwarfing him with that one gesture. 'Uncle, LJ has a right to know, too. You can't keep it from her. You shouldn't. Please tell her now. Tonight.'

Dad's answer was a low murmur that I couldn't quite catch and, to be honest, I didn't want to.

I went back upstairs in a daze. My mind reeling, my breath hitching. The guy I could maybe see myself liking, who was actually decent to me, had been talking to my dad, the man who hadn't spoken to me in two years, about me. *Me!* The inconsequential offspring. The worst daughter ever.

I didn't know what to make of all this, except here was another thing my dad thought I didn't need to know. It shouldn't have hurt me so much. I should be used to it by now.

But it hurt all the same.

# Chapter Ten

'Guess what? We are all under house arrest for the next ten days.' Atharva breezed in a little later.

I was struggling into my nightclothes. Actually, considering how many work-from-home days I'd taken at Toilethumour.com, the tee-flannel pants ensemble could easily double up as office wear.

'Shut the fucking door, idiot!' I clutched the T-shirt to my chest, while I hissed at him.

His eyes rounded and he quickly turned his back to me.

'God, couldn't you have done so in the first place?' he muttered. But he shut the door as I'd asked. Then he raised his brows at the sari mess artlessly draped on the mattress. 'My wife is a saint to put up with you, Kutty[29].' Atharva only used the dreaded nickname when he wanted to irritate me.

'Yeah, I know. Everyone knows I am pathetic and a loser, so you can just shut it. Also, is everything okay with Praaps? She isn't her usual, hyper-chipper self.'

As I was talking, I retied the drawstring on the plaid pants. They were old and comfortable, and contoured to my size-33 waist without judgement or the hassle of such things as buttons and zippers. I'd measured myself on Christmas eve because I wasn't masochistic enough.

By mutual agreement, we'd moved to the sari and were now holding the two ends like the workers of a dhobi ghat. We'd done this as kids too, folding Paati's or Mom's saris, after they had dried

---

[29]Little one

in the backyard under the crisp summer sun. Those saris were georgette too, or cotton, simple plain things that we'd loved to play catch-catch under.

'Prapti's just fine. Stop deflecting.' His words were clipped. 'And no one thinks you are pathetic or a loser. You can stop being a mopey brat anytime you feel like it.'

I glared at him. Atharva calmly continued folding the sari into halves, coming three steps closer to me.

'Ahalya didn't attack you in the living room. Our dad is still talking to you. In fact, I bet he wants to declare you his sole, living heir for being so amazing and perfect. So, don't call me mopey if I want to take a moment and wallow in the unfairness of it all.'

'You deserved all of that,' he shot back. I folded the next half and took two steps closer to him. 'And you can start by saying hello to Dad, you know,' Atharva muttered. 'He doesn't have to make the first move himself.'

'He was the one who threw me out of the house when the stupid book came out.'

'Yeah, because you'd written such a flattering description about him in the stupid book, right? What was it?' Atharva folded the last bit and tugged the square folded bit of fabric from me. '"My father was a distant, Messianic figure for most of my childhood. He gave us pocket money, tongue lashings, and absent hugs in equal amounts and considered it good parenting."'

He finished folding the sari, aligning the sequined borders neatly, so the edges were razor straight. My scowl should have melted the smirk right off his face. It didn't.

Atharva raised knowing eyes to me. 'Was that right?'

'No.'

'Of course, it was.'

'I didn't say Messianic. I said Machiavellian,' I replied stiffly.

My brother laughed. It was a harsh sound that echoed. 'And

you wonder why our father won't talk to you, LJ.'

'It was just a book,' I protested. 'It was fiction. Not real.'

'Is that what you told that *Times* reporter?' he asked me softly.

I had no answer to that. Because I hadn't told the *Times* reporter that. Or indeed any of the reporters who'd interviewed me back when *Spectacular* came out. Back when I had milked my family's alleged dysfunction for all it was worth. When I had been hot shit and arrogant with it.

'That's what I thought.' His soft words were condemning enough.

'I can't stay here for one more day if this is the attitude I have to put up with.'

I was dead serious. I couldn't. There was a limit to how much humiliation and debasement even I could take. And, admittedly, over the course of the last few months, my threshold had expanded. But there was a limit. Staying under the same roof as my family who wanted to stone me for my very many sins was that limit. It was the outer limit. Even Kiki wasn't above pushing back at me and calling me names when it came right down to it.

'You can't leave. None of us can. Not even Kiki, and she isn't making as much of a fuss as you are.' He was so logical I had to pause my pity party.

I might have a trenchant family that was, at best, tolerating me, but Kiki was missing out on marrying the love of her life.

'There's really no getting out of it? Gopal uncle is on board with it?' This seemed unbelievable. A piece of paper couldn't just make us stay where we didn't want to stay, with people we didn't want to. Not for all the money in the world.

Atharva sighed. 'He is. Appa and Deep uncle spoke to him and then Mom came and told me. We're having a breakfast meeting at 8 tomorrow. The visitors will start to arrive by 9. You are on tea-making duty along with Kiki.'

'What? Fuck. No. I am not making tea.'

He shrugged. 'Whatever.'

'Atharva,' I began, intending to ask him about the strange conversation Ben had had with dad.

'What?'

I shook my head. I couldn't. It was stubborn pride refusing me to scrounge for information about my father, like it had refused me to beg for scraps of affection in my childhood. No, if Dad didn't want to tell me whatever 'it' was, then I didn't want to know.

'Nothing.'

Before Atharva could attempt to pry it out of me, Kiki barged in, her eyes red-rimmed, and came straight to me. I hugged the life out of her, while she tried to control her tears. Atharva sighed and rubbed her back.

'I'm sorry. About the wedding.' My words of comfort were trite, but they were all I had. As if we didn't have enough to feel shitty about.

'Trilok's parents are flying back tomorrow. They figure there is no point hanging around with the wedding cancelled.' She sniffed.

I gestured to my brother to hug her too. With an aggrieved expression, Atharva put his arms around her. She stood stiff and unyielding between the both of us. I hugged her tighter. It helped that I had a lot more flesh to push back into her, although Kiki defined the word 'babe' in her cute navy-blue pyjamas with a matching bed jacket.

'You're way too obsessed with getting married,' I said. 'With a boyfriend you've known for as long as you've known Trilok.'

'I'm not a cynic like you. I'm a romantic.' She sniffled again and wiped at her cheeks. Then she looked critically at me, since we were in such close quarters. 'Dude, you look like shit. Actual shit. What happened to you?'

'I ugly cried after I came up,' I confessed to her.

'Ahalya's a witch.' Kiki rubbed my arm bracingly. And hugged me back tight.

'I deserved it.' I sniffled too.

'Yes,' Atharva added helpfully. 'She totally did.'

'Okay, we aren't going to cry anymore,' Kiki announced with determination, not all of it fake. 'This is dumb. Paati would kick our asses if she saw us being these weepy, mooning females. Then she'd make us write impositions.'

'Crying feels very productive right now. It is the proper way to grieve.'

Sounding older than her years, Kiki said, 'There's no proper way to grieve, babe. We can do whatever we want that helps.'

It sounded almost the same as what Ben had told me. And it made so much sense to me, who had so much grieving to do. I was the queen of endings too.

And it was that statement that haunted me for the rest of the night as I thought about my paati and the long, mostly amazing life she'd led—which *had* included making us write impositions, or pick tea along with the other workers or warning our mothers that their daughters were running wild and no one would marry us—the spectacular melancholy of living, and Ben and that almost-inappropriate kiss and the fact that maybe I *did* have to talk to my father. Even if he was Machiavellian and gave absent hugs, tongue lashings and pocket money and considered it good parenting.

Even if I felt like I didn't deserve any of it.

In the middle of the night, my phone buzzed and I picked it up out of habit. It was a text from Atharva: *We need industrial-strength Wi-Fi if we have to survive 10 fucking days. Right?*

Despite myself, I smiled. Here I was, undergoing a major

existential crisis, our grandmother's ashes were still cooling in the fancy urn we'd purchased for it, and all my brother could think about was a working Internet connection. I guess Dad had passed on his Machiavellian tendencies to us, after all.

## Chapter Eleven

'Hi, Dad,' I murmured under my breath as I took my place in the formal dining table, next to Vidhaant and far away from Ahalya. Vidhaant was in the chair next to Dad's, at the head of the table. Ben wasn't to be seen.

I felt funny because the seat next to Ahalya was taken by Atharva. Ahalya was sitting on the opposite end; Jo was playing with her hair, twisting it in curls. I used to do that too, years and years ago. Ahalya always had amazingly beautiful hair, which she took manic, religious care of by applying a paste of egg yolk, ground coffee beans and yoghurt. It shamed me that I was only now noticing how lanky her curly mane of hair had become. And the crow's feet at the corner of her tip-tilted eyes. Or that her lips were always pinched, as if she had too much to worry about.

And, of course, she did. Being a single mom to an energetic seven-year-old and working a demanding job with my father as boss would ensure that she was always stressed. I had always thought that working in the family business—she was the only one among us who did—would be a breeze. I'd forgotten to factor in my father.

Now, I judged my moment. He took his seat, pinching the bridge of his nose while he checked his phone.

'Hi, Dad,' I said loudly.

Dad looked up from the screen.

'Good morning,' I said equably.

'Is everyone here?' he asked of the table in general.

Our eye contact lasted precisely two seconds. Two seconds longer than it had been in two years. So I'd take what I could get.

'Trilok's still showering, but we can start without him. Prapti is getting the last batch of idlis. It will take her two minutes,' I answered. 'How are you holding up?'

'We can wait two minutes,' he said. Then he bent back to his phone.

Mom, who had settled on the other side of Dad, gave me a small smile. It was encouraging and a damn sight different than her eternal why-can't-my-kid-behave face. I took heart from it.

'I am doing okay too,' I continued. 'The job's alright. I have to call up Puru, the editor, and inform him of my change in plans. He won't be happy. But I guess we all have to suck it up.'

Dad gave me a long, wordless stare. I watched as a single drop of water dripped down the collar of his ironed T-shirt. He too had more greys than the last time I'd seen him, and clearly he was not patronizing the salon in Kochi that he had ten years ago, when the greys had first turned white. And did he always have that small bald patch right near the forehead?

*Say something,* I pleaded with my eyes. *Say anything. Tell me whatever 'it' is Ben asked you to tell me. Please. Give me some sign that you aren't going to hold the one thing I did against me forever and ever. Please.*

Dad slid his eyes away and nodded. 'Prapti's here. We can talk and eat at the same time. Then the vaadhyar is coming for the next round of pujai[30] at 9.30.'

Vidhaant put his hand up. 'Mama, do we all have to attend all the pujais?'

Dad's lips thinned and I caught Atharva's eye. He shook his head in an uh-oh motion.

'Of course, not,' Dad replied. 'There is no compulsion to attend any of the pujais and rituals. I know everyone has to log in to

---

[30]Puja

work or take con calls.'

'Awesome. Thanks.' Vidhaant dug into his tasteless idli and accompanying coriander chutney with gusto.

'I'd just like to say that I am thankful you all are here,' Dad continued coolly. 'I understand how busy everyone's schedules are. And that spending ten days cooped up in the house with us elders is not your ideal vacation.'

'It never was, Dad,' Atharva said. He was out of the kill zone, sitting on the opposite end too. So he could afford to be cheeky. 'We hated all the times you forced us to come here and vacation with the idiots we call cousins.'

'Back at you, Atharva anna,' Kiki said cheerfully.

'Krutika!' Subhadra admonished Kiki. 'Sorry, Anna. I apologize for my silly daughter's poor manners.' She gave her daughter a laser stare. Kiki stuffed a piece of banana in her mouth.

'Amma always loved a full house.' Dad's voice was not as strong as it had been a second ago. Mom squeezed his hand, much like I had Ben's last night. Except, Dad did the movie hero thing and held hers back tightly. 'So, she will be glad you are all here too. Gopal has informed me that Ben did a thorough job with the will and we can't contest it in any way, not without looking like squabbling fools.'

'No one is going to contest the will,' Deep grunted. 'We are civilized people. We don't squabble over family.'

'What about if we want to tweak some parts of it?' Ahalya demanded. 'Also, if I am stuck here in this house, who is going to oversee the contract negotiation in Chennai with our new logistics supplier?'

'We can postpone it, Ahalya. You can take a crack at it when we leave here.'

'Alright. And what about—'

Varun held up a hand. 'Ahalya, sweetie. You can schedule a

mini-meeting and talk work and assignments with Anna once he is done with the funeral rituals. Right now, let's just get through this family meeting?'

I wanted to cheer for him. Go, Chitta!

'Right. Family,' Dad murmured to himself. 'In accordance with the terms of the will, we can't leave the house unless it is for official funeral duties. We meet for breakfast, lunch and dinner and the women take rotations entertaining the guests. The local community is holding a small function on Friday, honouring Amma and all the little ways she has helped grow our mountain, so we will be attending that. The lawyer has already signed off on it.'

'I'm going to need help with the speech I have to give for the occasion,' Mom said. She said it looking at me, so I nodded.

'I know all of you are going to have to put your lives on hold, but I hope you don't mind.'

'Of course, we don't mind, Appa,' Prapti said. And, to her credit, she seemed like she meant it.

Dad gave Kiki a rueful glance. 'We talked it over yesterday with Trilok's parents and they are going to look for another mahurat, the soonest one. I am so sorry, Kunju[31]. I wanted to continue with the wedding as arranged. Even call all the guests.'

'That's alright, Uncle,' Trilok answered for the both of them, while he too squeezed Kiki's hand tightly. More in warning than anything else. 'Kiki and I have been through too much to give up now. We waited seven years for the big day. What's another month, right?'

He kissed the back of Kiki's hand and her eyes promised holy retribution even though she nodded stiffly. Kiki wasn't afraid of a lot of things, her tramp stamp butterfly tattoo was proof enough of that, but even she dared not cross my father.

'Sure, Perippa,' Kiki said through clenched lips. 'I don't mind.'

---

[31]Little one

'I would hope that your work, important as it is, would not mean everyone skipped meals. Show up for at least one family dinner, everyone.'

'We will, if you will,' Atharva said.

Dad silenced him with a single, piercing look. Atharva bent his head down and played with his idli. 'I stand by it,' he muttered to no one in particular.

'Mama works extremely hard, Atharva,' Ahalya jumped to his defence. 'God knows, it's not been easy carrying on everything alone. Especially when people want hep, cool brands like Chaayos with fancy names like Soy Chai Latte and not good old home-grown tea like we make it.'

'Then maybe we should merge with Chaayos and be done with it,' Atharva retorted. I couldn't decide whether I admired him for his balls or I was afraid for him.

A muscle ticked in Ahalya's forehead and Vidhaant gripped her forearm, as if to physically restrain her from going after my brother.

'Thank you for that lovely defence, Kanna[32], but it's quite unnecessary.' Dad gave her a warm, fatherly smile. I never got the endearment or the smile. 'Now, there is one last bit of news I'd like to share with you all before we end this meeting.' He waited a second to ensure he had everyone's attention. 'I'll be retiring at the end of the year. And I have actually decided to sell the company to the first prospective buyer who offers me full market price.'

'FUCK!'

Ahalya's expletive fell into the hushed silence like an explosion waiting to happen. Until Jo stopped sipping her chocolate milk and remarked, 'Mom said a bad word. She needs to go sit in the quiet corner.'

---

[32]Sweetheart

*Hello Puru,*

*Please accept this request for extending my work from home till the fifteenth of this month. I understand that asking for this extension is against official HR policy but we have a 12-day ritual to say goodbye to the dead and I can't, in all good conscience, not attend and ensure that my grandmother enters heaven through the fulfilling of our karma.*

*I will log in at my usual hour and finish all my tasks as required and be available on Slack, mobile and via video chats for any and all emergencies. Work and deadlines won't suffer in my absence.*

*You've always been a fair and understanding manager and we have always had a cordial relationship. So I hope you understand and accept my request in the same spirit.*

*Sincerely, Lasya*

I spell-checked the email a couple times and sent it off. I had a mail tracker app installed on my phone so I knew the second he opened it. As anticipated, my phone buzzed two seconds later.

'What the fuck, LJ?' Puru was his usual loquacious self.

'I know.' I injected some tears in my voice, not that it was super hard to do. My nose was still clogged from yesterday's crying bout and taking cold showers did not help my sinuses. 'I am so sorry, Puru. But it's a family emergency and I understand the anniversary edition is coming up. I promise I'll be online for as long as needed every day starting day after.'

I figured I owed it to myself to take a couple days off and mooch around the house while everyone else worked from home. Maybe catch up on those French films after all.

'I am trying very hard to be understanding here, LJ.' I could hear the clacking of keys, thumping bass and someone yelling, '*Ae, chai laana, bhai*[33] and I felt homesick for a second.

Then I remembered. I hated this job and the headlines and the gross frat-boy humour we used to peddle cupcakes and makeup to an uncaring audience.

'And you're doing a fantastic job,' I assured him. 'Best. Boss. Ever.'

Puru was only mildly flattered. 'Day after tomorrow. You'll log in at 10?'

'9.30'

'Okay, then. And I expect that French film piece by EOD on the sixth.' (Sixth being the day after.)

'Absolutely. You got it,' I promised him recklessly.

Dammit. Now I was going to be forced to watch the movies and come up with appropriate GIFs and memes that made the content 'relatable'.

I sat down on the overstuffed bed where Trilok sprawled, typing furiously on his laptop and contemplated my accommodation with a critical eye—now that I was going to live here for the next ten days. The attic covered the length of the rest of the house and was laid with the stone mosaic tiles that were in vogue in the late eighties and early nineties. The windows, there were four of them, opened up to stunning vistas of tea hills and mountain peaks as far as the eye could see. The glass panes were kept in immaculate condition.

It was January, so no fans were needed, and this was a good thing. There *were* no fans in the place. And it was slightly draughty because of the high ceilings. One wall was covered entirely with

---

[33]Hey! Get the tea, man!

dusty and broken cupboards, odds and ends and huge paintings. A tiered chandelier was balanced precariously on top of the paintings. It looked like a good puff of wind might blow it into a million pieces.

With all of us cousins milling about and claiming individual corners, the attic was suddenly super cramped. I smiled because Atharva and Vidhaant were both jostling for window space as signal reception was the strongest there. I blinked because I could clearly see Ben, in casual pyjamas, leaning down and sharing a joke with Atharva, his lips quirking in that half-smile that caused butterflies in my stomach. I liked to think I was too jaded to believe in something as ephemeral as attraction based on nothing but good looks, but dammit, I was now hallucinating the man. Especially because he and my father were keeping secrets from me about me. The curiosity, that need to know what my father knew, would disappear for a bit but it always returned, bringing with it a burning curiosity, a need for Ben.

I was even morphing him into the perfect family scene, just because I was lonely and alone and a little bit apart. But I didn't feel alone around him, like I was standing apart and observing. I was all there, even my skin tingled with awareness. But, he wasn't here now so I was back to being the observer.

All writers, the good ones who worked on their craft, understand this instinctively. Everything is to be experienced, observed and analysed in a quiet, always-working corner of our mind.

*Everything.* It was the wretched quality that had ruined my relationships with all of these people, in the first place.

I resolved to stick to my New Year's resolution and be kinder to myself as I started on the most important task—that of shopping online for clothes I couldn't afford just so I didn't have to wear the damned sari again.

# Chapter Twelve

*O*ver the next two days, we all occupied different wedges of the attic, creating our own niches. The elders wisely opted to stay downstairs and escape work. Varun was utilizing his vacation days, while Deep uncle had retired with honours from the Army. Dad was stealthily handing over everything to Ahalya.

She was a demon at work. It was downright inspiring and vaguely frightening how she handled emails and phone calls from irate vendors and planned marketing campaigns using nothing more than a working Internet connection, her razor sharp tongue and a laptop that was older than mine—by millennia. I learned a lot about the tea-producing and manufacturing business just by watching her in action.

All this while she was still keeping tabs on Jo, who wandered in and out of the attic every hour or so. Kiki had the bright idea of dragging the TV from Paati's room and rigging up a makeshift theatre opposite my bed.

Then, the party really started.

Between cartoons and educational programmes for Jo, and ridiculous soaps in Hindi and Spanish that were cast from someone's tablet, the noise was at a constant 7 throughout the day. Of course, we all had to take turns and go downstairs and socialize with the guests arriving in hordes.

'Socializing' included serving water or juice to the guests, followed by precisely seven minutes of conversation and moving onto serving dry snacks and tea before graciously escaping. Trilok, our resident scheduler, made up a spinning buddy-chore chart, pretty easy to follow once you gave in to the inevitable. Do the elders' bidding if you want to keep the peace. Even Ahalya was mildly impressed by the colourful, handmade chart. Jo had a ball spinning the thing.

Because I had the inside track with Trilok's fiancée, I was never stuck with anyone other than Kiki or Vidhaant for socializing duty. Kiki and I had a system that we perfected as kids when it came to dealing with unwanted guests—and, I am not sorry to say, most of them were. Please don't get me wrong, there were a lot of genuine well-wishers, people from the neighbouring estates and labourers mostly, whom Chandralekha had helped one way or another.

Stories of how she quietly fed an entire family for a dry winter, or sent some labourer's promising kid to school or bailed out a neighbour with their mortgage and grocery bills were now legion. She had set great store by education, having been yanked out of school at age fourteen.

One of my favourite memories of summers at Chakrapani Illam was Paati calling me to her room after dinner, where she'd be reading the newspaper with her Coke bottle glasses, line by painstaking line. She would then ask me about my exams and how I think I'd fared. If my answers pleased her—she was a stickler for the truth, while I was a bit more creative with honesty—she'd also direct me to open the almirah where Kiki and I had found the photo albums.

And there, I'd find them all.

*Enid Blyton, Nancy Drew, Amar Chitra Katha, Tinkle, Chandamama, Archie* comics, *Hardy Boys* and, one summer, a stack of *Tintin* comics. I dove into the books, the stories, the worlds. It was a magical, foundation-building time for me.

So, I wasn't really surprised when I heard these stories of how Paati had helped some other kid become a CA or a lawyer or get a job with a local MNC or, in a few cases, make enough so they could afford the jewellery for their daughters to get married. I was proud. Insanely, incredibly proud of my crotchety, curmudgeon, dragon of a grandmother.

When Thatha died, I'd been a child and I didn't have an exact recollection of the amount of people who'd come to pay their last respects to him. But, I did know this. He had been feared and respected. Chakrapani Iyer had been a pillar of the community and given lavishly to the town (there were two bridges named after my ancestors) and he'd even paid for a huge demo crane that could be deployed during the monsoon season when landslides and mudslides abounded.

He'd been a shrewd businessman who took guff from no man.

But, my grandmother was *loved*, in a way that I don't think is possible in today's Instagram-crazy world. She was too opinionated and stubborn and she'd managed to run a small lending bank from her personal savings account, especially helping widows and other needy women. All without my bear of a grandfather finding out. It was incredible.

I didn't even know how to process all the stories, anecdotes and memories. Everyone mostly spoke Malayalam and a smattering of Tamil. But affection and love transcends language and I heard it in their voices, the tears shining in their eyes, the reverent way they touched the garlanded portrait Kiki and I had selected for pride of place.

I am not ashamed to admit that I cried often, as I heard the stories during my rotation, and wondered what it would be like…to be universally loved. A towering success. A pillar of the community.

A woman who didn't care what anyone said about her. Who commanded a seat on the company board, yet insisted on wearing the traditional nine-yard sari until she became too physically frail to carry the weight of it.

My next social-chore rotation happened during lunch break at work. A fact I was immensely grateful for.

The flip side? I had to share it with Ahalya. She did not look pleased to be forced to socialize with me either.

With the magic of one-day delivery, I amassed a sweet wardrobe consisting of mix-and-match kurtis, tunics and ankle-length palazzo pants. I had also ordered three dupattas—one black, one grey and one light pink. They'd work for all the outfits. No more borrowing from Prapti.

Ahalya and I wore cotton tunics in pastel colours under sweatshirts we'd borrowed from the men. Ahalya had on warm leggings, while I wore sweeping palazzo pants that accentuated my non-existent, stumpy legs. Physically, Ahalya and I resembled each other a lot. She too was petite and curved, becoming heavier around the hips and waist after her delivery. But she did power yoga for forty-five minutes at 6 a.m. and ruthlessly maintained her figure as best as she could. Unlike me, the eternal slob who carried her water weight proudly like a newborn baby.

Her spine-length hair was curlier while mine just frizzed, badly, but our features were similar enough—round cheeks, bow-shaped lips and warm brown eyes. Our skin tones were shades closer to each other, so much so that, in her wedding pictures, everyone had commented how much we looked like sisters. Real sisters.

Because it seemed imperative to break the thick, resentful silence surrounding us, I asked, 'Is Jo enjoying the *Harry Potter* set I sent her for her birthday?'

She nodded stiffly. 'Yes. We are on book three now. We read two chapters every night. She's learning to spell "Alohomora" and "Dementors" all by herself now.' Then, as if the words were dragged out of her. 'Thank you. For the books. Everyone else just called. No one sent anything.'

I sighed. The Chakrapani clan was notorious when it came to

gift-giving. Our parents all claimed they had done without gifts in their childhood, so they couldn't understand what all the fuss was about. The second generation had also adopted the same slogan, apart from me.

I was a spendthrift. I bought shit: a BarcaLounger for my brother; the seven-book *Harry Potter* hardback collector's edition for Jo; a backpack for the chai-wala intern at work when his had gotten ruined in last year's Mumbai rains; an apartment for myself that I could not afford to keep anymore…

'She's my kid too, Ahalya. No matter what else is going on between us, I love Jo.'

Ahalya's breath gusted out. 'I never thought you don't care about my daughter.'

And I remembered the exact thing we had fought over. The exact thing I'd told her, when she had confronted me with evidence of her husband's perpetual infidelity. 'Jo deserves better than Sukumar, Ahalya. He is a part-time dad to her because he has another family in Nagpur you didn't even know about. What good will it do to your kid to have such a man in her life, even if he did contribute to her existence?'

I had been so convinced, so morally righteous of what I thought Ahalya should do.

Leave her husband. Leave the world and life she'd built for the last twelve years with the man she loved for the longest time.

Now, of course, I knew different. I knew that Ahalya was amazing and brave and strong in ways I couldn't even fathom. That leaving meant living with a person-sized hole in your heart for the rest of your life. Regardless of who did the leaving.

'I'm glad,' I said. 'I'm glad you still like something about me.'

'Doesn't mean I like the rest of you,' she said shortly, then she ran down before I could do anything to stop her. I descended the stairs at a slower pace, abruptly thinking about Ben and my father's secret, as I did at least twenty times a day. To distract myself, I sent a '*Help Me*' text to Kiki, who immediately sent me back a thumbs up, because she was such a supportive pal. What more could a woman ask for, right?

The middle finger emoji got a workout again, but an incoming call interrupted my rude reply to Kiki's unsympathetic text. Gordhan Vithaldas Real Estate Agent. While a part of me wanted to know why he was repeatedly calling me, I was also waspish enough to keep him waiting. I used the red button and sent him a message: *Busy. Call Later.* I wasn't exactly watching where I was going when I collided with someone on the landing.

'Oh, sorry, excuse me,' I murmured as I raised apologetic eyes. And froze.

'No need to excuse yourself for old friends, babe,' Ahalya said sweetly, while her warm brown eyes glinted at me. 'Gotcha!' they said. 'Right?' She squeezed the arm of the person I had collided with.

The last person on earth I ever wanted to see.

Mehul Jagtap. My ex. The guy who'd expertly played on all my daddy issues before dumping me for being super difficult and 'emotionally fragile'.

# Chapter Thirteen

*M*ehul was beautifully made, with perfectly chiselled cheekbones and a fucking chin dimple that still caused my stomach to dip.

'Hello, LJ,' he said quietly, hands in the pockets of his perfectly pressed jeans. The seams of his pullover stretched on sexy shoulders I'd loved to bite once upon a time. 'I'm so sorry for your loss.'

I was rendered speechless, as past and present and a future that would never be, collided sickeningly inside my head, my chest, my stomach. My very atoms.

'That's very kind of you,' Ahalya said smoothly, drawing her arm through his. He immediately stood up straighter, the gesture speaking to the manly heart of the Jatt he was. 'Why don't you come inside and meet the rest of the family? LJ needs to go to help in the kitchen. She'll come find you later, so you guys can catch up.'

He raised one perfect (styled?) brow in silent enquiry and I had no choice but to nod helplessly as Ahalya smiled venomously at me beside Mehul. Then, ever the perfect hostess, she ushered him to one of the couches where Varun was talking to a couple of local store owners.

My gut churned and I felt nauseous again, but I couldn't run off to vomit. All the bathrooms on the lower floor were occupied and I was not allowed on the upper floors till my shift was up. Besides, I realized with perfect despair, I didn't have anyone who'd follow me to the bathroom and make me feel okay about throwing up.

Ben Dewar wasn't here.

So I straightened my spine, jutted my chin out, took three deep cleansing breaths and walked into the kitchen. If Ahalya had wanted to devastate me, she couldn't have picked a more perfect weapon than shoving the love of my life in my face, someone I had lost due to my own stupidity. It just brought home how much she must really despise me, and what our relationship had spiralled into.

The Chakrapani clan in action was a tragedy in the making.

'I'm so sorry about Paati,' Mehul said an hour later, when he finally found me.

I was plastered to the side of the house, having taken the back door through the kitchen once I was done preparing three more litres of orange Tang and straining more tea than I ever wanted to in my life. I had also arranged cookies and digestive biscuits in large platters in a flower pattern, before escaping from the kitchen.

I did not think Mehul would follow me out here. I jumped, tea spilling down my tunic and staining it an ugly pale brown.

'Shit,' he muttered, 'I'm sorry.' He immediately reached out one long hand to wipe it down. I jumped away from him and hit the side of the door.

Mehul's face telegraphed distress and concern. 'Are you fine?'

I gulped the piping hot tea down; it burnt its way through my oesophagus. I wasn't fine. And he knew it.

'Yes,' I said, when I could finally speak again. 'I am absolutely fine. Never better. You? How are things?'

'Things are alright.' He sighed, running a hand through his perfectly styled hair. 'When did you get here?'

'On the third night. I came with Atharva and his wife.'

'How are they doing? Everyone must be so devastated.' He leaned against the wall, one knee propped up; a pose that was so dear and familiar to me, my heart clenched despite everything.

'She was eighty-nine. It wasn't exactly unexpected.' Then, 'Are you working here now?'

He nodded. 'I manage the estate for Manikuttan's BJ Teas now. Just took the gig last year. I was in Delhi when I heard the news. I wanted to come sooner but...I had things to take care of.'

Mehul's fascination with me, back when we first met in college in Mumbai, was that I was part of a beverage dynasty. Before you think, 'gold-digger', let me just clarify something. He loved the idea of being part of an old, established business—unlike a drone corporation—that was not wheat, sesame, cotton, sugar or the paddy of his beloved Punjab. Aka agriculture. So, that left coal mining, which he was against for moral reasons (something I'd found so hot), rubber plantations and coffee and tea estates.

We'd first become friends, I didn't even have a crush on him or anything. Although after he kissed me on my twenty-fourth birthday, he claimed he'd always liked me in 'that way'.

He hung out and came to the Illam on a couple of occasions and the family loved him. And who wouldn't? He was smart, he had charm and he could reach for things on the upper shelf. The trifecta when it came to deciding life partners in the Chakrapani clan.

Given everything I knew about him, I wasn't surprised at all that he'd taken up a job here in Munnar itself. He'd always told me he wanted to honeymoon here. It was his most favourite place in the world.

'Right.'

There was an awkward pause as we ran out of polite things to say. Finally, I said, 'I tried to call you. After...after the review came out. I wanted to talk to you.'

My heart pounded like I was in the middle of a marathon, pulse drumming in my ear. I figured, now was as good a time as any to get it all out. 'I know you think I screwed up and you were right. I was reckless with the money and overly ambitious writing the play based on the book myself. It would have worked better as a web series. You were right.'

He touched my hand. Just one small touch and my skin went hot with remembered desire. I clutched at his wrist.

'Mehul,' I said urgently. 'I'm so sorry about everything. I knew I took everything that happened out on you. I blamed you for things that weren't your fault.'

'I wasn't completely blameless too.' He gently disengaged himself from my hold. I felt deprived deep inside. 'I was seeing Mini for a solid year before I told you about it. Even though we were just friends in the beginning. I didn't lie about that.'

'I know.' My voice was now a whisper. 'I understand.'

Mehul had stood by me when the entire family nearly ostracized me for publishing *Spectacular* and the awful events that followed. He supported me when I went on a fifteen-city book tour, flying in from the palace hotel he was managing in Jaipur, as often as he could. We'd been together for so long by then, it was a given we'd be together forever.

We'd been together when we were both starting out, it seemed inconceivable we wouldn't be together when we made it.

But that's exactly what happened.

I tried working in Jaipur but I needed to be in Mumbai, where the action was. He commuted once a month but then it became once every three months. Then the phone calls turned into texts and then we only spoke when we missed each other.

Until, one day, I didn't miss him anymore. I still loved him. I will always love him. Mehul was the first man to have seen me naked, to have kissed me senseless, held me when I ugly cried and still wanted me. He was supposed to be my knight in shining armour. But, after five years, the armour wore off.

'I kept waiting for you to say something,' he said quietly. 'Anything. Ask me why I wasn't coming to see you. But you didn't.

You were so preoccupied with your brilliant play that I just didn't feel needed.'

'Oh, so you're saying that you felt the need to bang a twenty-four-year-old hotel receptionist named Mini while you were with me, because I didn't make you feel needed enough?'

Even saying the words out loud brought back those original feelings of inadequacy and disappointment that I could never quite dispel, not since childhood. Not when my father didn't come to watch me win the inter-school debate competition from standard five to ten, or refused to stand in line when I applied for a seat at Mumbai University for my Arts degree. Varun chitta came with me.

Whether knowingly or through unconscious and poor decision-making, I loved a man who had many of my father's characteristics. Withholding, slightly conservative, and so handsome it broke my heart just to see him move sometimes.

Mehul closed his eyes in utter resignation.

Something else I was familiar with. I knew this man. His nuances. The way his beard scratched against the skin of my neck, the shape of his toes. How he took his tea and called my name first thing in the morning.

'Of course not, Lasya. I have apologized endlessly for what I did to you and I know it's not enough. But don't be facetious. I am just saying, you were in a different place than me for the last two years—emotionally. You'd isolated yourself and I didn't know how to reach you.'

'You didn't even try.' It was an accusation. And it was the heart of why I'd never get over him. He'd found another woman, someone less complicated and less 'brilliant' as he'd put it, but he had rejected me.

He'd decided I wasn't worth it anymore. How do you live with the idea of not being worth it to someone anymore? How do you live with the idea that maybe that is your one true place in life?

'I was tired, I guess,' he said finally. 'I'd done it so many times. Picked up all your pieces every time you had a fight with your father. Like, when you defied family tradition and took out your nose piercing, or stayed up partying with your pothead college mates or you didn't accept a job at CP Teas.' I closed my eyes as I remembered each of those instances. 'It was worse when your book came out. When Ahalya wanted to murder you for outing her husband's affair. When you wanted to wait tables in that restaurant in Colaba and your mother thought it was unsafe. I was tired of all the drama.'

'Sorry for being so much trouble.' I stared unseeing at the vista spread before me. My legs turned to lead. *I was tired of all the drama.* Like, constantly having to defend your life and career choices was a hook I used to make my life interesting. Like, I didn't wish every night for things to be different.

Like I didn't wish every night to be *different*. Be anyone other than me.

'I didn't mean it like that.'

'Yes,' I said evenly. 'You did.'

When another awkward pause began taking root, I asked politely, 'So, how is Minika? Still going to the gym for three hours every day, like that's a legit career move? Do we even have gyms here in Munnar?' I couldn't resist my snicker.

This time, he held my wrist loosely. I was rigid and unyielding, even though my bones started melting. *Maybe he was leaving the home-wrecking whore. Maybe he'd decided our love was inevitable, like I knew it was.* 'Actually, LJ, we're expecting a baby. In July.'

The breath whooshed out of me and I clutched the steel tumbler in my other hand tight enough to hurt. 'That's awesome. Congratulations.' I was so proud of my cool, don't-give-a-fuck voice.

'I didn't want you to find out from somebody else,' he added. 'It's always better to break the news yourself, right?'

'Yeah, right.' I didn't know what was coming out of my mouth, but I assumed it made sense, because Mehul was still looking at me. Albeit cautiously.

'I understand if you're upset.'

I shook my head and tendrils from the loose braid I'd pulled my hair into fell on my face. 'Why would I be upset? Everything's fine. I am absolutely fine. And you're going to be a father. Everything is great!' I was babbling but it was imperative I made sounds, I kept doing *something*. Because if I paused, then I'd scream.

And I'd never stop.

I even gave him a sickly kind of smile. 'Congratulations, Mehul. I wish you two nothing but happiness.'

'LJ.' He took a concerned step toward me. I shook my head and whirled and ran down the slopes to the rows of tea plants that I trampled like a bull in a china shop.

'LJ,' Varun chitta called out from somewhere behind me. 'LJ, you there?'

Hard, little puffs of air were coming out of my mouth and nostrils. Tears dried cold on my cheeks and I wiped them angrily. I didn't know how long I'd been sitting here, in the middle of a row of tea plants, hidden beneath them. The ground too was hard, packed; it hurt my butt. But I welcomed the pain. It distracted me from the other, more real, more agonizing pain of the man I'd thought I'd love forever turning out to be a virile douchebag.

He'd knocked his wife up within six months of marriage.

I dipped my chin in the little hollow created between my knees and shuddered. The plants around me rustled as Varun tramped noisily through the area.

'LJ, dammit. Answer me. Where are you?'

'I'm here,' I said shakily.

'LJ?' He called out in my general direction.

Reluctantly, with no interest whatsoever, I raised one hand and waggled my fingers as high as they'd go. Considering I was so short, I barely made it past the clumps of four-feet-tall tea plants. But he must have spotted me because I could hear footsteps pounding the dirt and, finally, he parted the row I was leaning against and sighed.

'Darling, you nearly gave me a heart attack.' He pressed a comforting arm on my shoulder.

I nearly broke. 'It wouldn't be the first time I gave someone in this family a heart attack.'

Varun tapped his feet; he wore fancy, branded sneakers. They were a kitschy neon green, coloured in patches and incongruous against the sober cream kurta. Unlike the rest of us, Varun did not wear a sweater or an outer layer. He lived in America and braved subzero weather every year. This kind of cold was pleasant for him.

'I'm sorry,' I said softly. 'That was a terrible thing to say.'

Without warning, he dropped down to sit next to me, legs folded at the knees. He groaned. 'God. I am old. I can't do this as easily as I used to before.'

'What? Sit down?' I ventured a tiny smile.

He bumped shoulders with me. He also handed me a dirty black stole. 'Here's your cape, Cinderella. You dropped it in your mad dash through the forest.'

'I think you have your fairy tales confused, Chitta.' But I took the garment and held it against my knees. I'd taken this one from Mom, sneaking into her room when she'd gone for a bath. I'd wanted comfort clothing and wearing something of Mom's always made me feel better. Once upon a time, I'd been able to borrow actual clothes from her—kurtis and blouses—considering we had the same small shoulders and lean waists. Now, I made do with stealing her stole.

'I might, LJ. I am an old man.'

I leaned my head against his shoulder and automatically, his arm came around me. We both stared into absolute dark green and brown, while the air around us smelled like damp earth, manure and tea.

'You know,' he said after a few seconds. 'Amma would make Raghav anna, Deep and me wake up at 4 a.m. and help the workers during picking season. I think I was the only kid in seventh standard to have my very own knife.'

'That was a thoughtful gift.'

'Everyone made fun of me, though. Called me chaikutty[34] and other, less flattering names and your dad always came and punched the kids who did it. Always. Deep was a big coward back then.'

I chuckled. I couldn't imagine my strapping, military-man uncle cowering behind a school bench while my mild-mannered businessman father beat up a kid. It didn't compute. 'This is a very interesting if irrelevant anecdote, Chitta.'

'It's not irrelevant. The point is, people change, sweetheart.' He looked solemnly down at me. Varun didn't look like Dad or Deep uncle. He apparently resembled Chakrapani Thatha's dad. A man with a lean, poet-like face and a calm personality. 'Everyone changes. For the good. For the better. Sometimes the best. It's up to us to decide what we do with ourselves.'

'I can feel a lecture coming.'

'You're thirty-one now. You don't need me lecturing you.'

I winced. 'Ouch. Way to rub it in, Chitta.'

'Don't be silly, kid. You still have decades to go before you feel your age.' But he rubbed my back. 'I saw that Mehul came to pay his respects. You guys talked?'

I nodded. Varun was always supportive of Mehul and me.

---

[34]Chai boy

According to him, Mehul was the rock that would allow me to fly high and return to earth safely. Yeah, my youngest uncle was a closet poet alright.

'We did. He told me he and his bimbo were having a baby. And that he screwed her in the first place because I was emotionally shut down.'

'That's a terrible thing to say.'

'It's true.'

'If you were emotionally shut down, then he was responsible for it too. Two people make up a relationship, darling.' His smile was sweet, conspiratorial. 'You know this. You wrote the book on it.'

The book. The damned book that had begun and ended it all. If I'd not written the book, Mehul would not have married Mini and knocked her up. Ahalya would still be married to the cheating scumbag husband. And I'd have the love and approval of everyone I cared about.

'I was so arrogant, Chitta. I was so sure I was doing the right thing by exposing so many of this family's secrets and calling it art. It was so dumb of me to think there wouldn't be consequences.'

'Next time, stick to fairy tales, will you?' He was so non-judgemental, so understanding, I couldn't help sniffling softly, a lump forming in my throat. 'Also, don't be arrogant *and* stupid, Lasya. You didn't expose any secrets.'

I gave him a wry glance.

He shrugged. 'I am serious. You wrote a book. Was some of it based on your own experiences growing up? Yes. But did it actually bring about the destruction you've taken full responsibility for? Fuck, no. Sukumar was a bad man. A terrible man. And if you'd not had that showdown with Ahalya, I would have. I am so proud of you for that, by the way.'

'Yeah, but Dad hasn't even spoken to me after that.' *And now he won't tell me something that Ben wants me to know.* 'Ahalya hates my guts. And everyone treats me differently. I can see it. Like they want me to fail. And I have failed. On multiple levels.' He had no answer to that, so I continued. 'Sometimes I feel like I have screwed up so monumentally, with everyone—Dad, Ahalya, Mom too... I won't ever be able to make it up to them. I'll never stop disappointing them.'

'Lasya.' He kissed my temple softly. 'You silly girl. Stop being so hard on yourself. The rest of it will fall into place. And no one wants you to fail. We love you. We have strange ways of showing it, but we all love you.'

It seemed impossible to believe it right then. Love did not manifest itself like this. Love was kind and sweet and forgiving. Love accepted. We judged and made fun of each other and were selfish and reckless with feelings. Repressed did not begin to describe our dysfunction. If this was love, I was doomed.

But it was a nice thought to hold on to as I walked back with my uncle, ready to face the firing squad all over again.

# Chapter Fourteen

*A*lain Resnais is one of my favourite storytellers. Not filmmaker or director, but storyteller. His films have the three things that I consider mandatory for classifying any story as great.

- *Compelling characters—Motivations, moralities, behaviour aside, these characters live. Absurdly sometimes, sure, but they live. And they are always true to themselves.*
- *Linear timelines—Not often, but often enough that I can just immerse myself in the story and not wonder constantly if the threads need to be unravelled later. \*Not looking at you,* Hiroshima Mon Amour\*
- *Imagery—All good stories allow the audience to create their own imagery as the story moves forward. Resnais's movies do the same. For instance, in* Hiroshima Mon Amour, *the opening shot of grains of sand and two bodies writhing in the throes of passion are blended together perfectly. It's exactly as if a writer—*

'Move, na?' Trilok nudged me aside and flopped down on the mattress. I was alone in the attic, because everyone had dispersed during my mini-meltdown. Even Ahalya had taken off. I took advantage of the blessed quiet by quickly typing my article.

Trilok peered at my screen and started mouthing the words on the page. 'How do you pronounce Resnais? Rez-nay or Runnai?'

I buffed my reading glasses on the edge of my kurti. 'It's pronounced Rennay.'

'Sexy. I can never sit through these subtitle-y, arthouse films.'

'I know.' I grinned. 'Your idea of a good film is action and nudity. No?'

'I'll take a good storyline too!' he protested.

'Right. And that's why your favourite film of all time is *Shoot 'Em Up*. Because of the storyline.'

I continued typing my thoughts on Resnais's storytelling genius. I had to turn in the French Retrospective piece in a couple hours. Fortunately, I remembered most of the films, Goddard's and Resnais's specifically, from my college days. And so a quick refresher course was enough to get the juices flowing. That, and the threat of a looming deadline.

'Well. Monica Bellucci is a beginning, middle and end, isn't she?' He made a gross hourglass motion and I laughed out loud.

'I'd forgotten. You're a perverted man-child and my sister should not be with you.'

Anyone else and I would have filtered my responses, but Trilok and I went way back. He'd crashed at my place while he fought the jung-e-ishq[35] with Kiki's parents, trying to convince them he wasn't an unpatriotic terrorist/murderer/molester who'd get their precious daughter killed off.

My family pretended to be broad-minded, but we were the *slightest* bit bigoted about outsiders.

'You've forgotten me entirely. Why the fuck did you not call me on New Year's Eve?' Trilok was abruptly and totally serious.

He wasn't the only one with the complaint. Atharva and Kiki hadn't asked me about it because they knew me the best. They knew I didn't want to talk to anyone.

The rest of them couldn't understand.

I shrugged. 'Sorry, bro.'

'So, how you doing?' he asked me, as he switched my phone on

---

[35]Battle for love

(I'd placed it on charge once I came back from my meltdown). It would take forever to get powered up and then I'd be deluged with emails. Mostly from Puru. Mostly regarding the correct spelling of twat and wenker. *('It's wanker, FYI.')*

'All good. You know, the usual.'

Trilok shrugged. 'I guess.'

I patted his knee. 'I'm sorry about the wedding. I know how much this day meant to the both of you. Kiki's being remarkably calm about it and it's mostly thanks to you.'

He braced both hands behind his head and contemplated his toes. They were well-shaped but the nails were overgrown, as if he couldn't be bothered to clip them. For some ridiculous reason, I remembered the toes of the last man who'd occupied this bed with me.

Ben's toes. He'd been wearing open-toed leather slippers. His big toe had been kind of square and solid, with curling hair.

It was an odd thing to notice about a man. Right?

'I told her. I told her four years ago, we don't need all this drama. We could have stood in line at the Registrar's office and done the deed in like two hours, before lunchtime at work. I even had a guy all lined up at the Delhi Registrar office,' he said mournfully.

I laughed. Pushed my hair back into a messy bun and tied it with a stray scrunchie. It probably belonged to Kiki or Prapti. I devoutly hoped it wasn't Ahalya's.

'She broke up with you for that, didn't she?' I recalled the frantic phone call from my dear cousin, the first fifteen minutes of which had gone in deciphering her words between hiccupping sobs.

'She did.' He looked perplexed. 'What is up with chicks and weddings? Why do you care so much about lehengas and jewellery and the fucking flower arrangements? Do you know, she wanted to import calla lilies for the actual ceremony? What the fuck are calla lilies, anyway?'

'It's one of life's great mysteries,' I deadpanned.

Trilok tapped a cigarette out, offering his half-empty packet to me. I jonesed for one so bad, but I'd quit smoking socially and every other kind when I was twenty-six, and I was proud of the one positive life change I had been able to maintain for the last five years.

He lit his and I watched the smoke puff out. Then I grabbed the cigarette from him and put it out on the nearby tumbler he was using as a makeshift ashtray.

'It's 2019,' I said mildly. 'Quit smoking already.'

He pinched my arm and I yelped and punched him. He dodged the blow quite easily, Trilok came from a tall, well-built, khaata-peeta[36] family and he didn't care that I was female. It was refreshing, to tell the truth.

I tried to get under his guard, my thumb tucked under my fist like I was taught in my self-defense class. 'Not all women are obsessed with weddings.' I was breathless as we wrestled on the bed. 'Some of us just want a quiet, simple ceremony that causes no ripples whatsoever and just begin our lives with a man who wants us.'

'Did you go on Shaadi.com?'

The question was so random I stopped trying to hit him. I blew sweaty hair off my face. 'What the fuck are you talking about?'

'Ben wrote that. That exact same thing. About wanting a quiet, simple ceremony and begin his life with a woman who will understand him.'

I am ashamed to admit that everything inside me melted when I heard that. Everything.

'Very funny.' I had no interest in fighting anymore.

'I'll tell you what I love about the big fat Iyer weddings. The

---

[36]Well-to-do

murukku, man. As far as I am concerned, it's the only good thing about this entire shaadi drama.' He smacked his lips and sprawled next to me.

'Men and food. Now that's life's greatest mystery.'

He nudged my waist in a friendly way. 'You're one to talk, LJ.'

'This is true. I eat. Emotionally.' I sighed and adjusted the kurti that had ridden up in our wrestling. 'I've been feeling very emotional these days.'

'I wanted to punch Mehul for you. But Keeks held me back. She said your dad will only blame you for the drama.'

I smiled. It wasn't a happy smile. 'Keeks is right. If there is anything that can be blamed on me, my dad will go for it.'

'That is a gross exaggeration, LJ, and you know it.' But his voice lacked conviction. Trilok had been on the receiving end of his share of unfair blame. He knew how it felt like.

I checked my phone—all work-related messages and emails, e-commerce site discount offers. More work.

'So,' I said slowly. 'Ben Dewar wrote that he wants a quiet simple wedding on his matrimonial profile.' I shot Trilok a quick, assessing look. 'Why would a guy like him actually be on a site like that? Shouldn't women be throwing themselves at his perfect bod and stable life?'

Ugh, that was so cheesy. Trilok was going to tease me mercilessly. But instead, he said quietly, 'Yours is not the only family that's effed up, sweetie.'

'Oh.' I considered this new information. 'Anyway, it doesn't matter.' I sighed. 'The man has seen me throw up and cry. Like cry all over him with snot and everything. Secondly, Ahalya's into him, because he is perfect and he smells nice and he is good to her kid. Thirdly, he is off-limits because he considers me a pathetic headcase and I can't do that to Ahalya again.'

'He didn't follow Ahalya anywhere and see her throw up and

cry,' Trilok pointed out.

'I...' Fuck. That was a very good point.

'Exactly. Men don't do things they don't want to do. Especially men like Ben.'

'The stable, perfect kind?' I didn't want to sound dreamy and bitter at the same, but I did.

My phone buzzed loudly. It was Chanchal, my colleague at work, probably to check up on the status of my French Retrospective article. I let it ring till she gave up.

'I am not going to say anything more because it's not my place and I am not going to snitch on my pal,' Trilok defended himself. 'I think I'll have this conversation with Ahalya, instead. "Three Hacks to Winning the Heart of a Stable, Perfect Guy".'

Trilok nudged my shoulder and tapped another cigarette out. This time I didn't stop him from smoking it.

'Fuck. You,' I said, while I considered that particular headline.

It would make for a good story. And maybe if I helped Ahalya land Ben, she might start behaving halfway normal with me... which would go a long way in bringing my antagonistic father around. On the other hand, Ben *had* followed me and watched me throw up and ugly cry.

He'd been there with me. For me.

Maybe it meant something. Maybe he was trying to help out a pathetic headcase. The thought depressed me more than it should have.

My phone buzzed loudly. Really loudly. And I saw the caller. Gordhan Vithaldas Real Estate Agent. I picked it up hastily. 'Hello, Gordhanji? Sorry. *Phone silent pe tha.*[37]'

The man rambled for a couple minutes before he said the

---

[37]My phone was on silent mode.

golden words: *'Party ready hai, madam. Deal karna hai kya?'*[38]

I closed my eyes as quiet, desperate relief filled me.

I'd found a buyer for my home.

'Yo, Writer Girl.' Kiki shook me awake. Hard.

'Wha-what?' I came awake with a start. My dreams had been hazy and filled with big toes and curling masculine hairs. I hissed at Kiki's grinning face. 'What the fuck, woman? Why did you wake me up at—' I checked the time on my phone, '11 p.m.? We have to wake up at 6 tomorrow, right? For another pujai.'

'Stop being such a cranky baby and follow me.' Kiki bumped shoulders with me and I smelled it on her. A whiff of beer. What was going on?

'Kiki...' I said very quietly. 'Kiki, we can't drink. It's forbidden. And we can't go out of the house. The elders will kill us.'

'When has that ever stopped you?'

She threw a heavy jacket and jeans at me and I shrugged into them, because it was super cold. Not because I had any plans to break the house rules with my tipsy sister. 'Does Trilok even know you're here? Do the others know?'

'Everyone knows. Even Ahalya's coming. Jo's sleeping with your Mom tonight. Apparently, Gomti perimma loves *Harry Potter* now.' Kiki's grin was off-centre and goofy. I felt an immediate pang of alarm and foreboding. 'Now come on. Let's get going. We have to be back by 5. Or the elders will kill us.'

'Whatever this is, is a very bad idea, behena.'

'Wear some lipstick and gloss, behena,' she advised me sagely. 'Give me some, too. I'm in the mood to make out with my fiancé.'

---

[38]The party is ready, madam. Do you want to finalize the deal?

She winked at me.

I shook my head and handed over my Forest Essentials Rose Petals Lip Balm with the cute mirror. She dabbed her lips with it while I groggily applied brown lipstick and then applied the gloss over it. I had no idea why I was doing this but I didn't want to have a conversation with Kiki. The sooner we got out of here, the sooner I could huddle under a blanket somewhere and snooze.

Then, I arranged my pillows to resemble a lump, tossed the quilt over the mass and sneaked out behind Kiki, holding on to her waist so we could move. We snuck out the back door of the kitchen, and were immediately hit with a blast of frigid air. I actually shuddered inside my fleece-lined jacket and my sneakers were hardly protection in the middle of the night.

'Dammit, Kiki. It's freezing. Let's go inside,' I whispered.

She shook her head, some of her curls escaping the gray beanie hat she wore.

I raised the hoodie of my jacket and ran down the side of the house, panting. I caught up with her as she took the left fork outside the gate—which was open enough for a slim person to slip out comfortably—and then we jogged farther ahead to where I could see the SUV.

'You need to exercise more,' Kiki said, as I wheezed my way up.

I was bent over and my breath gusted out in cold curls. 'It's the elevated sea level,' I managed. 'My asthma's acting up.'

She rolled her eyes. 'You've never wheezed a day in your life.'

'We can't all ride the SUV, right?'

Kiki shrugged, giving me a wicked grin. 'Not all of us, no. Look who finally decided to join us. Sleeping Beauty has arrived, bitches. Let's get this party started.' She disappeared to the other side of the car.

Vidhaant poked his head out the driver's seat of the SUV and waved at me. 'Welcome to the party, Sleeping Beauty. It's houseful in here.'

Twin low rumbles startled me before I could say something snarky back. I gasped as I saw two helmeted figures bring two motor beasts to life, one on each side of the SUV, like outriders at a politician's motorcade. The sound was particularly loud in the dead of the night. I looked about in alarm at the deserted side road.

'*We* are going to get arrested,' I muttered.

'In that case...' A thoroughly familiar voice spoke from underneath one of the black helmets. My heart rate speeded up. The figure removed the helmet and shook his hair out. My heart stopped completely for a microsecond. 'It's a good thing you have a lawyer to bail you out, right?'

Ben Dewar, leather-clad sexy biker, gave me a slow burn of a smile.

## Chapter Fifteen

'They dragged you into this, huh?' I couldn't help smiling back. I just couldn't.

'They didn't have to try very hard.' He wore the helmet back and gave me this unfathomable look that warmed me from the inside out. In zero-degree weather. 'I was looking for a reason to come back anyway.' He snapped the helmet visor shut.

Ben patted the seat behind him, while Kiki settled herself behind Trilok.

'Do you need a formal invitation or are you going to get on the bike?'

A million smart answers rushed through my brain as I, a grown woman on the other side of thirty, contemplated climbing onto the back of a death machine and clutching this man's chest while I screamed in mortal fear. Nope. Not happening.

'I think I'd like to ride,' I said slowly.

Ben listed his head to one side and snapped the visor open. His eyes were curious, patient. 'You're sure? This is a heavy bike.'

'She doesn't ride, bro,' Atharva called out, rolling down the window on his side. He glared at me. 'You'll be risking arrest if you let her.' Prapti shushed him from the inside and he gave her a perplexed look. 'What?' he asked. 'What did I say wrong?'

'You don't know how to ride this thing?' Ben patted the handlebars of the chrome monster.

'I do.' I crossed my fingers behind my back. 'I'm just not very good at it. Are you an adventurous man, Ben?'

To my intense mortification and surprise and something else…

something I couldn't define in the moment but which added to the warmth spreading inside me, he considered my question for a long, drawn-out moment.

Then he balanced the bike on the stand, scooted back and handed me my own helmet. 'Never say I didn't give you anything.'

I wore the helmet in blank shock. My wayward hair was already packed inside the hoodie so it couldn't be in the way.

'This is a very bad idea, Ben,' Atharva warned. 'She will crash the thing and you'll have to bail her out for real.'

'That's alright,' he murmured, even as I threw my leg over the bike.

He kicked the stand away so I had to balance the bike on my own two feet. He was right. This bike, whichever make it was, was heavier than whatever I'd ridden before. My arms trembled on the handlebars and I tried to find my centre of gravity while the Hanuman Chalisa[39] ran through my head in a desperate bid for safety and courage.

Ben put his hands over mine on the bike and bent his head so our helmet heads knocked awkwardly. I pressed start on the ignition and it rumbled so loud, it felt like the sound of impending doom. I swallowed through a dry mouth and devoutly hoped I wouldn't crash the demon bike.

I could feel him behind me, every single part of us in close, intimate, almost sexual contact with each other. His chest against my back, our legs flanking the bike, while his gloved hands covered mine in a reassuring and thoroughly sexy grip.

I admit it. I was a goner right then.

Even before Ben said what he said: 'I'll take care of her.'

---

[39] A Hindu devotional hymn addressed to Lord Hanuman.

'Woman, speed up,' Ben yelled ten minutes later, through the damn helmet. I winced and bent low as we took the next bend down the hilltop on our way to the Vivanta. 'A snail passed you at the last bend. Drive faster.'

'I am not going to murder you on the way to this totally pointless and ridiculous party that I didn't even want to go to,' I shot back.

Somewhere after minute three, when he'd realized I wasn't a terrible rider in imminent danger of crashing the bike, Ben let go of the bars and I had settled in to ride behind the SUV. If I felt the slightest bit deprived that he'd let go of me, it was buried fathoms deep under the sheer terror of actually controlling the heavy machine.

'If I am going to die of anything, it's going to be boredom,' he muttered in a voice designed to get a rise out of me.

I gritted my teeth and continued riding on.

A stray dog crossed my path before the next bend, caught in the low headlights, and I screeched before braking hard.

Ben was thrown against me, our helmets banging together. He yelled something unintelligible and inappropriate. But he used his superior height and strength to control the bike's dragging motion, immediately putting his hands on the handle bars, his palms digging into mine.

When we finally rested on the safe side of the road, he let go of the bars and got off the bike.

I opened the helmet visor with shaking hands.

He was furious. 'Are you nuts? Why would you stop in the middle of the fucking road with no lights? Someone could have come from behind and hit us. We'd have really had an accident, you fool.' His voice kept getting colder and colder with each sentence. I gulped.

'If you didn't know how to ride the fucking bike, why did you ask to ride it?'

'I'm sorry,' I whispered. 'I didn't mean to...'

'Oh yeah. That's your standard excuse, isn't it?' He cut in with cruel irony. 'I didn't mean to cause any trouble. It just happens to me. I am pure as the driven fucking snow. It's never my fault.' He took a deep breath, while I saw his frankly impressive shoulders shake just a bit.

I bit my lower lip hard to stop it from trembling. Ben was right. There was no excuse for what I'd just done. There never really was. I got off the bike, my thighs screaming in protest, still trembling from the effort of handling the machine. I hung the helmet by the strap on the back bar.

'Now what are you doing?'

'I'm walking. It's safer for everyone.' I kept my voice even with effort. Visions of what could have happened flashed before my eyes. A truck could have hit us. We could have stumbled on a rock and been thrown into the ravine. We could have hit the dog! Oh God...

His curse echoed, a lewd, offensive one involving mothers and the sexual act. 'Don't be silly, LJ. Get on the bike.'

'I don't think so. I don't like bikes. This was a mistake.' My voice broke on the last word and I was appalled at the tears rushing to my eyes. This whole crying-at-the-drop-of-a-hat thing was so weak. I couldn't do it. So I straightened my back, jutted my chin out and started walking, fighting back the tears.

No. More. Crying.

Ben cursed again. 'I'm not going to apologize for what just happened.'

'I'm not asking you to.' I continued walking. Slowly. My shaking legs impeded my progress, but I liked to think it was anger and indignation too.

I so wanted to hurl accusing questions at him about the conversation he had with my father. But I gnashed my teeth and plodded on.

'LJ, please.' The words were a long sigh. 'It's late and I am insanely tired. Get on the damn bike. Everyone will wonder where we are. They'll probably send out a search party for us.'

'Atharva's probably calling the local hospitals already. He has a lot of confidence in my motor-riding skills.' I was justifiably bitter.

'Yeah, well. I don't blame him.'

I shot him an indignant glare over my shoulder. And he indicated the bike. 'Come on,' he said. 'Please,' he added.

I wanted to think it was the two pleases and the quasi apology he gave me, but truthfully?—I couldn't walk another step. My legs were shaking so.

So I settled gingerly behind him, wearing the helmet, and gripped the back of the bike where I'd hung the helmet. I kept a sedate 2 inches of distance between us, taking care not to brush against him in any way. Ben gave me that unfathomable look again in the side mirror, but kept his silence.

I was only half-grateful for that while we roared off.

The backlot of the Vivanta, Kiki's cancelled wedding venue, was set up for a bonfire. Beach loungers with umbrellas dotted the immediate radius of the fire, someone's Bluetooth sound bar pounded mellow rock and I could see a huge blanket full of snacks.

As I made my way to the fire, walking ten feet apart from Ben who'd not spoken for the remainder of the ride, I was caught up in a maelstrom of memories.

Past and present mashed together in a kaleidoscope of half-forgotten incidents and the sounds of laughter and shrieks. We'd done the bonfire thing as kids one winter in Punjab where Deep uncle had been stationed, celebrating the harvest festival of Lohri in early March. All of us, even Ahalya, had dressed up in traditional outfits, while we pigged out on motichoor laddoos and steaming aloo parathas. It was a happy, uncomplicated, joyful memory.

The bonfire was roaring, giving off a nice orange blaze. Everyone huddled around it. I saw Atharva and Prapti huddled under the same blanket, his head bent attentively towards her as they spoke. In that moment, I envied my brother his perfect life with his perfect wife. They were together. It meant something monumental. That they were together despite thoughts of homicide and the everyday annoyances and daily detritus that make up a relationship.

Add in the stress and annoyances of maintaining your space in two different families, of which one family was mine, and the odds of anyone making it was astronomical. Yet, here they were, my brother and his bride. Three years and still going strong.

God. To have that with someone.

Kiki and Trilok were dancing, swaying on the other side, while a group of youngsters—I recognized a few neighbours' kids and the under-forty shop owners—swigged beer from a blue and white cooler. I took my place on a beach lounger, perching on the side and huddled inside my jacket.

It was freezing.

'Yo.' Vidhaant slid into the seat beside me and handed me a beer bottle. I took it with a wrinkling of my nose. 'We don't have your fancy Cabernet Sauvignon here. So suck it up and drink.' He expertly twisted the top off and watched me take a small, cautious sip.

I was not a beer fan. It tasted funny and it had too many bubbles for something that did not rhyme with campaign and it was meant for balding uncles with pot bellies.

'I sold the house,' I blurted. 'I mean, someone made an offer. Unofficially. They want it. I haven't told anyone about it yet.'

'That's awesome, LJ. Congratulations.' We did a quick sideways hug and Vidhaant awkwardly patted my back. 'I am glad the house is off your head. I think it was driving you crazy... Being in that much debt and unable to do anything about it.'

It was. Being in debt did not suit me. But that wasn't what I wanted to talk about.

'I like the lawyer,' I continued.

My eyes roved restlessly across the fire. Kiki and Trilok were making out. Hard. It should have bummed me out. But it didn't. I felt happy for the first time in months, hopeful, as I saw my cousin and the love of her life kiss like their lives depended on it. They'd made it. Through everything.

'I like the lawyer,' I said again, in a stronger voice.

'You what now?' He almost spewed his beer out. 'You like Gopal uncle?'

I grinned. 'I mean Ben. The younger one. Not bald Gopal uncle. My taste is not so bad, is it?'

Vidhaant was not convinced. 'Ben Dewar?'

I nodded. 'Yes, Ben Dewar. And he seems to like me too. When he isn't rescuing me or yelling at me or...'

I stopped talking. My words went cold because I saw Ahalya.

She was embracing Ben, going up on her tippy toes. Looking a damn sight more put together in her skinny jeans and boots and sweatshirt than me in my pyjama top and fleece-lined jacket with the dirty sneakers. Looking years younger and as pretty as she'd always been.

And Ben, that sneaky bastard, was embracing her back. Bent almost in double, his solid, reassuring arms wrapped around her while his nose was buried in her hair.

That was no ordinary hug. That was a full-on pre-coitus embrace.

'LJ.' Vidhaant saw what I saw. 'I don't think that means anything,' he said. But I heard the doubt in his voice. And, when I glanced over at him, saw the vague pity he quickly tried to mask.

'Sure,' I said. 'It means nothing at all.'

But we both knew I was lying.

## Chapter Sixteen

'Summer of 1999,' Atharva said lazily, a couple hours later. 'I think it was my upanayanam[40]. And Reshmy aunty had just started her snacks business here, with the fried jackfruit chips. God, they were delicious, weren't they?'

The music and mood was decidedly mellow. Most of the snacks—apparently 'borrowed' from the stack back at the Illam—were gone and the fire was giving off blessed, lovely warmth. We were all gathered around it. I was snuggled on a lounger next to Vidhaant, my sweet, beloved cousin who'd decided to stick by me in case I fell to pieces and created a scene with the lawyer who preferred Ahalya.

'Yeah,' Kiki slurred. She was four beers down and cuddling next to Trilok who was already out like a light. But he had his arm wrapped around Kiki and they shared a blanket, so bully for them. 'Wasn't that the year we held the chips-eating contest? Remember, LJ? We beat the boys, two plates to one.'

'I remember the epic diarrhoea. That's what I remember,' Vidhaant shot back.

I smiled. Surprisingly, I was enjoying myself despite the seesawing emotions. It was a huge blow seeing Ben and Ahalya together, after dealing with Mehul today. Even now, they were sitting next to each other on a lounger, and she kept whispering things to him and he laughed softly. But I was determined to not

---

[40]Traditional boyhood ceremony among Brahmins to signify their entrance into the Brahmacharya life.

be pathetic even if that was my natural state.

Today was a good day for me.

I'd faced Mehul and the news of his unborn baby with dignity, if not grace. I'd finished a 3000-word feature, complete with images and GIFS and it had been approved with minimal fuss. I was in talks with an interested buyer for my house, the albatross around my neck. *And* I had ridden a bike without causing or sustaining any physical injury.

Never mind good, today was awesome.

And I wasn't going to allow any one, not even the lawyer I liked and who obviously liked my older, more appropriate-for-him cousin, to wreck tonight for me.

I'd earned the right to be happy.

'I actually remember seeing Atharva cry for the first time, when he had to wait to go use the toilet. Remember that, bear?' Kiki snickered.

'Ewwww.' Prapti shuddered.

The rest of us laughed. The sound was especially boisterous in the still night. Fog drifted around our ankles, setting us all in a weird dream-like space, cocooning us.

I felt oddly at peace, considering everything.

The outer crowd had drifted off once the booze dwindled down to the last few bottles and the food got over, so now the real skeletons started coming out of the closet.

'This is nothing,' Kiki said. 'How can you forget the Great Bombay Pool Incident of 2001?'

Atharva yelled, 'We aren't going to talk about that in front of my wife.'

'*Poda ni!*'[41] Kiki shouted back in Tamil and that started a swearing match between Atharva and Kiki that I tuned out.

---

[41]Get lost!

Vidhaant chuckled as he heard the insults and leaned back, contemplating the stars.

Despite my best intentions, I watched Ben and Ahalya. Their faces partially in shadow, partially blazing orange from the bonfire. His half-goatee looked sinister, giving him a sexy villain look. I felt a spasm of heat in my belly as I watched him talk. Ahalya was murmuring something to him and his badly cut hair fell forward when he bent towards her. The heat turned tundra cold inside me. They fit together, made sense. Like the other couples here—two adults who had their shit together and were determined to make it work.

Tamping down on my needless grief, I murmured, 'How did you guys arrange this?'

'Actually, Ben made all the arrangements,' Vidhaant said. 'He flew down to Kochi in the afternoon and then drove up and managed the rest with the hotel people. It was a lawyer thing where he got a partial refund on the wedding reception and utilized the rest of the money to give Kiki and Trilok a night out.'

'Oh.' I blinked. Shit. I did not want to like the man anymore. But that was a pretty sweet thing to do.

'I can't believe Trilok is still here. That man has the patience of a saint. Two saints.' Vidhaant shot the snoozing Trilok a speculative look. 'Or he has ED or something.'

'Yuck! That is an awful thing to say.' I shoved him and snatched his blanket. 'I am happy for them. They have what everyone is looking for.'

'What?' Vidhaant burped as he finished off his beer. 'A really expensive honeymoon package they can't utilize anymore because they are stuck here?'

'You think you're so funny.' I pinched Vidhaant's arm and he howled soundlessly. 'No, I meant, they have each other. They have the kind of love that lasts. Like you and Gargi.'

'Dude, I would not be married to Gargi if she'd made me part of all this family drama. That man *is* a fucking saint.'

'But you love her, don't you?' The question was largely rhetorical.

'I do.' His answer was short, typical. When it came to talking about his own feelings, Vidhaant was just like the rest of the Chakrapani clan. Closed off and brief. Yet, I heard it in his voice. True affection for another person. The willingness to put up with their crap no matter how bad life got.

Everything inside me yearned to have that.

'Don't you miss Gargi?'

'I miss sleep. I miss having breakfast in peace, honey.'

'Well, she is staying home and raising your kids, you ungrateful jerk.'

'Hey, don't get on your smash-the-patriarchy soapbox,' he said equably. 'I am just saying, after having the twins, normal, sexy things such as missing my wife became impossible. I don't have the energy to miss her anymore. If you talk to her more often, she'll tell you the same.'

'That's a better answer.' I drank more of my chilled beer. Both the weather and the ice cooler had made it colder. The half-demolished plate of jackfruit chips between us had made it go down smoother.

'What's it like? Marriage. Kids. Being that much of an adult.'

'Like the hardest job in the world combined with the most boring routine of all.'

I rolled my eyes. 'Be straight with me, Vidhaant.'

'I am serious,' he insisted. 'You know, I'm so glad you and Mehul didn't marry in the end. You need someone who'll give you the wings to fly and yet pull you back when you're flying too close to the sun.'

'Meaning what?' I frowned.

'Meaning, you are capable of making terrible decisions just to defy whichever authority you hate at the moment. This could be theatre company owners or your father or a shitty boss. You're self-destructive, sweetie. You need to come with an instruction manual.'

My first instinct, asking him to fuck off, was smothered by the slightest buzz the beer gave me and the semi-serious notion that maybe he was right.

'You can't self-destruct in a serious relationship like marriage. There are other people to consider,' he said softly.

Ahalya had been married before. She knew how to behave in a relationship. I couldn't even hold onto a career without destroying it. The thought astounded me.

'I'm going to go for a walk up the hill, okay? I need the exercise.'

I took the blanket and plate of chips and walked away from the bonfire and the ribbing match between Atharva and Kiki.

'So they sent me to find you,' Ben said. I nearly fell off the rocky ledge I was sitting on.

My answer was a rude four-letter word that would make my mother wash my mouth with soap.

He smiled, that half-smile thing he did around me, hands stuck inside his jacket pockets. 'Sorry if I startled you.'

He didn't sound sorry at all. He stood ridiculously close to where I was sitting, legs folded up under the blanket as I stared at nothing. I'd been so engrossed in my own thoughts, thoughts Vidhaant had incepted, I'd lost track of time.

Was I really so naïve and stupid as to believe that teenage rebellion was cute in my thirties? Did I not want to live in the real world, like both Mehul and my father had more than once accused me of?

'May I join you?'

I shrugged. 'It's a free country.'

Taking that as his formal invitation, Ben sat down, swinging his legs down the ledge. Because I was a somewhat-gracious host, I handed over part of the blanket to him and he placed it carelessly on his lap. Our knees brushed and I moved away under it.

He shot me a long sideways look.

I ignored it as I focused on his hands. The left one was curled in a loose fist, the fingers long but stubby at the tips. I'd seen him do that before. When we were sitting on my mattress bed. It made me feel squishy inside to know such an intimate detail about this man. And slightly possessive.

'I get the feeling you're mad at me about something.' Ben was quiet, cautious.

'I'm not. I have no reason to be mad at you.'

'That's what I figured.'

Ben sighed and rubbed his hand over his face. Our knees bumped. I shivered inside the damned blanket. It was the cold, I reasoned. It had to be.

Then he said, 'You're not the world's worst bike rider. But you definitely need lessons in speed.'

'If that was your attempt at making up with me, I'd give it zero points. Also,' I added pointedly, '*I* didn't total my Ferrari because I was too drunk to see where I was going.'

His glance was utterly startled and I shrugged. 'Trilok talks.'

'That asshole. Also,' Ben was amused, 'it was a BMW, not a Ferrari. And I wasn't drunk, I was on pain meds.'

'I sense another story coming.' I wanted to tell him to fuck off, to not entertain me and make it up to me because not two hours ago he'd been canoodling with Ahalya, but Vidhaant said I was a self-destructive masochist, so I didn't. 'You can't leave it at that,' I said.

He looked at his hand resting loosely on top of the blanket. 'I'd had my appendix removed the week before. And the hospital let me out because of my parents' anniversary party. Where my father brought his thirty-two-year-old girlfriend and Mom fainted so I tried to drive her to the hospital. But I was on painkillers and they made me dizzy and...'

'And what?'

He rolled his jacket sleeve back and I saw a long and ugly scar run the length of his left forearm. It was jagged and thick, the skin raised as if it hadn't healed properly.

I touched it, morbidly fascinated like any normal human would be. Tingles ran through me at the contact.

'I ran a red light and a car came from the other side, dashed against us. I dislocated my shoulder and the pain was so horrifying that I put my hand through the windshield. It required twenty-five stitches.' He made his left hand into a fist. 'And it still pains like a mother most days.'

I eased my hand back. 'I'm sorry,' I said awkwardly.

He smiled, a crooked little smile that did not reach his eyes. 'Yours is not the only family that's fucked up.'

'No,' I said slowly, recalling Trilok's words. 'It's not.'

I was split in two. Half of me wanted to order him to leave me the fuck alone. It wasn't fair of him to follow me around when he had zero interest in me. The other half wanted to grab him by his curly, badly cut hair and kiss him.

I was so fucked up.

'Ben,' I began quietly. It was on the tip of my tongue. *What were you and Appa talking about the other day when you mentioned me?*

He beat me to it. 'Your family is always this boisterous?' Okay, he was a lawyer. Asking questions was probably textbook for him.

'Yes,' I murmured. I drew my knees up to my chest and rested my chin on it. My hair flew past my cheeks; I'd discarded the hoodie. It wasn't the wisest thing to do, given the weather but you only live once.

'I actually escaped before Kiki and Atharva began their thumb-wrestling match. Apparently, old grudges need to be revisited.' He looked up at the clear velvety sky dotted with a million stars. So close, you could just reach out and touch them. 'You guys have no boundaries whatsoever, do you?'

I couldn't help the questioning glance. 'What do you mean?'

He shrugged. 'I grew up with cousins too. I am not an only child but my sister is eight years younger, so the cousins were sort of my substitute siblings. And we had some good times, but you guys had *childhoods*. You have secrets and inside jokes the rest of us don't get. Especially the four of you. Even Ahalya feels left out, did you know?'

'That's what you guys were talking about?'

I felt gooey inside when he nodded shortly. 'She is not on the same wavelength as you four.'

So, they hadn't been flirting with each other, or murmuring sweet nothings. They'd been discussing my family's gross history. 'Yeah, Ahalya's older than us and she helped out her mom, my Sujata athai, so she had her own thing going back then.' My voice was softer and less defensive than it had ever been. 'So, she was always on a different wavelength than us.'

I pulled a blade of grass as I casually posed the next question. 'And you two are?'

'We two are what?'

I shrugged. 'You two, you and Ahalya, are on the same wavelength?'

'Someone has to be on her side, man.' The non-answer was depressingly vague. 'You guys are brutal. I haven't seen such clan-like behaviour in a long, long time.'

I looked up at the sky too. A strange melancholy filled me.

Then, I reached my hand up and touched one shining star. *Bing*. I smiled. Touched the next one. The air felt cool and kind of sexy against my fingertips.

'We all lived in each other's pockets for a long, long time. It's why we don't really have any best friends outside the family.'

'That's nice. That's really nice.'

I made a sort of swooshing motion and watched several stars blink in and out, one by one. This was fun. And sweet. I was going to go back home and do this in my apartment building's terrace. Then I remembered. My house was being sold off. I was shortly going to be homeless.

My hand froze on a big star. I blinked and it winked away. Reappearing the next second.

Could I be a bigger failure if I had actually set out to be one?

Out of nowhere, Ben raised his hand and captured mine, tucking my cold fingers between his warm palms. 'You'll get frostbite if you don't watch out.' His murmur was husky.

I glanced at him. His eyes had the same velvety, endless quality like the night sky. This time I could not mistake that look. It said, *I want you like crazy*. My breath hung suspended in my chest.

'Ben.'

'LJ.'

He dipped his head closer, and then I moved the last inch and our mouths lined up. 'I'm not thinking about projectile vomit now,' I whispered.

'Shut up, LJ.'

Then he shut me up with his lips.

A little later, I stirred from his solid, tree-like arms, cosy under the blanket. The rocky ledge was an uncomfortable place to make out but we'd managed just fine. Although making out was as far as it had gone.

Our legs were tangled together, jutting out of the ledge. I was burning up inside my open fleece-lined jacket. He still wore all his clothes but my pyjama top was open. My lips were chapped, my breaths shallow and it felt like I was on an erupting volcano.

'You kiss very well for a lawyer,' I whispered, as I traced Ben's goatee, and he kind of hung suspended above me. He was doing his own tracking above my jeans, below my navel. The man had moves. Some serious moves.

'I went to kissing camp.'

I chuckled at the deadpan humour. Traced his wet, chapped lips and we kissed some more. His hands tunnelling under my hair, shaping my skull, as he pressed closer to me. It was illicit and dangerous and all sorts of wrong, kissing out in the open where anyone could find us, but that just made it all the more exciting.

Then again, I'd kiss him in a bathroom filled with vomit. I wasn't particular like that.

'Your hair drives me crazy,' he confessed as he traced a line of kisses down my chest. I shivered slightly at the hot-cool air contact. And held him closer, for body warmth. Mostly.

'It's unmanageable.' I have tried everything to get the curls to tamp down. Leave-in conditioners, spa treatments, coconut oil and serums and straighteners. The thing had a mind of its own.

'I know. It's sexy.' Ben trailed a little bit of it down my shoulders and above my shoved up bra. It was a pretty sexy move and the man knew it. He grinned, a very boyish expression on his face. 'This is sexy too.'

'I don't want to bring this up right this second but Ahalya knows, for sure, you're not into her, right?'

I played with the curls on the back of his neck and he hissed. He actually hissed. My moves were driving him crazy enough to hiss. I was ridiculously proud of myself. So I did it some more. He did something to the inside of my ear with his tongue and I groaned.

Okay, he had some serious moves.

'Before we get any further...'

His hand wandered into my bra and I arched into him. 'I think we've gone as far as we can get tonight,' he murmured as his lips followed his hand.

'We have to talk about Ahalya.'

'I'd rather we didn't talk about your hotter cousin.' He kissed my frigid nipple, then did it again and I hissed.

'I saw you two earlier and it looked like...'

'Woman.' Ben lowered my T-shirt to its proper place and I felt deprived. 'What kind of a man do you take me to be if I am hitting on two cousins at the same time? What kind of a woman are you if you think like that?'

I had no answer to that. I turned my head away and considered the grass tickling my nose.

'LJ.' His voice was soft but firm. 'Answer me, please.'

I didn't want to.

He sighed, slid off me and took most of the heat with him. I shivered and it wasn't just from the freezing temperature.

'I'm thirty-six, Lasya,' he said quietly. 'I don't play games. I don't lead women around. Not you. Not your cousin. It's what I wanted to tell you the other day. If I wanted Ahalya, I'd be with her. Not you.'

'I didn't say...'

'Yes,' he said quietly. 'You did.'

'I didn't mean to.'

'Yes,' he said, still in the same quiet voice. 'You did.'

I sighed and reached for his hand. The damaged one. His palm was hard, the fingers still and unyielding. But I persisted, even though a voice inside my head whispered, *he may want you now but it doesn't mean he'll want you always.*

'I'm sorry. I should not have brought Ahalya up.'

'No.' He returned the pressure on my hand slightly. 'You shouldn't have. Why did you?'

Tears filled my eyes. And I sniffed, a very unromantic move. 'I don't know. I've been told I am self-destructive and that I have real problems with male authoritarian figures.'

'Uh huh.' He unbent enough to twine our fingers together.

I nodded. 'I look for ways to fuck things up because I am really good at endings. Apparently.'

'Sounds like a very professional diagnosis.' His thumb started to circle the back of my hand and I shivered once again.

'It is.' Our mouths aligned once again and Ben's eyes glinted with intent like they had a little while ago. I suspected my eyes said the same thing. *Kiss me now or die, mister.* 'I came up with it myself.'

'God, you talk too much.' His lips brushed mine in mini-kisses that melted my knees even though I was lying down. Then he crushed his lips to mine.

And then we didn't talk at all.

I'd like to say that we ended up doing it on the cold, damp, jutting ledge of the Vivanta back garden, but that would be untrue. Even with a blanket and his jacket and mine to shield us from the hard ground, things poked into us—our spines, knees, butt, among other body parts—and it wasn't worth risking back injury to indulge in outdoor sex.

So, after lots of making out, we went back down to where the bonfire burned on. The orange flames had petered out and gave off very little spark but it made for a pretty sight at 4 in the morning.

I could swear my skin glowed. The man was a phenomenally good kisser. And I bet he knew what to do with a clitoris too. I couldn't wait to find out. Like most men, Mehul had been a little clueless when it came to the G-spot and surrounding areas and most of the time when he'd gone down on me, it felt like I was being lapped at by a very enthusiastic puppy.

Lots of spit, not much tongue and definitely no finesse.

When Ben kissed, he used his tongue. Quite effectively. And with much finesse.

'Where's everyone?' I looked around the empty campsite.

All the loungers were vacant, but the half-empty plates of food and empty drink bottles were neatly stacked on the side of the bonfire. Ready for garbage collection.

'I guess they either went back without informing us or decided to give us some privacy.' He sounded pleased at the notion of being stranded on a small hilltop with me.

I stumbled as a tiny shiver of delight ran through me. I felt like singing an Arijit Singh song. One of the happy ones. Or even that damned Ed Sheeran number.

Ben pulled me close to him, his arm stayed on my waist and I couldn't resist the small, delighted smile I gave him. He didn't smile back. Ben wasn't the always-smiling kind, but his arm stayed on my waist.

It felt nice. For one single moment, everything was perfect.

'What?' he asked.

I could hear the smile in his voice. That delighted me too. I shook my head. 'After the profoundly shitty day I had, I can't believe it ended with you kissing me.' I winked at him.

'As I recall,' he pulled me up by my jacket collar, 'you were the one who kissed me.'

Just before we were about to lock lips, he murmured, 'And

what do you mean by "profoundly shitty day"?'

'Does it matter?' I did my best to bat my lashes and sound sexy. I also brushed my lips against his. His goatee tickled my chin and it was deliciously gooey. His hands tightened around the back of my neck.

'It should,' Ahalya said coldly, breaking the perfect moment. 'Her ex came to visit her yesterday and left her crying.'

I froze mid-kiss. Ben's hands tightened fractionally around me before he let go entirely and stepped back.

The worst part? He gave a sigh. A resigned sigh, exactly like the one Mehul had when we had talked yesterday.

# Chapter Seventeen

'Sorry,' Ahalya continued, sounding not-in-the-least sorry. She was bundled up inside a jacket and a shawl, so only her boots peeked out from under the layers. Her hair was covered by the shawl too. 'I didn't mean to interrupt.'

'That's fine,' Ben gave her a formal little smile. 'Good morning, Ahalya.'

'Morning, Ben.'

They did a quick one-arm hug that made me feel awkward. And a tiny bit envious. *I* didn't merit a good morning hug from my cousin but apparently he did. And he was also very cool with hugging my older, hotter cousin back. No problem.

Everyone was so evolved. So adult.

'Where's everyone else?' he asked.

Ahalya shrugged. 'They wandered inside at around 2 a.m. and it's not peak season so they got the suite. They're sleeping there.'

I couldn't resist the jibe. 'And I suppose you couldn't sleep.'

Ahalya gave me a hot look. It wasn't as effective because she didn't tower over me like Kiki, but it did make me feel small and petty. 'I was worried about...things.'

'Right.'

Even Ben shot me a surprised look at the sarcasm coating my voice. 'I'll just go check up on the others.' He made a show of looking at his watch. 'It's nearly time for you all to wake up anyway.'

'Please,' Ahalya drawled, not taking her condemning eyes off me. 'Stay. Don't let me spoil your pre-dawn cuddle.'

'I wasn't...' I stopped, drawing a deep breath. I tried to remind

151

myself that Ahalya really had cause to worry about things. My dad's announcement had sent her semi-ordered world into a tailspin and there was always Jo to consider. 'Let's try this again. Good morning, Ahalya.' I even gave her a small smile to go with it.

'Morning, LJ. How does it feel to get laid in two years?'

Ben's eyes widened at the open hostility and his brows shot up. 'I'm just going to leave...'

'No.' I shook my head, curled my fists. 'She wants an audience. Please oblige her.' I stared daggers at the woman who would not give me one single inch because of her misplaced sense of injured pride.

Ben touched my arm briefly and leaned down. 'LJ,' he murmured softly. 'Let it go. This is not the time to get into an argument with your cousin.'

I glared at him, feeling unreasonably hurt. 'You're taking her side? What happened to "I like you, LJ. Not Ahalya"?'

Ahalya gasped. 'You said that to *her*? Why would you say that?'

Ben cursed under his breath. 'Ahalya, I'm sorry I didn't mean it like that.'

'You're apologizing to *her*?' I couldn't believe he was doing this, choosing Ahalya over me, when I was the one he'd been wrapped around like a Kashmiri quilt for most of the night.

Ben cursed some more under his breath and his left hand curled into a fist. And it wasn't a sexy gesture anymore. It meant he was mad.

'He is a gentleman. Like Mehul. Unlike my husband,' she said bitterly, defending him.

'Ex-husband,' I gritted out. 'And Mehul was not a gentleman. He came home just to tell me Mini is pregnant. They're having a baby in July. So, thank you very much for making sure that conversation happened.'

She smiled, all acid sweetness. 'I was just trying to give you some closure.'

It was a throwback to the statement I'd made when I tried to have Sukumar meet her one last time after the big fight when she had stormed out of the house and my dad had disowned me.

'I didn't need any closure.'

'Me neither,' she shot back. 'But you, in your infinite literary wisdom, decided that I did and I had to watch that lying coward pretend to beg me to take him back. I actually had to consider taking him back for my baby's sake.'

I'd never thought of it that way. I'd just been trying to do the right thing by Ahalya and Jo. And my dad, who considered me a partial homewrecker anyway.

'I—'

'That was not closure, Lasya,' she barrelled on. 'That was you interfering in a situation you had no idea about. And you acted like you always do. Thoughtlessly. You don't think I know you wanted to write more of my sad pathetic story in your next fucking book? That I was just a social experiment you wanted to use for more fame? You think I am that dumb?'

My jaw dropped. I was vaguely aware of Ben standing next to me, his neck swivelling back and forth between us. I didn't want to know what his face looked like. The way my cousin, the woman who had been happy to call me little sister, her Kunju, once upon a time, was pouring all her vitriol on me.

'Ahalya, I—'

'Did she tell you, exactly, what she did to me?' Ahalya rounded on Ben, suddenly including him in the conversation.

He looked as taken aback as I did. But I had a bad feeling about what she was going to reveal.

'Ahalya, please, calm down,' he said, trying to soothe her. He even put a consoling hand on her arm.

But she shook it off and continued, in that same hot-cold, venomous voice. 'Tell him,' Ahalya said. 'Tell him or I will.'

'I didn't do anything,' I said staunchly. 'I didn't do anything and you know it. I told you this a million times. I told Dad too and everyone else. But none of you listened to me.'

The disappointment and anger of that moment still remained with me, a puckered scar that never really healed.

Ahalya looked Ben in the eye and said, 'Lasya knew about Sukumar's second wife but she waited till she wrote the book and got famous and the world came to know about it before she told me about it.'

Ben looked thunderstruck. And his left hand was clenched so tight, I could clearly see the veins sticking out. I put a trembling hand to my forehead as a deafening roar started filling my ears. Like when you're at the beach and the water hits the shore.

'She told me that he'd come to see her after he'd read the book,' she continued remorselessly. 'He wanted to know how she knew about his affair. About his bigamy. How the fuck did she find out? That's what I wanted to know. It's what I always wanted to know.' She switched her basilisk gaze to me. 'You'd never tell me.'

I wet my suddenly dry lips and said nothing. I'd answered her a million times. But it wasn't what she wanted to hear, so she never listened.

'LJ,' Ben said, awkwardly. 'I should go.'

I shook my head. Because Ahalya would drag this out and I was damned if I'd let her. 'I'll finish the story. I told Ahalya about the horrible confession Sukumar had made to me. She didn't believe me. So, I told my dad and he didn't believe me either. But he confronted Kumar who admitted to everything. And Ahalya left him a month later.'

I turned to my cousin, the woman who had once ditched her wedding anniversary and helped me get over a crush's rejection back in college, by spending her whole salary on a cute pair of jeans for me. She'd even had dinner with me instead of her husband.

The lying, cheating, selfish son of a bitch.

Ahalya had loved me like only an older sister could and I missed it, missed *her*, with a consuming sadness I'd never let myself feel before today.

'Kumar was a bastard and you didn't deserve what happened to you. And I am *sorry*.' I stressed on the last word. 'I will apologize till the end of time for what happened to you but I didn't cause it. I swear to you.'

You'd think I would shout, that I'd raise my voice. But I was just tired. My voice was too.

'You did,' she whispered. 'You and that damned book of yours.' Tears shimmered in her lovely brown eyes, stressing the fact of her exhaustion, adding to it. But they didn't fall. It was just one more thing we had in common, Ahalya and I. We avoided such things as crying in front of company.

I raised one hand to touch her, maybe even hug her, but she batted it off. 'And I'll never forgive you for it, LJ.'

And then she walked away from me in a gesture of stunning and total dismissal.

That Ben *was* a gentleman became clear two minutes later when he hugged me briefly. My battered heart just about broke in two at the gesture. It was a perfunctory hug. I knew the difference between perfunctory and the real deal, having experienced the real deal with him.

'Are you okay?' he asked, quietly.

'Say it,' I evaded his question.

'Say what?' He sounded confused but wary.

'Say what you're thinking.'

'What am I thinking, LJ?'

'That I did it. That I knew about Kumar's affair and I wrote it in the book and conveniently broke the news to my family afterwards when it suited me.'

'Did you do that?'

I shook my head so violently, my neck snapped back. 'Of course, not. I would never do that. They try my patience and my sanity but I love them.' My voice trembled now. Humiliatingly. So I jutted my chin out and straightened my spine. Looked him in the eye. 'I'd never sell my family out like that.'

He looked thoughtful. Not judgemental. Just thoughtful. 'Alright.'

'Alright?' If I sounded disbelieving, it was because I was.

'Alright, I believe you.'

Hope flared a bright, burning path through the disappointment and disbelief. 'You do? Thank you very much.'

Ben gave me a wry look. 'You can sound less sarcastic, you know. It's a lot to process at 5 in the morning.'

'I can.' I reached for him. And we held hands for a second. 'It's just really hard when I have spent the last two years being treated like a leper for something I didn't do. And I am tired of defending myself over it.' I admitted my most shameful truth to him.

'Is it true, though? What Ahalya said?' he asked, instead.

My brain couldn't connect the dots. 'Didn't we just establish that she doesn't believe the truth?'

'No.' Ben let go of my hand and stuck both of his hands in his back pockets. His voice was casual but his eyes were carefully blank. 'Not about her bastard ex's despicable behaviour. About yours.'

'My what?'

'Your ex, Mehul. Is he really having a baby with his wife?'

I nodded slowly. 'Yes, he is. He came to pay his condolences yesterday, when Ahalya helpfully invited him over. And we ran into each other.'

'I see.'

I wondered what he saw. Why his voice sounded so quiet, so distant. 'It doesn't mean anything,' I continued. 'She just brought it up so she could mess with my head.'

'And did it?'

I considered lying. Telling him what I thought he wanted to hear. But I wasn't built like that, no matter what my family thought of me. I couldn't lie. I nodded, slower than before.

'Things didn't end well between Mehul and me. I…was in pretty bad shape for a long time.' I hesitated. 'I haven't dated in more than a year after he left.'

'I see.' His eyes, so warm and brown moments before when he'd kissed me, were flint hard.

'You don't.' I couldn't stand still anymore. So I started pacing toward the Vivanta. My legs striking the ground in hard, angry thuds. Ben's long legs easily kept pace with mine, even though he kept his distance from me.

'Mehul was seeing his wife, the woman he left me for, for a full year before he left. Ahalya thinks she's the only woman who's suffered.' I kicked at a clump of grass, clenching my fists inside my jacket, the bitter, corrosive anger filling me all over again. 'She isn't. If anything, she has the full support of the family. My family. She has Jo. I don't have anyone.'

'I see.' He had an expression that I couldn't identify. It was thoughtfulness and…regret?

I stopped short. 'What do you see?'

'Why you had a "profoundly shitty day" yesterday.'

'What?' I turned to glare at him.

The man was talking in code and I was operating on zero sleep and zero coffee. It wasn't precisely his fault but he was a handy target. Besides, he deserved it. He'd hugged Ahalya. He'd apologized to her. And he found her hotter than me.

I don't know why I ever believed for a single second that he wanted me. Obviously, I was just conveniently available.

'What do you mean by that?' I demanded.

He shook his head, rubbing the back of his neck in a weary gesture. 'I should have known better than to think this meant something. Something real.'

My glare should have withered him on the spot. 'It was plenty real last night.'

Ben gave me a small, sad smile. 'Let's not confuse lust for a deeper connection, shall we? We're too old to play those kind of games.'

I saw red. Without thinking, I raised my hand and punched him square in the gut. It bounced harmlessly off of him, of course. His chest was muscular and defined, a product of disciplined gymming and good genes, as he'd shared with me last night.

'Damn you,' I gritted out. 'That was a terrible thing to say.'

'It's true, isn't it? You wanted to distract yourself from the drama and chaos of your life and I was handy. And last night...I was your rebound too.'

'You said you liked me. Was that just something you said to get into my pants?' I couldn't believe this conversation. That we had quickly devolved into accusations and arguments. A part of my brain, maybe my common sense, was quick to point out that all my relationships went exactly this way.

That I always brought it upon myself.

That I deserved this.

Ben's eyes widened again, then his face shuttered. His eyes went remote and a small muscle ticked in his jaw. 'I'm not going to dignify that with an answer.'

'Of course not.' I turned away from him, hugging myself with suddenly leaden arms. 'I do want to know one thing, though.'

'What?'

'Why were you and my dad discussing me the day of the will reading?'

If it was possible, his eyes went colder than before, like bits of obsidian. Nothing came through from them—not feeling, not warmth. Nothing. 'That's not for me to reveal, LJ. I didn't come here to talk about that anyway.'

'Of course, not. You got what you came for. Mostly.'

There was a dreadful moment of silence when I could only hear my own angry breaths.

Then Ben spoke, 'If you truly believe that then you're right. You don't have anyone. Especially not me.'

I didn't have to turn around to see him walking away from me with full and absolute finality. Not when I could hear the hard, angry thud of his footsteps over the deafening roar in my ears. They sounded like the death knell of a beautiful dream I didn't even know I'd wished for.

They sounded like yet another person leaving me when I needed them to stay.

'Are you okay?' Prapti asked me sotto voce, as we rode back in the SUV.

Vidhaant had quietly accepted my seat exchange, riding tri-seater with Kiki and Trilok while I went with Atharva, Prapti and the remainder of the food. Usually, it would irritate me seeing my sister-in-law in pressed jeans, matching pullover and a plaid scarf that was wrapped artfully around her neck at 5.15 in the freaking morning but, for once, I couldn't work up the necessary outrage.

I was squished in the back seat, my head stuck to the glass window, resolutely turned away from the rest of the family. Particularly, my beloved cousin, Ahalya, who was driving us all back. Like the competent superwoman she was.

'I'm fine,' I told Prapti. 'I just need some coffee.'

Ahalya took a sharp hairpin bend and the fog parted for her, like Moses parting the Red Sea. The vista of early morning in Munnar lay before me in all its splendour across the ravine. Little houses dotted the plateau, surrounded by slopes of tea plants, green and glinting with dew. Small fires glimmered, giving off little sparks as they puttered out in the light of day.

If I really strained my eyes, I could even see people moving about, wrapped in layers and monkey caps as they began their day. Having their morning kaapi, sending their children off to the local school, cleaning up their yards before they began their jobs at the local stores or businesses or the estates themselves. They were probably fucked up in their own individual ways but, for today, I'd trade places with any of them in a heartbeat.

'You don't look fine,' she continued. 'And I didn't see you at all, last night. Atharva was worried you'd catch pneumonia in this weather.'

I shook my head. 'I didn't catch pneumonia, honey. And I was…busy last night.'

'With Ben?' Her question was soft, non-judgemental. It tore into me with the force of a hurricane.

'It doesn't matter now.' The cold of the window pane seeped into my cheeks, my bones. My very marrow. 'He isn't what I thought he was.'

Just saying the words out loud made me realize how deluded I had been. To think that a man like him, a successful, good-looking, very single and attractive man would want to end up with me. I hadn't been able to make my father or Mehul love me. Thinking Ben Dewar could was just compounding the naïve, tragic stupidity of it all.

She sighed and rubbed my thigh. 'If it's any consolation, he looked like hell when he came to wake us up.'

I attempted a smile; it was probably a grimace. But I couldn't care too much about it right now. 'I'm sure it was just the cold.'

'LJ, no.' She patted my knee. 'Don't think like that.'

I sighed and gave her a look that betrayed all of my inner turmoil and misery. 'Praaps, can we please not talk about this? I really need some coffee if I have to face the rest of the day. And Ben Dewar is not part of it.' *Not anymore, at least.*

I spoke in a low, furious tone, so the front seat couldn't hear me. I didn't want Ahalya to know she had succeeded in destroying me once more.

'I was just trying to help.' Prapti's lips thinned at my unnecessarily curt words. 'I'm sorry if I overstepped.'

I closed my eyes. God. When would this family stop making me feel like pond scum? 'I'm sorry, Praaps. I didn't mean to make you feel bad. I'm just having a rough morning, okay?'

She sighed. 'Tell me about it.'

I was startled. 'What do you mean?'

Prapti opened her mouth, as if to say something. Finally she shook her head and patted at a few flyaways in her hair. 'Nothing. Just trying to make you feel better.'

'You're sure?'

'Of course, I'm sure.'

Her answer should have reassured me. Prapti, after all, was the one woman I knew who had her life together. One time, she'd cooked a four-course meal—complete with sambhar, raita, fried chicken for those who wanted a more Western meal, and gulab jamun for dessert—while dictating a market analysis report on her phone for a presentation. She'd still managed to accessorize her outfit with proper jewellery and shoes by the time the guests came.

I was one of the guests who'd arrived early, so I had actually seen her doing multiple tasks at the same time, without losing her calm or breaking a nail. It was terrifying. Unreal.

So when Prapti dismissed my honest concern, I should have been reassured. But the last few days had made me reassess everything I knew about the women in this family. None of us were what we seemed to be.

Maybe the same applied to Prapti too.

# Chapter Eighteen

$W$hichever god—out of the 33 crore gods and goddesses we had been taught to worship—was supposed to protect wayward, slightly hungover adults and small children, did so when we arrived back at the Illam. The SUV was stashed in the next lane and the bike was wheeled in with minimal fuss. We'd even piled the food containers and empties on the back of the bike so we could dispose them.

All in all, it was with a profound sense of relief and numerous yawns that we made our way up to our respective rooms. Ben had elected to settle up at the Vivanta before driving back to Kochi.

It depressed me that we'd not said goodbye. It hurt even more to know he was right. Confusing lust for a deeper connection was unrealistic and naïve on my part, regardless of age. Besides, the rest of my life was in utter chaos. I did not have the emotional bandwidth to handle disappointing yet another person like I would Ben, eventually.

There was a reason why I had not gone out with a man for more than a year.

I wasn't very good at it. And, as a thumb rule, I tried to stay away from things I wasn't very good at. Like regular salon appointments or writing my next novel or going out on a date with a man who might expect me to have my shit together. Amongst other things.

And the only reason I even considered giving myself a chance with Ben was because he was here. Trapped in this house with the rest of us youngish adults.

In the real world, back in Mumbai, if we had met at a party or a bar or something, I would have been intrigued—he was undeniably everything any woman would instantly want—but dismissed the possibility of us. Because, he was everything I couldn't be. Starting with being about 10-inches taller and able to talk in coherent sentences without the aid of caffeine.

Yeah, sooner or later, Ben and I would have crashed and burned.

Ahalya had just expedited the process. I didn't have to thank her for it, though. And, if anything, in this particular case, I could actually blame her for the whole debacle. Something I'd never been able to do before.

I should have felt better about it. About having someone else to blame my pathetic love life on, but I couldn't. And, either way, I had a last rite function to attend in precisely thirty-five minutes. So it didn't matter much at this point.

Sipping my second mug of epic filter kaapi, I contemplated the contents of my new wardrobe. I had exactly one more kurti, a soft sky-blue apple-cut linen that actually flattered my figure. The rest were already worn and we still had four more days to go.

Today was day ten of the kaariyam[42].

According to what I had been able to Google and what I had caught from snippets of conversation with the elders, we were entering the last and most important stretch of the thirteen-day ritual. The rest of our relatives, my mother's father and Subhadra's mom, were arriving today to participate in the activities of the next four days.

Apparently, days ten and eleven would be when my father would begin the final preparations to send my paati's soul to its heavenly journey and day twelve would be the first-ever shraddh ceremony.

Shraddh was the ritual where we invoked all our ancestors and asked them to bless the departed soul and surviving members for

---

[42]Funeral rites

the rest of the year by providing them with food prepared without any spices, except salt and pepper. The shraddh, which Dad and both the uncles performed for my grandfather, would now also be performed on an auspicious day for my grandmother.

I chose the sky-blue tunic and matching Patiala pants. I was going to wear it instead of saving it for a later date. I needed to feel good about something today.

Saying goodbye to Paati felt very real today, after yesterday's upheavals.

'There you are,' my mother said briskly, as she walked in.

Mom carried a small piece of paper and the edges of her shawl dragged against the floor under her crisp lemon yellow sari. She was petite in a way I always aspired to be, but could never attain and, even now, with lines on her face from age and lack of sleep—she woke up at 5 everyday with my father—she was terrifyingly beautiful.

I suppose all kids felt that their mother was the prettiest woman in the world. And that they could never measure up to her in any way that mattered, no matter what they did. The protagonist in *The Spectacular Melancholy of Living* certainly had.

'Yes.' I finished off the last of my coffee and dumped the day's outfit on my bed. 'I am here. Going nowhere.'

Mom raised her brows at the lumpy pillows and the quilt dumped on top of the pillows but didn't comment. I cursed mentally and casually patted at the quilt. 'Just trying something new. It's pretty fucking cold here, no?'

'I've told you to stop using that word, Lasya.' Mom's censure was conducted in a quiet, even voice.

'What is up, Mother?' I asked in a flippant tone.

Her lips tightened when I was being facetious and it struck me, as it sometimes did, that Mom and I were the same height. She had miraculously managed to avoid the delivery weight that plagued most women and looked petite and pretty for the most part. She was regal too, never raising her voice when she needed to make a point.

She was also the only one my sexist, workaholic father bothered to pay attention to. Growing up, if we had fucked up too badly or we needed something desperately—namely money to buy stuff or permission to stay out late or both—Mom was the conduit to make it happen.

Atharva and I had even perfected the technique we used to get her consent.

First, we'd do something we usually avoided, like clean up our rooms or do the homework or set the table and clear dinner utensils without being asked, then we would make Bournvita for her with a single marshmallow, her one weakness, and then, when she was full on hot chocolate and obedient children, we'd strike a deal.

It worked. Most times.

But, when I was writing *Spectacular* and recounting a particular incident that involved me totaling the second-hand Maruti that Atharva was gifted, it struck me—Mom was no dummy. She knew what we were up to. And she let us get away with it anyway.

'You know, it wouldn't kill you to make more effort with your father and me.'

I shot her a disbelieving glance. 'You're joking, right?'

She shook her head. 'I'm not. I'm dead serious. Appa is harsher than most dads, granted, but he is not a bad man and you shouldn't punish him till the end of time for what happened two years ago.'

I shook my head. 'I am not doing this with you, Mom.'

'Of course, not. You'd rather fight with Ahalya in front of an absolute stranger.'

I shook my head even more vehemently, preparing an opening statement to defend myself.

'Save it, LJ. I know what happened last night.' Mom held up one hand. It was perfectly manicured with clear polish laid on oval nails. 'And Kiki and Trilok deserve the party you guys had last night. But I raised you better than what you're doing, LJ. I just thought you should know that.'

'I can't do this early in the morning, Mom. Let's drop it.' I sounded like the petulant thirteen-year-old she'd compared me to on my last birthday. But, whatever. I didn't have to listen to yet another laundry list of defects from my mother before 6 in the morning. 'Let's agree that of your two offspring, one is the nice one, the good one, the one who makes you proud. And I am the dirty little secret. Now, is there anything else or did you come here just to make me feel bad?'

'You're not so old that I still can't whack you, Lasya.'

'I probably deserve it too, right?'

Her swift intake of breath made me realize, belatedly, that I might have gone the tiniest bit overboard in my desire to make my point. Mom, after all, was only pointing out facts and observations.

'I don't know what I did to make you feel this miserable and defiant both at the same time, but no, I didn't come up here to make you feel bad.' My mother was dignity personified while she spoke quietly, firmly. Without any inflection. 'I needed your help. I thought I'd come ask for it.'

She handed me the piece of paper with trembling hands. Guilt and shame lashed my insides, taking away what little buzz I'd gotten from the coffee.

'What is it?'

Her handwriting was chicken-scratch on the best of days. It was outright illegible right now.

'It's the speech I have to make for Paati day after tomorrow. I don't have any ideas or pointers…I was hoping you'd write it for me.'

Now I felt doubly bad. 'Oh.'

'It's okay if you don't want to do it.' She made to take the paper away from me.

I held on to it with a clenched fist. 'No,' I said. 'I will write something awesome. For Paati. I'll do it. Don't worry.'

'You're sure?'

'Yes.' I nodded emphatically.

'The vaadhyar is coming in twenty minutes. Please come down on time.' It was the closest she could come to offering an apology. Couched in mom terms. At least, that is how I consoled myself.

Especially today.

*Dear Lasya,*

*The HR department has been trying to contact you for the last two days regarding the terms of your WFH, which you have not fulfilled to the fullest extent of your capabilities and your manager's expectations. And, therefore, are not eligible for anymore.*

*Given below is a list of all tasks that were assigned to you that remain incomplete or unfulfilled, on Asana as well as on private chat with your manager.*

*Please let me know when will be a good time to talk to you about the matter. Please do treat this grave issue with the attention it deserves.*

*My number is...*

The words swam before my eyes and my head pounded as I scrolled through the rest of the email. It had appeared with nothing more than a silent, vibrating buzz two minutes ago. The subject of which read: Concerns Regarding WFH Extension. It read like a lengthy, airtight excuse to fire someone.

All neatly and very precisely documented on a Microsoft Excel sheet.

The basic gist of the email was that I was only logging in about ten hours every day, not responding immediately enough to emails and calls from colleagues and generally goofing off. Bottom line? I had to shape the hell up or expect to be fired at a moment's notice for a long list of infractions and transgressions.

I closed my eyes and tried to pay attention to the monotone of the vaadhyar as he droned on in Sanskrit, reading mantras from one of the four Veda Puranas and hastened my grandmother's departed soul on its journey to heaven. Of course, considering she had spent the last year completely bedridden, unable to even go to the toilet without assistance, I figured she had suffered her own version of hell while still on earth.

It should have put my own life in perspective, thinking about the hard, harsh life that Chandralekha Chakrapani had led. Thinking about the fact that she had to die in order for her family—extended, near and far—to gather under one roof.

But, honestly, I was seized by panic. Consuming, unassailing panic. I couldn't get fired. I could not *afford* to get fired. I still had the remaining mortgage to pay off on the house that was almost sold. I needed to be productive, useful, contribute as an employed human being to a structured society. This job, shitty as it was, and as much as I despised it, was all I had.

I needed it.

I needed the daily human contact it provided and the monthly salary that pinged into my bank account and the fact that, even if it was a stupid potty-mouth website as far removed from pop culture as the local newspaper was from *Rolling Stone* magazine, it validated me. In a very real and meaningful way. Now, I had truly struck rock bottom.

Because, now even the job I hated was in jeopardy of being taken away from me.

# Chapter Nineteen

'*M*om's calling you,' Atharva muttered as he helped me wash the dishes after dinner.

We might have had wait staff to do domestic chores for us when we were growing up, but living alone had made my brother and I self-sufficient in a few ways. An affliction no one else really suffered from, given how they'd chosen to not help us.

'Calling me for what?' I was in no mood to chat with anyone tonight.

After the disastrous, extremely short conversation with Puru and the general sombre mood of the day—I had never seen Deep uncle cry before—I just wanted to snuggle up in bed under three layers of blankets, ready for the sweet oblivion of sleep. I had even bought a nice romance online to cheer myself up.

Yeah, I was that cheesy sap who believed in love and the happily-ever-after as depicted in books. And tonight, more than anything else, I needed to believe in something.

'I don't know.' My brother had perfected the art of shrugging without shrugging. It was one of many things I lacked. 'She didn't say. She just wanted me to tell you to go to Paati's rooms when you're done cleaning up.'

'Alright.'

A second later, he said, 'So, do I need to talk to you about spending the night with a semi-stranger or do I hope you guys used protection?' He playfully flicked a drop of water at me.

I elbowed him. Hard. He howled.

I scrubbed vigorously at the rasam stains on the ceramic plate.

'You stay out of my love life and I'll stay out of yours.'

'I was just trying to help.' His mutter was defensive but his tone was sheepish. He stopped flicking water at me.

We washed the rest of the dishes in silence while I desperately tried to come up with a plan that would save my job, help me pay off the loan on my overpriced house and magically fix everything else wrong with my life. Unfortunately, liquid soap and scrub could only do so much and, pretty soon, I shucked off the dish towel and apron I was using to clean the dishes. I made my slow way over to the only part of the house I hadn't visited since that first day.

Chandralekha Chakrapani's rooms.

The menfolk had retired for the day. I didn't blame them. Sleep sounded like heaven right now.

A small burst of female laughter caught me by surprise at the corridor that led to her suite. Was that Kiara? Jo squealed next. I was now intrigued. I wished absently for my phone, the familiar heft and comforting weight of it in my palms. But, refreshing my email inbox was not going to get me any closer to a miracle than washing dishes. What would happen would happen.

I smiled a little. That homily sounded exactly like something my grandmother would say. Chin up. Get the work done. That's something else she would say.

I pushed open the old-fashioned carved wooden door.

'Hey,' I said as I took in the scene before me. 'Did we decide to have a sleepover or something?'

'LJ atha!' Jo shrieked when she saw me, and jumped three feet down from the bed where she had been jumping, a little trail of her mother's dupatta dragging on the floor as she dashed towards me and into my arms. 'We are painting our nails and gossiping,' she informed me, smiling widely.

I noticed that one of her upper front teeth was missing. 'Jo baby.' I pushed affectionately at the gap in her teeth. 'Did the tooth fairy visit you last night?'

Her head bobbed like it was on a spring, violent and enthusiastic. I almost got whiplash as her curls swung forward with the force of her nods. 'Yes! And I got twenty rupees from the fairy too.'

I caught Ahalya's eyes, diligently applying a demure brown nail paint on my mother's toenails. 'Someone has a very generous tooth fairy.'

Her shoulders twitched. But at least she didn't outright bark at me. I'd take what I could get at the moment.

'Come on, LJ atha.'

Kiki waved me over while blowing on the nails of one hand. 'I need your help painting my left hand. Jo baby has picked out really pretty colours.'

Jo nodded again and some of her hair went into my eye and I blinked back tears. 'I'll pick the colours for you too, Atha.'

She wriggled off me like the little monkey she was and bounded over to where Kiki and Prapti had a small manicure kit, complete with a buffer and pointy scissors. Prapti pulled Jo onto her lap and cuddled her close, closing her eyes while a small smile played on her lips.

On the other side of the huge bed, Kiara and Subhadra were flipping through a fashion magazine, their heads bent close together, one blond and one grey-haired. Giggling like a couple of schoolgirls.

My mom saw me, standing 3 feet apart from the familial scene. Something that happened often, when I was younger. I'd stand, either in a corner or in the centre of a room, while the aunts, uncles, my parents and siblings gathered for meals or a family photo and I'd make up stories about how I felt right then.

I'd make up stories about how a stranger would see the scene unfolding in front of them. All of us talking one over the other, shameless and a bit offensive too. Just like any other Indian middle-class family. And, after a few minutes, my mother would catch my eye and beckon me towards her with a small smile.

A heavy, suffocating wave of love filled my chest, spilled out of me in a shaky breath. I blinked again. This time a very real ball of tears was lodged in my chest because I realized that I really and truly loved my well-meaning, condescending and judgemental family.

'God,' I whispered. 'I love you all.'

Mom tilted her head a bit to the side and waved me over. She smiled tonight too. 'I'm sorry,' she mouthed.

'For what?' I whispered back.

She patted the seat next to her, beckoning me to come forward.

'LJ, come on. Kiki won't let me touch her precious nails,' Prapti said. I shook my head, gave Mom an apologetic smile, and perched on the side of the bed that Prapti and Kiki occupied.

'I'm done with the speech,' I said aloud to my mother. 'You can read it if you want to.'

'You can read it for us,' Kiara said, addressing me directly for the first time in days. 'Can't you?'

I immediately shook my head. 'No. It's not mine. It's Mom's. She can read it if she wants to. I'll make any changes required.'

'Sure. Hold it for me, then. And get my glasses, Kunjalam[43]? There is a spare in Paati's big cupboard.' Mom ran a fond hand over Jo's hair and Jo scampered to the almirah and scrounged for the glasses. She found them and brought them over while I handed Mom the one-page speech I'd written for her.

I settled next to Kiki, looking critically at the bottle of gold polish she held up for my consideration. 'You don't want silver?

---

[43]Dearest girl

It's more muted, isn't it?' Kiki shook her head, much like Jo had, vehemently and with great force. 'I am sick of muted and circumspect. I want bright, bold colour.'

Prapti and I shared a quick, knowing grin, then I started applying the paint. Behind me I could hear Mom clear her throat and then she started reading in a low monotone.

'Manni[44], louder please,' Subhadra said.

'And with more inflection,' Kiara added.

I moved on from the little finger to Kiki's ring finger on her left hand. The diamond solitaire Trilok had given her three years ago and which she'd finally worn last year in a formal engagement ceremony had lost some of its shine. Constant use had dulled the warmth of the gold and the facets weren't as sharp as they used to be.

But, that ring symbolized commitment. Everlasting love. Two people who had made it, despite every possible obstacle thrown at them. That ring meant Kiki had made a promise to someone to be there for them. And to have someone be there for her.

It was priceless.

*You don't have anyone.*

I shook my head because I didn't want to hear Ben's calm voice echoing there. As if underscoring the fact that maybe, just maybe, I had made a huge mistake letting him walk away. That maybe I'd been too hard on him because I was running scared...

'LJ,' Kiki hissed, waving a hand at me. 'Pay attention. Your mom is reading your speech.'

I tuned back in.

'...Chandralekha was a beacon of hope, a fair but tough businesswoman and a compassionate human being.

'When I was newly married, and we spent our first harvest

---

[44]Older sister-in-law

season here at the Illam instead of back in the city, I had my first real conversation with the woman I only knew as mother-in-law. It was evening, the air smelled of tea grounds, rain and hope. And the streetlights were not what they are now, so my husband and his workers would guard the crops through the night in turns.

'Chandralekha, Ammamma[45]', Mom smiled, because I'd used the term everyone in Munnar called Paati, 'always stayed awake till we made the first batch of tea for the guardians.

'One night, the night I am talking about, I requested her to go to bed. I'd do the needful. Make the tea and send it for my husband and the other workers. I was cranky, there was nothing much to do here back then. The TV didn't work, we didn't even have electricity through the night.' Everyone chuckled at this bit, on cue.

'So, there I was. A newly-wed bride whose husband preferred to spend his nights with the tea leaves than me.' Mom raised a brow at the slightly risqué language but continued on, 'And my mother-in-law did not trust me with making tea. I don't exactly remember if I cried, or if my frustration was evident on my face. So, Ammamma sat me down on the chair in the kitchen while she brewed the aromatic tea our business is known for. Elaichi and spices ground with ginger to make the most intoxicating scent.'

Mom sighed a little and pushed the glasses up her nose. I continued to apply nail paint on Kiki's toes as carefully as I could.

'And she said, "Gomti, these men will never admit to needing us. But they do. It is up to you to make him see that. It's backward but then no one ever said men were particularly smart, right?" I was shocked at the casual words and the wisdom behind it. So, I asked her, "Aren't you including your son in the not-smart category?" Ammamma winked at me. "He was smart enough to

---

[45] A respectful way of saying Amma.

find you. The rest of it is up to you." They were crude words. But effective. They were something my own mother should have said to me, but didn't. My mother-in-law did.

'It was the day she became my amma. And I can't believe she is gone.'

Mom's voice trailed off as she raised stunned eyes to me. Tears glistened in them, fogging the glasses. The paper rustled in her hands as she lowered it. My heart thumped loudly in my chest.

'How did you know?' Her voice creaked. So, she cleared her throat and said again, 'How did you know about this? I never told you about this incident.'

I shrugged. 'Paati told me years ago. When I was asking her about the harvest season.'

'And you remembered it?'

'It's my job to remember stuff like this, Mom.' I paused before continuing, 'Paati said, that night was the first time she realized you weren't from this world. You were a city girl and you had married into an agrarian business family. You needed help. Like her own daughter would.'

Subhadra sniffled and Kiara patted her back.

'That was some speech.' Prapti sounded amazed. 'I didn't know... It was so real. As if it was happening in front of me. Right, Kiki?'

Kiki squeezed my knee. A silent gesture of support. 'Yeah. Right in front of me.'

'Gomtimma, don't cry.' Jo hugged my mother.

Mom crushed the little girl to her chest, unmindful of wet paint on her fingers. Tears seeped out of her closed eyes.

'That was a good speech, Kunju.' For the first time in a long time, my mother looked at me with something other than disappointment, regret and bewilderment.

'It's in English,' Ahalya said in a so-helpful voice. 'Most of the locals won't even get the fancy words.'

Yep, my moment of fragile peace with her was over.

'I'll translate it,' Mom murmured.

'Yes, Ahalya,' Kiki said. 'Ever heard of the words "good job"? You should try saying them sometimes.'

'Why?' Ahalya rounded on Kiki, with fire in her eyes. 'Anyone can cobble together a few chosen words. It doesn't require skill and talent. Showing up and working eighteen-hour days through crises and disasters requires real guts. The kind Lasya doesn't have.'

'Dude, in case you missed the obvious, people are crying here.' Kiki angrily dashed off a thumb under her own eye. 'That wasn't just cobbling together a few chosen words. That sort of thing moves people. Something you're incapable of.'

'Mommy. Can you not fight with Kiki atha?' Jo said in a tiny voice while I sat there, mute. Incapable of defending myself. Only hearing Ben's condemning words in my head: *You don't have anyone.*

'Be quiet, Kiki,' Subhadra hissed at her daughter. Kiara looked at all of us in distress. 'Don't talk to Ahalya like that.'

'Why not, Amma?' Kiki shot back. 'Someone needs to. She's been picking on LJ constantly since she got here and I am so pissed at her.'

Ahalya's eyes filled and I felt it like a punch to my gut. I squeezed Kiki's knee. Hard.

She threw my hand away and looked me square in the eye. 'Tell her. Tell her how shitty your day has been.'

'What happened, Lasya?' Mom asked.

I shook my head. 'Nothing, Mom. Kiki's raging for no reason.' I squeezed her knee again, digging my nails in. 'She'll stop now.'

'Are you sure?' Mom insisted. 'Is it because we fought in the morning?'

'Of course, she fought with you in the morning, Mami,' Ahalya jumped in. 'Today of all mornings, when Mama is already so exhausted and you have a fever.'

It stunned me how scared I was in that moment when I heard my mother was unwell. 'Mom, you have a fever? Why didn't you tell me?'

'It's nothing.' Mom dismissed her health as if it was of no consequence. 'It's just all the hair baths. I am fine. I had strong tea and pepper milk. Are you upset because of me?'

'Manni, we should sleep,' Kiara said, awkward as hell in the middle of all the family drama.

I shook my head. 'No, Mom, I'm not upset because of you.'

'Why didn't you tell me you fought with Perimma?' Kiki demanded, while she blew furiously on her nails.

I could already see Ahalya raring to scream some more at me.

'I am sorry, Ahalya,' I told her. For the millionth time. She didn't hear me. As always.

Subhadra and Kiara talked to Mom, prescribing home remedies for her.

'Hey!' There was a loud clap and we all quietened down. The yell and clap was from Prapti. She held a bottle of red nail paint in her hands and waved it once. I could see that two of her fingers were unpainted, the thumb and index finger. It was oddly jarring to look at, vivid red against her fair skin.

'What is wrong with you all?' Prapti spoke through clenched teeth.

Mom looked shocked. Prapti waved the bottle in her direction. 'Not you, Amma. Or Subhadra aunty or Kiara. But you three.' She withered us with her glance. 'You can't go five minutes without screaming at each other?'

'Prapti—' Ahalya began in a huff.

'Don't even bother, Ahalya. I have listened to you bitch about how LJ gets everything she asks for just because she asks for it for the last goddamn time. How impossible it is to raise Jo alone with no help whatsoever and how you wished everything was different.

Have you even bothered to ask if Gargi is doing okay? She is alone there while Vidhaant is here. And she has twins!'

My jaw dropped open. Ahalya said what? She thought I had it easy? What planet was she living in?

'And you,' Prapti rounded on Kiki who cowered behind me. 'Be kinder to your mother, will you? She's just lost her mother-in-law, your freaking grandmother, and she is paying for an expensive wedding that will now not take place. So she is worried and tired and needs a fucking break.'

'I...' Kiki shut up after Prapti's skewering look. Prapti moved on to me.

'Praaps,' I began uncomfortably.

'And you...you're so blind, LJ. You haven't even bothered to ask Atharva if everything is okay with him. Do you know he wasn't given his promotion, the one he worked his ass off for? He's crushed. He's been crushed since June. And he is still worried about you, the sister who cannot get her life together. Instead of me, his wife. I am exhausted with all your family drama, with coming second with my own husband. And I just...'

'Prapti,' Mom said quietly.

Prapti dragged her shattered eyes to my mother. 'I'm tired,' she repeated, defiance in every line of her brittle body.

Mom held her arms out and Prapti crawled into them. Kiki and I stared at each other in utter shock. Even Ahalya looked mildly concerned, while Jo's eyes rounded to the size of saucers.

Mom rubbed Prapti's back, murmuring soothing words, and Prapti held on to her and sobbed like a baby.

'You can't keep fighting like this. All of you,' Subhadra said, tearfully. 'You're family. You're all you have.'

'Come on, LJ,' Kiki said decisively. 'I need the blow dryer to dry my toes. It's in my room.' Then she leaned down and gave her mother a quick, hard hug. 'If that's okay with you, Mommy.'

'Don't be cute, Kunju.' Subhadra's chuckle followed us out of the room.

We walked up the stairs, our slippers clacking on the cold floor. Kiki and I looked at each other in utter and absolute misery when we reached the first-floor landing.

'You knew?' Kiki asked. 'About Atharva?'

I shook my head as hot shame and guilt assailed me. 'No. I didn't.'

She sighed. 'He didn't tell anyone, I think.'

'I should have known.'

'Yes,' she sighed. 'You should have.'

I glared at her. 'Thanks for that, Kiki. It's real supportive of you.'

'Hey.' She nudged my shoulder. 'I bitched out Ahalya in front of the moms for you. My middle name is supportive.'

I gave her a sideway hug and she said, 'Want to come in and crash with me? I don't want to sleep alone.'

'Yeah,' I said. 'Me neither.'

We snuggled together under the blankets, after shucking off our shoes and squealing at the cold, cold floor. My phone buzzed.

*Hey. Sorry for this morning. ~ B.*

My heart stuttered. But I wasn't sure. I didn't know what he wanted, what he was apologizing for. My sister's bad behaviour, his own ambiguous comment or the fact that we had been together. And I didn't want to find out tonight.

'What are you going to do?' Kiki asked quietly. 'About the job? You can't go back till we're done here. And you know it's not for the money. We have to do this for Paati.'

I sniffed, but I attributed that to the unholy cold. No more tears. 'I know. I know it's not for the money. But the money will be good for us all. You have another wedding to pay for.'

'Trilok's right, you know.' Kiki was mournful. 'We should just do a court marriage and be done with it. We are cursed with the wedding gods, anyway.'

'You're just saying that because Prapti laid a guilt trip on you. You don't really mean it.' I paused for a second. 'I don't think she gets it…us. You, Ahalya and me.'

'Yeah. It's why she feels like she is competing with you for Atharva's affection.'

'I'm going to have to apologize to her too, aren't I?'

'She's probably pregnant,' Kiki said, rubbing my shoulder for comfort. 'Her outburst is just hormones acting out.'

'You know you're a doctor, right? You can't make such casual, sexist, and blatantly stupid assessments without checking the patient out.'

I turned to face her while my phone buzzed again. Another text message. I resisted the urge to check it. It buzzed once more. He was calling me now.

Kiki saw the caller ID and rolled her eyes. 'You had to screw things up with him too, didn't you?'

'I didn't…I don't know if I did.'

'Do you want to fix it?'

'He thinks he's my rebound after what happened with Mehul.'

Kiki asked the most logical question: 'Is that what you think?'

I looked at his name. Stored on my phone as Ben the Lawyer. I could picture him, clear as a bell, in my head. Those endlessly dark eyes, which never really smiled, the break on his longish nose. The texture of his hair. The shape of his lips right before it curved into a smile and he leaned down and kissed me.

How he'd sounded when he'd spoken about his own fucked-up family. Lonely. And yearning.

Like me.

'I don't know,' I whispered. All the lonely yearning rose up inside me like a tidal wave, threatening to drown me.

'Then it's time to find out, behena.'

Kiki's sleepy words hit me where it hurt. So I opened his message thread and wrote: *I need your help in figuring something out.*

His reply came gratifyingly fast: *What?*

I thought about Prapti's comments to all of us. How right she was. Especially about Ahalya, who was a single mother to a very demanding seven-year-old. About Subhadra who had spent in the seven figures for a cancelled wedding. About Gargi, Vidhaant's wife, who was single-handedly managing twin toddlers.

And my own twin brother, the boy who had stepped in front of me and taken bullets with my name on it when it came to my father. The man who had sat and poured whiskey into me for four hours the night my play bombed. The man who put my happiness above his sainted wife's.

And I thought about Paati and how she'd been crude and brusque and helped so many, *many* people with her words and deeds and money.

*It's legal stuff. Can we do a call tomorrow morning? Whenever it suits you?*

His reply was quick: *I'm staying at the Vivanta. Working here. Come see me for breakfast?*

I mulled over his offer. While a small part of me was ecstatic that he was still here, that we could still touch if we so wished it, common sense and sheer empirical evidence indicated he wasn't here for me. It was Paati's legal business.

*I'll buy you the largest mug of coffee known to man.*

I sent him a smiley face. It was a non-answer, but screw it, I was entitled to a little ambiguity myself at this point.

'Stop texting so loudly,' Kiki muttered in her sleep.

And then, for good measure, she took my phone and threw it across the bed so it landed on the opposite side. Since it was exactly what I needed so I wouldn't type 'YES, YES, YES' in bold, large font to follow my smiley emoji, I let it go this one time, without any retaliation at all—physical or verbal.

Besides, I was distracted with planning my next few steps. And, hopefully, making things right with everyone I loved.

# Chapter Twenty

*I* was dreaming. I was on stage at the NCPA, with an armful of bouquets, waving my arm like a pageant beauty queen, in slow motion. For the plebes out there, the NCPA, or National Centre for Performing Arts, is a prestigious place of theatre history, with the greats of this country, such as Dr Mohan Agashe, Alyque Padamsee and Naseeruddin Shah, having played out their magnum opuses on its circular stage. The tickets cost a pretty penny too and the lighting board on the stage is nothing short of fantastic.

Also, for the record, the stage production of *Spectacular Melancholy of Living* was not staged at the NCPA. It was a little off-town playhouse, which, unfortunately, got shut down a couple weeks after the play closed on the opening night. The tickets had cost ₹100.

As producer-playwright, I'd even bought four tickets for Prapti, Atharva, myself, and a Tinder date who never showed up. We were preceded by a couple who sat in the last row and made out quite loudly for the entirety of the play. And, of course, the *Time Out* critic who tore my little play, my baby, into pieces in his online review and ensured that the thing couldn't survive day two.

This was reality, how it happened.

But, in my dream, it was the NCPA. I was being feted with a crown and my arm ached from holding the flowers. I bowed, along with the rest of my cast, and a warm hand slipped into mine. I turned. It was Ben. I smiled goofily. He smiled back. And we bowed together.

'This is for you,' he whispered in a really clear voice that I could hear over thunderous applause.

I smiled some more and tried to balance the flowers and my tiara when I bowed. The stage, where the most famous theatre personalities of India had performed, was spotlit. It was a hardwood parquet that still contained yellow tape for marks and blocking for the smashing play that *I* had written, for which I was receiving a standing ovation.

The play that starred the most handsome, most solid man I had ever met. A man who kissed like a biker boy on steroids. My lips tingled in anticipation of his kiss and I smiled some more.

*Plop.* Something white and square-ish fell on the hardwood floor. I was confused. *Plop.* A second white and square-ish thing fell on the hardwood floor. I looked at Ben and his features pinched in horror and disgust.

'Your face,' he said.

I let go of his hand and touched my face. My jaw felt lighter. A bit hollow. I watched in numbing, mounting horror as one more white and square-ish thing fell out. This time, from the cavity of my mouth. I put a trembling hand to my lips. Felt nothing where my front molars should be.

I looked down again.

They were teeth. *My* teeth. Oh GOD! Oh dear God! More teeth fell out, turning me into an old crone of a woman right where I stood—ugly and desiccated. Sort of like my grandmother, but with more body mass and horrified eyes. I opened my mouth, to scream, to yell, and all my teeth fell out, every last one of them… and I could only watch their doomed progress as gravity had their way with them…

The flowers fell down mixing with the teeth and I felt huge, bulbous tears fall down my cheeks, while Banjeet Dewar walked off the stage into the waiting arms of a heavily pregnant woman who looked like Minika, the hotel receptionist, with her huge breasts and fake smile.

I felt around the inside of my mouth, my heart pounding so loudly, it was echoing in the auditorium, and I could only find gums, plain gums worn smooth by teeth long gone.

And a scream erupted that I could neither contain nor hide. I opened my mouth for a sound that was raw and aching and dull and never-ending...

'LJ, wake up. Wake up!'

Kiki shook me violently awake and I opened my eyes with a short scream. My breath sobbing inside my lungs. I immediately touched my jaw and felt the sharp, poking set of teeth against my fingertips. I heaved a relieved breath.

'What? What happened?' I whispered.

'Ahalya's screaming downstairs. We have to go.' Kiki pulled off the comforter even as she spoke. She shoved her feet into mismatched slippers.

I almost drifted off. She shook me harder. I struggled to stay awake. 'I don't know if I can deal with Ahalya right now.'

'JOOOOO!' Ahalya's scream could be heard ringing through the rafters now.

The word penetrated my foggy brain and I sat up straight, shoved my feet into my own slippers and followed Kiki, who was way too awake for 6 a.m.

All the lights in the whole house were ablaze all at once. I blinked to adjust my eyes to the sudden blinding light. I tried to process the reason for why my upper middle-class, but decidedly frugal, family would light up the house like Diwali at dawn, but I was still back at the NCPA stage. With my falling teeth and a smiling Ben.

Nothing made sense to me.

We ran into the living room; into utter and complete chaos. Everyone was in varying states of nightdress and Ahalya was crying at the dining table. Silently, in heaving sobs. In a way I had only seen once before—when Sukumar had confessed his adultery to her.

A pang of premonition struck my already panicked brain.

My mom held her tightly, her face a mask of fear and unprecedented worry.

I was afraid of the answer even as I asked, 'What happened?'

Vidhaant answered grimly, 'It's Jo. We don't know where she is.'

At that, Ahalya's sobs turned into a wail. A never-ending, horrified scream of your worst nightmare coming true.

And the ground fell from underneath me yet again.

'Tell me what happened again.' I gulped down piping hot coffee that I had to prepare myself. It was just Atharva and me in the kitchen, as he had followed me, half-aware and following the magic words, 'I need coffee.'

Not-so-perfect Prapti was out there, consoling Ahalya, still weeping inconsolably.

'I don't know myself. I woke up about half an hour ago when Ahalya banged on our door. She had a note in her hand, from Jo. She was wild and incoherent. It took me a minute to understand what she was saying. There was just so much crying. I thought I was dreaming.'

'That makes two of us.' My mutter was only half-fearful.

I still couldn't fully believe that Ahalya was out in the living room. Crying. Talking about her missing baby…my missing niece.

It seemed frankly incomprehensible.

We paused to finish off our coffee and I rinsed the glasses. 'Okay. Then?'

'Then she showed me the note when I couldn't understand her.' He closed his eyes and shuddered; his shoulder muscles quivering in a quick, jolting movement. 'It said she was sorry she was so much trouble and that she was going to go live with her daddy. Love, Jo.'

'Oh God.' My knees felt rubbery. I clutched the back of Atharva's chair. He clutched my hand. 'What was she *thinking*?'

'Prapti told me,' Atharva said bleakly. 'She told me what happened in Paati's room. How she yelled at Ahalya and said some pretty harsh things. She blames herself for all of this.'

'Of course, it's not Prapti's fault. She is just reacting badly to this mess.' Then, I voiced the one thought running rampant in my head: 'Are we even sure she is missing?'

Atharva gave me a grim look. 'It's a seven-year-old kid, LJ. She has taken her favourite lunch box and Ahalya is pretty sure she changed clothes in the middle of the night. At this point, let's assume she is missing.'

'I wasn't trying to be hurtful.'

'I know.'

I sat down next to Atharva and laid my head on his very dependable, tree-like shoulder. 'I am sorry,' I said softly.

He laid his cheek against my temple. 'What are you sorry for? This isn't your fault.'

'Not for this.' I shook my head. 'For the promotion thing.'

He gave me a surprised look. That was a feat. Atharva was rarely, if ever, surprised. Chagrined, bemused, amused and confused by me. But I never surprised him. Not when it came to birthday gifts or planning bachelor parties (we did a Goa trip on a casino boat; he ended up lending me money to come back to Mumbai) or cheating off exam papers in school.

'Who told you about that?'

'Prapti, you big dummy.' I mock-punched his arm. 'You're supposed to tell me if stuff is worrying you. Stuff that is not me-related. It helps to talk, you know.'

'Like you've talked?'

'We aren't talking about me. We are talking about you. And your wife. Who, by the way, gave a very good impression of being on the verge of a nervous breakdown. What is going on with you two?'

He sighed and rubbed the spot on his arm where I'd landed a punch. 'She's just overworked. We were counting on my promotion, so she could take a sabbatical. But that fell through, so she is feeling the pressure. Plus, people won't stop asking us about a baby.'

'What? Who?'

Atharva's look was cynical and droll at the same time. A non-eye-roll eye roll. 'Everyone, LJ. Haven't you seen how much Prapti hides in the kitchen when the guests come?'

'I just thought she really loved helping Mom and the aunts out.'

'She does.'

I rubbed the spot where I had punched his arm. 'I didn't know all was not well in paradise.'

'That's because it's not paradise,' he said shortly. 'Nothing ever is. No matter how much it looks like it.'

His answer was pithy and on-point. And made so much sense. It made me instantly rethink how much I'd judged Perfect Prapti, and the ease and grace with which she handled everything life threw at her. Not-so-perfect Prapti was a lot more likeable for the eternal screw-up that I was.

And I suppose it made me a horrible person that I preferred a messed-up relationship than the bubblegum glow of my brother's marriage.

'Are you thinking of quitting?' I knew how hard Atharva had worked at his present job. The long hours he put in, the crap he took from his present boss when the man called with all sorts of unreasonable demands, the weekends he sat with his laptop instead of taking Prapti out for a date or whatever it is that married couples did. Grocery shopping, maybe?

'I don't know. I have updated my resume. Maybe I'll ask Dad for a job.' He smiled mirthlessly. 'You think they'll let me back in?'

'I—'

'There you both are,' Subhadra said briskly as she walked in to the kitchen with all the pride and purpose of a military general. 'We are organizing a search party within a 5-kilometre radius. Raghav anna is calling up all the neighbours and asking them to be on the lookout for Jokutti. You two need to go join the others.'

I shook my head while Atharva waggled his brows. Of all the people to take charge and not wail today, Subhadra was not at the top of my list. Yet, here she was. Taking charge and not wailing.

I followed my brother's tall, lean, pyjama-clad form out.

We split into several different groups with Ahalya, Subhadra and my mom electing to stay back and man the fort, so to speak. They were each armed with two phones and the numbers of everyone they could think of.

My father had spread a huge map of the estate on the dining table and Trilok, our elected cartographer, had marked it into grids of a quarter of a hectare. Even with so many of us and a few volunteers including Giridhar uncle and his two sons, who also doubled as the family drivers, it was a fuck load of ground to cover.

Everyone looked grim enough, so I didn't have the heart to point out the obvious flaws in this plan. The ground was too vast, the tea crops too thick and Jo too small, for us to have a realistic chance of finding her. Especially since it wasn't even broad daylight.

I knew why we were doing this.

We had to do something. *Anything*. Staying at home and looking at Ahalya's wailing face was not an option.

Not even for me.

We worked out a system of texting in the family WhatsApp group, formed expressly for this purpose and, armed with flashlights, watch caps and sturdy boots, set out in search of one tiny seven-year-old girl.

By dumb luck, I ended up with Atharva and Prapti for the first leg of the trek, hiking up the trail that led below Paati's personal tea garden. The ground was fragrant and mulched under my feet and I held on tight to my brother's comforting grip as I slithered my way down the slope. Finally, we reached level ground and spread out as we yelled Jo's name. In all its variations.

Jo. Jothika. Jokutti. Jo darling.

The chirping and cawing of morning birds and the beeps of phones greeted our cries.

I remembered how Paati had brought Atharva and I to her tea garden and given us one tea plant each to plant for our fifth birthday. We'd been bored children, not interested in our legacy or a lengthy explanation of how the hybrid tea variant that she had developed against my grandfather's wishes was now the top bestseller due to its organic nature, its fragrance ratio and its tannin content.

She'd made us water it daily for the remainder of our summer here. And we had done so because it was easier to do what she wanted than refuse.

I couldn't remember what happened to those plants now, but they were one more reminder of this link that I had to my childhood, my legacy. My family and the matriarch and who'd held it all together for decades on end.

Paati had been too ill in the last two years to do the same with Jo; she would never know what it was to grow something, to pat down the earth and water it and watch it blossom into something pure and alive in a way nothing else quite was.

I squeezed Atharva's hand again. 'Hey, bear,' I said softly.

He stopped yelling Jo's name and looked quizzically at me. 'What's up?'

I shook my head, reached up on my toes and kissed him on his unshaven cheek. He smelled of early morning dew, tea leaves and some cologne he'd splashed on. Probably Prapti's doing. She was particular about things like that.

'I never thanked you, not once, for being there for me.'

'LJ—' He cleared his throat.

'Atharva, you've done so much for me,' I said gently. 'All my life. You've looked out for me and shielded me against Dad's wrath.'

His eyes, so like mine, filled, and he cleared his throat. 'I haven't been able to shield you against Dad's wrath for two years now. I failed you. Both of you.'

My jaw dropped. As I considered the utter bullshit my brother had just stated. Why would he think any of what had happened between Appa and me his fault? Then it struck me. Of course, he would. Because I'd always put him in the middle. I *had* expected him to shield me. Except that last time.

That time I had stood up for myself.

I'd had to. My father's accusation had been too enormous, too personal to hide behind Atharva anymore.

'You idiot,' I whispered furiously. 'That is between Appa and me. That is not your fault. It never was. Do you not understand that?'

He made a noise that sounded like a grunt. I growled back. Prapti was a few steps ahead of us, the only thing visible about her was her cute muffler, in Gryffindor red and gold.

I dug my nails into Atharva's buff arms. He winced but he paid attention to me. 'We don't have all that much time to get into this right now but listen well, Anna.' I never called him Anna. *Ever.* 'You have to let go of me, now. I can't be the first thing, the first person, you save. That has to be your wife… Who loves you very much, God knows why.' I smiled slightly, even as his face fell.

'LJ, I'm so sorry—'

'No.' I shook my head. 'No, this is not the time for you to go on a guilt trip. That was not why I said this to you. So you're not going to make this about that.'

His lips quirked at the corners. 'You know how to be brutal, don't you?'

'I learned from the best—our dad.' I winked.

Atharva sighed and regarded his wife, clomping through mud and mulch and rows of tea crops, immaculately dressed as always and not one word of complaint. 'She's incredible, isn't she?' he murmured.

'She is. I sincerely hope when you have kids, the only thing they inherit from you is your height and our eye colour. Golden brown is so sexy.' I batted my own lashes.

He laughed softly. A second later, I joined too. But only for a moment. The calls of Jokutti and Jo pierced the air and cut short our moment.

We joined the hunt and tromped through the hills and valleys in two more grids before I cautiously made my way to Prapti's side.

I'd made up with my brother. It was time to befriend my sister-in-law. For good.

'Hey.' I tapped her shoulder, right before she let loose one more 'JO'!

I winced as my ear drums vibrated from the noise.

'Hey. Is it my turn to report to the group?' She'd already whipped her phone out, ready to do the needful.

Because there was so much area to be covered and about eighteen of us on the prowl, having everyone ping with an update every two minutes was counterproductive to the actual search. So, we'd elected Prapti to handle the communications part of our search while Atharva and I bent and looked under every possible tea crop and side alley to find one little girl.

Fear had coalesced into an ugly black mass in my stomach, so every breath was painful. It could be because of the kilometres of trudging I'd done in the last three hours, but I knew better.

We'd all screwed up. With the kid. With each other. It was time to set at least one thing to rights.

'No, it's not your turn yet.' I lowered her phone and gave her a brief hug. She was too surprised to do anything but return it. Bending at the neck and shoulders to do so, but she did.

'You're so good for my brother,' I told her without preamble.

Prapti raised one finely shaped brow, but said nothing.

So, I had to continue talking. 'Ben said something the other night. He said that anyone who didn't know us would find it hard to break into our group. He said that Ahalya's always felt out of depth with us. And that's true for you too, isn't it? Especially with Atharva and me.'

She didn't answer but her eyes were a little sad, a little wary. 'I don't understand where you're going with this, LJ.'

'You were right last night.' I sighed and felt snot drip down my nose.

Prapti dug into her tight jeans pocket and came up with a tissue. *Of course, she'd have a tissue. Of course.* But, this time, instead of resenting her for it or thinking her superior to me by being Perfect Prapti, I smiled at her. Delighted to have someone in my corner, who was always so prepared.

'Thanks,' I said and blew loudly into it. I crumped the tissue in my hand.

'LJ, we don't have to—' she began.

I cut her off with a shake of my head. 'My timing always sucks but, Prapti, you've got to hear this. You were one hundred per cent right about all of us Chakrapani women bitching out at each other instead of working things out. And you were right that Atharva's paid a lot more attention to my life and my problems than he should have.'

She gave an uncomfortable shrug. 'I didn't mean it exactly like that, LJ. And I'd never imply that you're not important to me too.'

'Prapti, sweetie, shut it, will you?'

Because I'd never used that particular tone of affection mixed with authority, she did as I ordered. It was the tone my grandmother used with me when I went on one of my pointless, argumentative tangents.

I squeezed her hand. 'I have been a bad sister to Atharva and, worse, I've been a sister-in-law to you when I should have been a sister to you too. Or,' I added with a lump in my throat, 'at the very least, a good friend.'

Her eyes filled and two large, perfect tears rolled down her cheeks. She wiped them away immediately. 'I'm sorry,' she sniffed. 'I shouldn't cry now, when we are searching for Jo. I just...'

'You don't have to be perfect every single minute, woman.' I grinned and handed her the cleaner half of my tissue. She accepted it gratefully.

'When we get back to our regular lives, I'd love to come down to Pune and we can have a girl's weekend, if you're up for it? I'd ask for Kiki to join us but I think she's exhausted her quota of leave with the wedding that never was.'

Prapti sniffed some more.

'Of course, only if you're really up for it,' I rushed to assure her. 'This is not a duty thing or a family thing. You can ask me to fuck off if you want to. I deserve that.'

She gave a watery chuckle and hugged me again. Tight. With arms and her whole heart. And I hugged her back.

'I'd love to hang out with you, Lasya. And not for duty or family. I'd love for us to be friends too. But I only have one problem with this scenario.'

'What's that?'

'Why the fuck would we hang out in Pune when I could come down to Mumbai and we can go to all those fabulous designer places and spend shit tons of money we don't have?'

I laughed too, as my heart sank. I remembered that I had a tragedy of a life in Mumbai to return to. I would have no roof over my head once the apartment was sold and a job that I was more or less fired from. Plus, a mortgage that I didn't know how I'd be able to pay off.

But this was not the moment to think about that. This was the moment to celebrate a turning point in my relationship with Prapti, my friend. So I said, 'You know what? It sucks but you're absolutely right. Like you always are.'

But this time, we both laughed at the statement because I was grumbling for form's sake. Underneath my bitter tone was affection.

# Chapter Twenty-One

We continued the fruitless search for an hour more. The sun went higher and higher in the sky, so we sweltered inside our layers. I'd hooked up with Kiki and Vidhaant once I'd had the heart-to-hearts with my brother and his wife, and I told Kiki the whole thing in whispers, amidst periodically screaming out Jo's name.

She approved whole-heartedly *and* promised to be there the first weekend she'd get free to help initiate Prapti into our tight-knit group. I hugged her too. I could always count on Kiki to do the right thing when it really mattered.

My heart was lighter than it had been in years but we were still empty-handed as we trudged back up through Paati's tea garden and towards the Illam.

I stopped short as I saw Ben, pacing the verandah, talking on his phone. To the cops, from what I could hear of his conversation. He stopped pacing as soon as he saw me.

By tacit agreement, Kiki and Vidhaant went ahead and left me alone with him. Vidhaant nodded at Ben, and Kiki reached up and kissed his cheek while he whispered something to her, to which she shook her head.

Then it was just him and me.

'Hey.' I pushed my hair inside my beanie. My nose was frozen pink from being out in the cold and possibly dripping with more snot. And I had a headache at the base of my head, from screaming myself hoarse for a lost little girl.

'Hey.' He came down the three steps off the verandah. He wore a puffer jacket over a brown pullover and jeans. Solid, comfortable clothes for a solid, comfortable man. 'How are you doing?'

I shook my head. 'I can't believe she's missing. Jo's not like that. She is a sensible, level-headed little girl. She can't be missing.'

'She's a *little* girl. They do silly shit sometimes.'

Tears, never far away, threatened to spill out at his gentle, pacifying words. 'I can't believe that. I can't.'

'We have the cops looking for her too. And all the neighbours are checking their roads and bylanes. The Vivanta people have offered to help too. She'll be found in minutes, LJ.'

I put a shaking hand to my forehead. 'I won't be able to live with myself if anything happens to Jo.'

'Don't be ridiculous. Nothing is going to happen to her.'

I got my tears under control at the sharp, acerbic tone of his words. No doubt, what he'd intended in the first place. I am sure Ben had had enough of me crying on his shoulder for the next decade or so.

'You're right. Like always.' My tentative smile faded under his intense scrutiny. I fidgeted, my toes squishing inside my running shoes. 'What are you doing here anyway? Did the Vivanta people inform you of Jo's disappearance?'

He shook his head, his hair sliding forward with the movement, and put his hands inside his jacket. I could see the outline his fist made inside the pockets. It unnerved me and saddened me a little that I knew his gestures so well.

'I waited for you to show up for coffee till 8 a.m. Figured you'd want to escape the pujai madness if you could. When you didn't show up I thought I'd come find you myself.'

'Why?'

Ben seemed about to say something when he thought better of it. Maybe it was because my eyes glinted or my breath was suspended on the word 'why.' Maybe it was because we'd drifted closer and closer till we were just inches apart. And when I asked 'why,' I was looking at his lips moving and he knew it.

'Because you said you had legal stuff to discuss with me? I don't come cheap, you know.' His lips, the ones I had been overtly ogling, quirked in a half-smile. 'But I owe you one, so ask away.'

'It's some legal and financial stuff, actually.'

'Sounds very business-like.'

I shook my head. 'It is. Kind of. I think. I don't know. Can we do this later? When everything is not so chaotic?'

'Sure.' His hand brushed against mine. I wanted to think it was deliberate but I knew it wasn't. His voice was perfectly cool, his face expressionless. 'We can do it later.'

Before I could stop myself, I said, 'You're not my rebound.' The words rolled over one another.

He paused mid-step. 'What?'

'You said, before...that you were my rebound. You're not.' I shook my head to emphasize how much he was not my rebound. Mine or anyone else's.

'You're handsome and your smile is killer and your kisses make my knees weak. And you're this successful lawyer with his own business while I am a thirty-one-year-old washed-out novelist and failed playwright who managed to alienate her entire family in one fell swoop. You see why this won't ever work out, right?'

Once the words started, they refused to stop. I held my breath as I looked at him, at once hopeful and despondent and crazy and wanting. This was the worst possible time to have this conversation but I wanted him to know anyway, in case we never spoke again.

'It wasn't you,' I said quietly. 'It was me.'

Ben's face shadowed, his eyes darkened, deepened with real emotion. The uppermost emotion was uncertainty.

My breath caught in my throat before whooshing out.

'Lasya,' he said in the same quiet voice as me. And the earth itself stopped rotating for a second.

Then, Prapti yelled from the door. 'Lasya, come in. Please. Now!'

I ran in, aware that Ben followed me, his eyes boring a hole in my back. I stopped short at the living room, and Ben almost collided into me, his hands gripping my waist for balance.

Ahalya held the tattered copy of *Spectacular* from Paati's room in one hand and a lighter in the other, the flame flickering wildly. Her hair was unbound, unfettered around her shoulders and her eyes were filled with unadulterated hatred. Her whole body was shaking with suppressed rage.

'You,' she spat at me. 'You're the reason my kid ran away. You and this awful, fucking book.' She held the flame close to the book and it quickly started burning.

I stood rooted to the spot.

Miraculously, Atharva and my father wrestled the book away from her. Flame curling at its ends, curling into my words. Words I had written with so much love and hope and wonder, being consumed by fire.

Ahalya was unhinged. I could process that, but, in truth, I was mesmerized by the flames burning my book. The only copy I had given my dead grandmother.

Finally, Dad pried the lighter away from Ahalya while she screamed names, accusations at me, at the book, cried for her daughter and generally proceeded to act the demented mother. Atharva tried to put out the flames, but bits of burnt paper and ash fell down. I followed their progress.

In a dim corner of my mind, I was aware that Ben's fingers were digging into my waist, whether for support or to stop me from rushing into the melee, I was unclear. I heard Prapti and

Kiki and my mom yelling at Ahalya to stop acting so childishly, to stop behaving like this. I could hear Deep uncle's threats in a separate, distant part of my mind.

Most of me was occupied in watching my words burn.

When the second piece fell down and broke into a thousand bits of dust and ash, never to take form ever again, something inside me snapped. Maybe it was my sanity. Maybe it was anger. Or my poor self-control. I wrenched free of Ben's hold and rushed forward.

My arm shot out and I slapped Ahalya.

The sound echoed in the suddenly still room…or so it felt like to me. Ahalya looked like a painting of a demon that I had seen in my childhood. Matted hair on teary cheeks, eyes red and bitter from crying, chest heaving with anger and agony.

But just for a second.

In the next second, she punched me. Right in my gut. I wheezed and doubled over.

'How dare you, gundu maami![46]' she taunted.

She punched me again in the kidneys and I doubled over. I hooked my arm around her waist and rushed her out of the stunned group and into the next available room.

She screamed. I growled. She kept trying to land punches and jabs anywhere she could while I grimly controlled her movements, breathing through my mouth while she tried to choke me. I head-butted her a couple times and Ahalya squealed. And then she pulled my beanie off, along with a few hairs off my scalp.

'FUCK! That hurt!' I yelled.

'Good!' She brandished my silver-grey beanie like a sword. 'It was meant to.'

'God, Ahalya! Do you want us to kill each other?'

'Yes. If that's what it takes.'

---

[46]Fat aunty!

She came after me but I was better prepared. We went at it, kicking, pulling each other's hair, smacking whichever body part we came in contact with. I kicked her between her legs and she smacked my boobs. The pain made my eyes cross.

Finally, seconds or maybe hours later, someone pulled me off her and someone else kept a struggling Ahalya away from me. I didn't know and I didn't care. My eyes were all on the she-demon hell-bent on murdering me.

'Let me go,' I gritted out. 'Let me *go.*'

I took a healthy chunk of someone's arm with my teeth. I think it was Atharva and he howled. But he let me go and I went after her again. I ran into my dad's arm, which shot out and kept me in place with an iron hold.

'Stop it this minute. Have you *lost* it?' My father asked me in a furious voice. The first words he had spoken to me in over two years.

'She started it!' I yelled back. Uncaring, unheeding of anything except this rage inside me.

Ahalya deserved it. She'd burned *my book!* She would not see reason and needed to be taught a lesson. It was past time I did something about her.

Way past time.

I struggled against my father's hold while Ahalya struggled against Deep uncle's.

'Let her go, Mama. We need to end this,' Ahalya yelled.

'She's your sister,' Dad told her.

Ahalya shook her head vehemently, more of her hair sticking to her cheek. The cheek I had pulled and slapped was slowly turning a mottled shade of purple. 'Sisters don't do what she did to me. She destroyed my marriage.'

'I didn't,' I shouted. 'I am telling you for the last time. I *did not* end your marriage. Kumar did. You did. He fucked around on you for five years and you didn't even notice. Some marriage you had, Ahalya akka[47]?

She stopped struggling as her breath hitched and weaved. She still glared at me with wild eyes. But she had stopped struggling.

'I don't know how many ways and how many years you want me to apologize. But I am sorry. I really am. I wish I'd never written the damn book. The only thing, the *only thing* I was ever good at. And you guys hate me for it. All of you.'

I glared at them all. My lovely, judgemental family who'd decided that the flaky writer was mercenary enough to twist her sister's failed marriage for her own commercial ends. Who had not even bothered to come see me fail at creating a play out of the said book.

'You all,' I whispered again. 'I know you all are happy to see me fail. That you all think I deserve it. Well, guess what? I failed. I failed spectacularly at everything.' I glared at my father. At Deep uncle and Varun chitta, who had the grace to look chagrined at their feet.

'I am a terrible daughter. A horrible writer and I will very soon be homeless and jobless. I am also hopelessly single. So there you have it. Whatever terrible fate you wished for me, Ahalya, it's fulfilled.'

I dashed angry tears off my cheeks, my own chest heaving with the force of emotions battering me inside out. I knew I was being unreasonable. That this was not the moment to lose it. But, then again, I had lost it a long time ago.

This was just a culmination of a chain of events set in motion years ago.

'I am a failure. And I failed at everything. And there's nothing, nothing you can say to me that could hurt me far worse than how I've hurt myself.'

---

[47]Older sister

Mom tried to engulf me in an embrace but I shook her off. Her hurt look ended me, but I refused to back down. This time, I was standing up for myself.

'You never told Dad to believe me,' I told her. 'You sat there and let him accuse me of lying and manipulating Ahalya for my own ends. You never stood up for me, Mom. Not you, not Atharva. None of you. And Paati didn't even leave me a small piece of jewellery. You didn't say anything then too. Am I less than Kiki or Gargi or Prapti? Am I such a terrible daughter, Amma?'

My mother's tears ran unchecked down her face. And I should have felt awful at having caused them. I didn't. I felt vindicated. Hollow with victory.

'Am I?'

Mom shook her head desperately, but I couldn't believe it. Believe her.

'I have to go,' I said. 'I have to go. I can't be here anymore. Not when you all want her and not me.' I said this, looking at Ahalya, and would have lunged at her again if not for a small voice asking, 'LJ atha, why is there blood on your lips?'

I whirled around, as did everyone else. As a group, we saw Jo standing at the doorway, rubbing her eyes and giving a small yawn.

'Jo,' Ahalya breathed. Then she pushed past everyone and snatched her daughter into her arms. 'Where did you go? Where did you go?'

'I went up to cuddle with LJ atha because you fought with her and she was sad, but she wasn't there. So I watched "Shape of You" and fell asleep on the sofa. It was cold, Mumma... Why are you crying, Mumma? Why are you all crying?'

I sagged against the person next to me. It was Ben, by some bizarre twist of fate. He slipped his warm, solid hand into mine and squeezed it. I didn't have the energy to squeeze back, but I held on.

With everything I had.

# Chapter Twenty-Two

'How's your lip?' Ahalya asked me a little while later. I was struggling to wear my kurti because every bone in my body hurt like hell. And then some.

Ahalya might have been small, but she threw a mean punch. She limped a little as she closed the door and came farther into the attic.

'Where's Jo?' I asked her shortly.

'Playing with your mom. I don't think Mami is going to let her out of her sight anytime soon.' She added a small smile, then winced as if the action hurt her cheek.

Yeah, I'd nailed her good too.

'I don't think any of us are.' I winced and zipped the kurti up as best as I could and groaned out loud.

Ahalya sighed aloud and shambled forward to where I was struggling with the zipper. In an efficient and slightly painful movement she tugged the zipper up with a whoosh sound. She tied the dori[48] at the nape of my neck deftly and then stepped back.

We stared at each other in the faded cheval mirror. My busted lip and her bruised cheek stood out in stark relief, as did the shape of our eyes and our similarly stubby noses. She'd showered and taken a hair bath so the greys were a bit more pronounced at the roots. But, otherwise, we did look like sisters. Our genetic resemblance was unmistakable. Especially as we both wore salwar kurtis. Hers was a warm lemon yellow colour and mine was the

---

[48]Fancy thread

shocking pink one I'd worn the first day I got here. The one with the busted button.

'LJ,' she said tenderly. 'How's your lip?'

'Why do you care?' And before she could answer me, I rolled on. 'Please don't think I am going to apologize for what I said down there. You deserved it.'

'I know.' Misery contorted her face into an aged mask. 'I know and I am not asking you to.'

'I can't believe no one thought to check the attic.'

'We all thought you'd come from there and it was empty.'

'Great.' I wore the matching dupatta around my neck while my elbows creaked from the movement. 'Let's blame me for not finding Jo sooner too.'

Ahalya held my elbow in a death grip. 'I don't blame you for that.' Her voice cracked.

A part of the icy bitterness in my heart cracked too. Much as I didn't want it to.

'If you're here to make nice, don't bother. I don't care. I am leaving tomorrow and you don't have to see me ever again.' I was proud that my voice didn't quiver. That my chin jutted out and my spine was ramrod straight.

'LJ.' Her voice cracked again and tears poured down her cheeks. 'Can you please, *PLEASE* let me apologize? Please.'

'You have nothing to apologize for.'

She shook her head and hugged me tight, while I stood stiff and resisting in her arms. 'I don't care. I still need to.'

'This doesn't change anything.'

'I know.'

'You've been a total bitch to me for two years. Appa doesn't talk to me because of you.'

'I know.' She was full on sobbing now. 'I know and I am so horrible because I was glad for that. I lost Sukumar and you lost your dad. It seemed like a fair trade.'

'You're insane. Who thinks like that?' I tried to break free of her embrace and she let me.

Ahalya wiped her eyes valiantly and faced me with a quiet dignity that grated against my insides. 'A woman who's lost everything. Her husband. The future she had built in her head since she was sixteen. The father of her child.'

She held up a hand before I could say something cutting back, and continued, 'I know. It doesn't excuse anything. I am not asking for absolution. I don't deserve it. I am just…'

She closed her eyes and swayed.

I grabbed her arm reflexively.

We sat with our backs against the mattress, the floor abnormally cold for the middle of the afternoon.

I was the first to speak. 'You just what?'

'I don't know. I wanted to punish someone. Anyone. Kumar would have been a handy target. But he moved to Singapore and I couldn't. You know he doesn't even bother keeping his weekly Skype phone calls with Jo.'

I swallowed at the forlorn desolation in her as she admitted that. 'Shit, Ahalya. That is awful. I hope you've told the lawyer that.'

She shook her head and twisted the edges of her lemon yellow dupatta together, over and over again. 'I am okay with it. And, most days, so is Jo. Anyway, the thing is, with Kumar gone, there was no one to blame. No one I could take my anger and frustration out on.'

'Ahalya, don't take this the wrong way. But Kumar is a piece of shit and you are well rid of him.' I placed my hand over her fidgeting fingers.

'Yeah, but what does it say about me that I loved that piece of shit and didn't even know for the longest time that he had another family. A whole other family, complete with a kid. How much of a failure am I? As a woman. As a wife. A mother.'

I was appalled, because she sounded like she actually believed this rubbish. 'You're kidding, right?'

She shook her head and I could see wet stains where the ends of her damp hair had touched the kurti. 'I am not. Kumar told me he wouldn't have looked elsewhere and loved someone else if I was enough. I am not enough, LJ. I failed at everything way before you did.'

Ahalya sounded so defeated, I couldn't process it.

'You're not a failure, Ahalya. Don't think like that.' I leaned in and gave her a sideways hug and we stayed that way for a bit.

'I am,' she said, finally. 'I blamed you for ending my marriage because it was easier to do that than admit I was a failure. And worse, I turned Mama against you too.'

'You didn't do anything he wasn't already prepared to do. Don't be a fucking martyr now and blame yourself for the ISIS too.'

She gave a watery chuckle. 'Paati would have a fit if she saw us sitting here like this. Whining about our problems and martyring ourselves.'

'Yep.' I squeezed her tighter. 'She totally would. So let's not.'

'I missed you,' she said baldly. 'I wanted to come see the play; Atharva had sent me tickets and everything, but we had an important vendor meeting the next day and I couldn't make it. I'm sorry about that.'

I smiled, a small sad smile. 'It's okay. It was a tragedy. You didn't miss much.'

'Yeah, but I would've loved watching you flop.'

I rolled my eyes at her and she grinned sheepishly. 'I have a lot of anger to process.'

'Yes.' I bopped her on the side of her head. 'You fucking do. Also,' I moved my aching shoulder away from her head, 'you're scrappy. You fight dirty. My scalp will never forgive you for what you did to it.' I gingerly rubbed at the spot on the side of my head where Ahalya had yanked my hair out from the roots.

'I'm sorry about that. I think Jo's a little afraid of me too,' she confessed.

'That's good, then. Maybe she won't pull stunts like this anymore.' I huffed out a breath. 'I cannot believe she wanted to come and cuddle with me and knows how to operate the USB controls on the TV.'

'She's seven, you know. And she's smart.' Ahalya rubbed tenderly at the spot where my scalp still hurt. 'God, I am sorry about this. I'm sorry about everything.'

I sighed. 'Maybe I shouldn't have written a book about the family. Maybe I deserved it.'

'You didn't. You wrote a book about every family ever. It's just unfortunate that a lot of families are like ours.'

I grinned and she grinned. 'Nah,' I said. 'I don't think any family is like ours.'

'You know what?' Ahalya said slowly. 'You might be right.' She made to get up and I tugged at her wrist. 'What?' she asked.

I felt that I could gain some sort of even footing with her. With everyone. With myself. Stranger things had happened.

'I am sorry too. For slapping you so hard.' I nodded at the mottled bruise on her cheek and she poked at it with one finger.

'You fight like a girl,' she said finally.

'So do you.'

And that was how Ahalya and I knew we still loved each other. We didn't say it, but we didn't have to. That was not how we expressed love in this family.

And I think it's what makes us so unique.

Ben was already gone by the time Ahalya and I came down, tactfully and correctly giving all of us some much-needed family time. Ahalya went to check up on Jo; I went into the kitchen to grab coffee.

I found Mom at the stove, stirring something appetizing in a large copper tureen. She looked small and a little lost as she stared out the window, her shoulders drooping a bit as she resolutely cooked. Before I could second-guess myself, I ran up to her and hugged her around the waist.

We were the same height, so I could lay my head on her shoulder.

She patted my hair and sighed loudly. 'I really screwed up with you, didn't I?'

'I did plenty of screwing up on my own, Mom. Let's not get too carried away.'

She squeezed my hands, linked at her slim waist. 'I love you so much, LJ. I don't know if you know this.'

I blinked back more infernal tears, because I might have known it in the bottom of my heart, but verbal confirmation was always nice. 'I do,' I whispered. 'I love you too.'

'Then I hope you'll forgive me for not making your father see reason all those years ago.'

Now it was my turn to sigh. 'You know as well as I do that I have more than my fair share of stubborn Chakrapani pride. I could have always forced Dad to talk to me, couldn't I? I didn't. I didn't want to. It was easier to wallow in the injustices done to me than face them like an adult.'

Mom gave a watery chuckle and wiped under her eyes. 'When did you become so wise, Kunju?'

'I don't feel very wise,' I confessed.

'Well, you must be a little wise to have snagged that nice lawyer boy.'

I gasped soundlessly. 'I haven't snagged... How did you know?'

Were there no secrets in this family? Was nothing sacred?

Mom snickered, a happier brighter sound than I'd heard in ages. 'I am your mother, LJ. I do know your heart even though I don't understand why it wants what it wants.'

It was as close to a blessing as I was going to get from my mother, but it was enough to strengthen my resolve. I stepped back from her after one last squeeze. 'My heart wants coffee. A really huge mug of coffee at The Vivanta.'

I had only once been inside The Vivanta's reception area, a quiet, dignified space with indoor potted palms, a huge marble desk and a tiered crystal chandelier. It was a little embarrassing that I didn't know Ben's room number and I was apprehensive of asking the receptionist who'd also probably want my ID and my bank account statement before I was allowed to fraternize with the hotel patrons.

Because I'd forgotten my wallet back at the Illam in my haste to come down and see him.

I was about to bite the bullet and call him when he exited one of the elevators. His eyes smiled, even though he didn't as he spotted me. I couldn't help myself, I kind of walked-ran towards him, meeting him under one of the potted palms.

'What are you doing here?' Ben asked, quite logically. 'Is everyone okay? Jo?'

'Everyone's fine. It's all fine. I just...' I looked around the reception where the woman was shooting me suspicious looks. Immediately, my back stiffened. 'I came for coffee.' I looked straight at him. 'If the offer still stands. I'd like you to buy me the world's largest cup of coffee.'

'That works for me.'

We ended up in the nearly deserted Tea Room, in a secluded booth also hidden by an indoor fern. I thanked God for the dense foliage because I really, *really* wanted to lean in and kiss his half-goatee chin. After the waiter had taken our order (the menu had fifteen different types of coffee), I looked around furtively to check for any prying eyes, then proceeded to do exactly as I wanted.

I kissed him on the chin. Except, he moved his face a little lower and I caught his lip. The kiss that followed reminded me, all over again, why I was so into this man. *He could kiss.*

I opened my clouded eyes and regarded him with something close to wonder. 'I was not expecting that.'

'Neither was I.'

I knew, we weren't talking about the kiss. He leaned in to kiss me again when I pushed him back. He blinked.

The waiter appeared, so we had to untangle ourselves from each other.

I couldn't help moaning as I looked at the giant mug of the world's most fragrant coffee. It had a mix of Sri Lankan, Indonesian, Colombian and Indian beans ground coarsely and the slightest touch of milk to give it a caramel colour. It was, in one word, perfect.

I sipped at my delicious coffee as slowly as possible. Wrapping my hands around the soup mug—that's what it was—trying to get warm.

'What a morning.' Ben shook his head as he sipped his own cardamom-flavoured masala tea. 'I think I nearly had a heart attack a couple of times.'

Intermittent shudders still ran through me as my mind conjured up awful scenarios of what could have happened. 'I am never going to get over it. Not if I live to be a hundred.'

Ben nudged my knees with his. It was probably accidental, I told myself, but it didn't stop me from leaning forward when he did so. He had shaved. I could see the small pores on the left side of his jaw where his razor had missed a few scraps of beard. It was very sexy.

'So,' he said slowly. 'You said there's some legal stuff you wanted to discuss with me.'

I blinked, trying to think past wanting to scrape my nails over his beard. Touch him everywhere. 'Yes,' I said. 'I do.'

'What kind?'

I took a deep breath. 'I bought a house, a very expensive house with a loan I can't afford to pay anymore. It's being sold for fair market price.' I named the sum; it was in the high seven figures. Almost touching eight. 'I did the math roughly. And I think I'll have some money left over once I pay the bank what I owe them.' I named another sum.

'Why are you selling your home?' He used his non-judgemental, lawyer voice.

'Because...' I took another fortifying sip of the coffee, 'it's time to give it up. I can't afford the mortgage with my job situation. Also, I am definitely, maybe, but almost certainly about to lose my job because I couldn't handle working from home in the middle of my grandmother's funeral.'

'That's discrimination. You don't have to put up with that.' Ben was instantly indignant.

I smiled. 'It's nice that you want to rescue me, but I need to sort it out myself. Puru, my boss, made some fair points. And I don't blame him for wanting to phase me out.'

Now, he did wrap his fingers around my wrist. Gave it a quick squeeze. My skin tingled where we touched. 'Don't be so hard on yourself, LJ. Everyone screws up. Everyone makes mistakes. We don't crucify ourselves forever over them.'

'You have not met Chandralekha Chakrapani if you can say that with utter confidence.' My smile widened, nostalgic.

*If you want anything done, do it yourself.*

'I did meet her. Remember? I'm her lawyer.'

'I keep forgetting.'

We shared a grin, which faded slowly the more our eyes held contact with each other. I could see two smiling me's reflected in his dusky brown eyes. In the ridiculous pink kurti and the missing button. It felt a little like falling.

'So, anyway, I was wondering if you could set up half the leftover money in some sort of trust for Jo?' I elaborated before he could ask why. 'So she can have a nest egg if she ever decides to go to college or travel the world or...I don't know...start a theatre production company in the middle of a recession.'

'Cool. That can be arranged.' I wondered if I detected the faintest bit of respect and admiration on his face. Or maybe I was just looking for it because I wanted it so badly.

'I read your book, you know,' Ben said slowly.

'Oh.' My heart slowed down as I anticipated his reaction. I drank some more coffee to hide my trepidation.

'I read it last week and it's good. It's really good. You know how to tell a wonderful story. Your words...' He hesitated, quite uncharacteristically. 'They live. Outside the page. You should do it again someday.'

I shrugged, uncomfortable with the words. The compliment. The intent behind them. 'Someday. Maybe. I don't know.'

'I'm serious,' he insisted and held my hand tighter. His fingers warmed me faster than the coffee had. 'I don't know why you thought you should stage a theatre production of your book, and you're obviously not a failure just because you made a few poor decisions, but the book was great. Ahalya was right to be mad at you.'

'She was?' God, I sounded so breathless. Then his words sunk into my brain. 'She *what*?'

Ben smiled. 'Yeah. She was right to be mad at you. I'd have believed it too. Like I said, your words live, Lasya. For better and worse.'

'I'll take that as a compliment.'

'You should.'

'Thank you, Ben.' I finished half the coffee, without breaking eye contact. I figured now was as good a time as any to tell him. After all, I was riding on a high. I'd made up with my sister, my baby girl was safe and all was as right in my fucked-up life as it could be. The worst he could do was break my heart.

I'd lived through worse.

'I was thinking—' he began slowly.

'I like you,' I blurted out in the same exact moment.

His eyes widened while his hand clenched into a fist again. It was absurd how that single gesture made me feel strong and weak at the same time.

I put the coffee down and said, 'I like you, Ben. I know that we just met and we know, like, nothing about each other but I want you to know the other night was one of the best nights of my life. And I just wanted you to know that I like you.' I trailed off, in a whisper because he was so still, so quiet that I was sure I'd made a big mistake.

I picked up my mug and took a huge gulp of the coffee. It didn't work.

'LJ?' He said my name so gently.

I thought of a hundred different excuses I could invent to leave right now and never return. When I only took one more sip of the coffee, he reached out and pushed the cup down so I was forced to face him.

'Yes?' I smiled brightly at him.

'Did you believe me when I apologized to you last night?' He wrapped his fingers around mine and I felt those damnable tingles shooting through my system again.

'You mean, when you texted last night? What were you apologizing for? When we were together, or later, when you were a rude, defensive jerk?'

His lips quirked in the familiar smile, but his eyes remained quiet and watchful. 'I don't know. What would you like it to be?'

'Hey.' I took my hand back from him. 'You know what? You were right. I am too old to play these kinds of games with you.'

'That's a shame,' Ben murmured. 'I was looking forward to playing all sorts of games with you.'

'Oh.'

When I didn't say anything more, he curled his hand into a fist. And I knew. Something pretty monumental was about to happen.

'Let me put it this way.'

'What way?'

'I hate texting. And I never use emojis. But I'd use them to apologize if that's what you need.'

'I don't need emojis or an apology,' I whispered.

'Then what do you need, LJ?' he asked in all earnestness. 'Because I'd like to try and give it all to you. For as long as we both shall live. I hope that works for you.'

I grinned. Because, I knew. It wasn't perfect, it wasn't anywhere close to being perfect, but somehow, in some magical, unique way that even I couldn't have predicted or written about, it was going to be alright. Everything was going to be alright.

'Yes. I believe it does. For now.' Then I did the thing I'd fantasized about.

I scraped my nail over his beard patch and his eyes narrowed, sending heat rushing through all the cold, cold parts of me. He caught my fingers and nibbled on the ends while I squirmed in my seat.

Then he leaned over real close to me and whispered the most romantic words ever. 'Let's get out of here once you've finished your coffee. Okay?'

# Chapter Twenty-Three

**A few days later…**

'I can't believe your parents are cool with you staying with the lawyer at The Vivanta,' Kiki muttered her favourite complaint of the last few days, as we adjusted the pallus of our saris. 'When I merely suggested living with Trilok after we got engaged, Mom fainted. She *actually* fainted.' Kiki snickered. 'As if the very idea of her daughter having sex was anathema to her.'

We were getting dressed for Paati's memorial ceremony in Kiki's suite, because it contained three floor-length mirrors. The whole room was filled with the detritus of women getting dressed. Makeup tubes and pots were open on the cherrywood vanity, our track pants and tees were bundled together at the bottom of the bed, while a huge plate of jackfruit fries lay half-eaten in the middle of the bed.

I made a mental note to clear the food off the bed, all as part of the new and improved LJ Raghavan I was determined to be. Besides, if my mom found the plate on the bed, there would be hell to pay.

I gave up pleating the pallu of the lovely, deep green georgette sari I'd borrowed from my mom and which actually worked for my current body type, and just pinned it up to the blouse as best as I could. The remaining fabric trailed along the floor but at least I managed to look presentable in it.

I grinned. 'Your mom is traditional.'

Ahalya snorted from the back of the room where she was

dressing Jo up in a traditional paavadai—a floor-length skirt made from peacock green kanjivaram silk—and a cutesy designer kid's dupatta we'd overnighted from a store in Mumbai. She was already dressed in a sedate yellow Chennai silk and, of course, her pallu pleats were military straight.

'What's so funny?' I asked idly, while I navigated the 5 feet to the bed and bent down to pick up the plate.

The pallu picked that moment to slide down my shoulder and slithered right into the fries. I cursed and jumped back, bumping into Kiki and we both cursed.

Prapti rushed in from the bathroom where she'd been cleaning off her home-made tea leaves, yoghurt, banana and honey face mask. She looked around wildly, trying to pinpoint the source of the commotion. 'What? What happened? Is everyone alright?'

Jo burst out laughing. Ahalya's lips twitched at Prapti's harried expression, while Kiki and I grinned sheepishly at each other.

'What's so funny, Jo?' Prapti demanded.

'Your face,' Jo answered, between giggles. 'It's brown. It's like cake.'

Prapti put a hand to her cheek and came away with a bit of the dried-up mask. Her expression cleared and she started grinning. 'Yeah, it is. It tastes gross, though.' Then she glared at the two of us and we attempted to keep a straight face. 'What were you two yelling about?'

'Nothing,' Kiki said.

'We yell in this family for everything,' I said. 'You should get used to it, Praaps.'

Prapti shook her head and went back to the bathroom to clean up.

Ahalya left Jo to play with the fancy dupatta and came over to the both of us. 'Turn around,' she ordered us and then, kneeling down, started fixing all the little bits that make wearing a sari such a pain, and also such a joy. Joining the pleats at the bottom so they were even and only the toes peeked out, tucking extra flab inside (in my case) by expertly draping the sari around my waist and so on.

'Subhadra is not traditional,' Ahalya said, while she adjusted my pallu and draped it tighter so it felt like I was wearing a really constricting seat belt. 'I remember one time in Amritsar, she wore this really scandalous mini dress and slutty red lipstick and she belted out "Laila Main Laila" like a rock star. Everyone was stunned but Deep uncle just grinned proudly, like he knew something the rest of us didn't.'

'I didn't know Mom did that,' Kiki said.

'Exactly. Your bra strap is visible.' Ahalya tapped her shoulder so she leaned to the other side and Ahalya shoved the strap under the blouse sleeve. 'We don't know anything about who our parents really are, so we shouldn't judge them.'

I shot her a sideways glance, while keeping half an eye on Jo who was still preoccupied with her peacock green dupatta. Ever since the incident, I'd become the slightest bit paranoid about the kid's whereabouts.

'Is that comment directed at me?'

Ahalya shrugged and stepped back from the both of us. We looked much better than we had five minutes ago, with everything in place and *staying* there. If this wasn't a 'big sis' thing, I don't know what was.

'It's for all of us.' Then she wrapped her arms around our waists and squeezed in between us. The oldest of us all. The three mirrors reflected three sari-clad women of varying heights and sizes. We wouldn't win any selfie contests, but hot damn, we felt like princesses.

And we all had the same kind of smile—relief mixed with corny affection.

'But I am glad Kiki brought up you living with Ben, LJ.' Ahalya turned serious in a heartbeat, squeezing my waist. 'I hope you know what you're doing with him.'

'I don't,' I said quietly, while Kiki rolled her eyes. 'I don't know what I am doing with him. And I definitely don't know what he is doing with me.' I made a restless movement with my shoulders. 'But it doesn't all have to make sense right away, does it? We can just live in the moment for now?' I grinned. 'Pun totally intended.'

Ahalya smiled back and I was relieved. I didn't want her to disapprove of Ben, just when I'd gotten her back. They were two of the most important people in my life. I needed them to get along.

'Of course, if that's what you want.'

'It is.'

'She's lying,' Kiki declared. 'She just wants multiple orgasms. And Ben seems exactly the kind of guy to deliver them.'

There was a moment of humming silence when they both looked expectantly at me. Finally, Prapti said, as she came out, 'You know, I need to have a talk about acceptable social conversation with you three.' She had already discarded her wet T-shirt and stood like a svelte model advertising plain underwear.

We all shook our head simultaneously and said, 'No, you don't.'

But I wisely kept my mouth shut on the subject of a delicious and very capable Ben Dewar and everything he could do to me.

There was a knock on the door and Jo opened it before Prapti could cover herself up. She squealed and snatched the blanket from the bed, discarding our piles of clothes, so the floor looked messy.

Incredibly, it was my father.

'Thatha, what are you doing here?' Jo asked innocently, climbing up his veshti[49]-clad leg with all the agility of a monkey.

Even more incredibly, my father looked me in the eye. 'I'd like

---

[49]Dhoti

to talk to you,' he said.

I looked around, just to be sure. Ahalya and Kiki both had goofy grins on their faces. Sentimental fools that they were.

'Me?' I asked Dad.

He nodded. 'Yes, you. If you're dressed, we can talk now? In Paati's room?' He unravelled Jo from his leg and patted her head absently.

Kiki gave me a push ahead. 'Go,' she hissed.

Feeling more mystified than ever, I slipped into the block-heeled sandals I'd paired with the sari and clopped my way to where Dad stood, just inside the door. He smiled fondly at Kiki and Ahalya and nodded at them. 'You girls look gorgeous.'

Tears pricked my eyes at the honest compliment and I swallowed them back.

We walked in silence over to Paati's suite. Dad even held my elbow while I navigated the stairs. He didn't say a word but he was there. With me. Helping me. It was so much more than I'd ever gotten from him in years that it felt like a watershed moment. It was even more surprising to find Mom and Ben, chatting quietly in Paati's sitting room.

They looked at ease with each other. Mom was smiling slightly at something Ben had just told her. And they were just themselves in that one moment. I wished I could write it down so I could remember it forever.

They stopped talking when Dad and I showed up, of course.

Ben came up to me immediately and took my free hand, the one that wasn't holding the pallu. 'Hey.' He squeezed my palm, his eyes so warm and brown it was like gooey chocolate. If I had to hazard a guess, my eyes were probably gooey too.

'Hey back!' I slid my fingers through his, the weight a comfort to me. 'You look hot,' I whispered to him. And he did. He wore a formal three-piece suit in severe black, with an open collar and no tie. A dressed-down lawyer look, which went incredibly well with his half-goatee and dreamy eyes.

'I can't wait to unwrap you,' he whispered back, his eyes turning sultry and hot.

We grinned at each other for a second before Dad cleared his throat.

'Uhm, what's going on here?' I asked Dad, who was strangely subdued. He stood next to Mom, dressed in a very fancy MS Blue Mysore silk sari that Paati had gifted her for her twenty-fifth wedding anniversary; it had real Swarovski crystals sewn into the hem and pallu.

I looked at Ben who just shook his head. My heart sank for a second before it started pounding really loudly.

Ben was here. So were my parents.

Ben was *here* with my parents, obviously having spoken to them beforehand. Did this mean he was going to propose marriage to me? My heart jack-knifed out of my chest at the notion. My palms went slippery with sweat. And I couldn't breathe.

'Someone better tell me what's going on.' *Right fucking now.*

Mom looked expectantly at Dad. 'Well, what are you waiting for? You wanted to do this now. It couldn't wait till we came back from the function.'

I glanced again at Ben. He gave me an encouraging nod. 'Go on. Go to them,' he said.

I went forward on wooden legs, keeping my back as straight as possible in a vain attempt to bolster myself. Inside, I was a shrivelling coward. I didn't want to go forward. I didn't want to face my parental unit. We'd done and said too much to each other already. But I had Ben now, and my parents *had* been cool with me moving out of the Illam and into Ben's room at The Vivanta.

Maybe, we were all capable of change.

'Alright, you guys.' I reached them and fidgeted with my sari end. 'What is going on?'

Dad sighed and ran a hand down my hair, dislodging three pins that held the bun together. It was the exact same gesture he'd made to Jo. 'I have been very hard on you, Lasya,' he murmured. 'I wish I could say it was because you were always so different, but maybe it was because I was afraid of how different you were.'

The damned tears came back. I swallowed a couple times, not wanting to ruin my makeup by crying.

Mom made it worse by leaning in and hugging me fiercely. 'I never told you, not ever, how proud I am of you, LJ. You're the best and most shining example of what Paati wanted you to be. And I am so grateful that you never changed.'

I looked over my shoulder and Ben smiled broadly. He knew what was going on, the rat fink. And he wasn't telling me.

'It's okay, Mom.' I patted her back and stepped back, afraid that I'd somehow unravel the damn sari by stepping on the pleats.

I sighed inwardly, a huge breath. And let go of all the hurt and resentment and sadness and fucking grief I'd carried inside my chest like a beloved friend. It didn't immediately dissipate, but I felt lighter for having done it.

'Its fine, you guys. We don't have to do this,' I told my parents. 'We aren't this family. We don't talk about our feelings.'

'But we should,' Dad said. He also held a plain white envelope in his hand. He handed it to me. 'I'm so terribly sorry, LJ. I should have given this to you when Ben asked me to on the day of the will reading. But I couldn't. I'm sorry, Kunju.' His shoulders heaved and tears gathered in his eyes—eyes like mine—and before I could think or talk myself out of it, I leaned forward and hugged him tightly.

He embraced me back while Mom patted us on our shoulders,

and I smelled my father, Old Spice aftershave and detergent powder. I sniffed and valiantly battled back tears. The envelope crinkled against my back and I eased back a bit. Dad handed it to me.

It was addressed to me.

*To LJ Raghavan, from Chandralekha Chakrapani.*

I raised stunned eyes to my parents. 'What is this?'

'It's a letter from Paati to you. Detailing your special inheritance,' Dad answered.

I gripped the envelope hard, crushing the paper and felt something small and solid bite against my palm, but I couldn't help it. My mind was reeling. My grandmother had left me a special inheritance. She hadn't forgotten me. I was important to her.

I didn't know how to look beyond that fact.

Mom wiped at her streaming eyes with the tips of her fingers. 'We'll leave you two alone. Come out in five minutes, okay?'

Then she took Dad's hand and left the room. Ben bent down and hugged her and shook hands with Dad. Dad smiled at him. 'You were right. I'm sorry, Banjeet.'

'Water under the bridge, sir.'

Then they left and it was just Ben and me and the letter.

Ben walked towards me and gave me a wordless hug. He had to bend down to do it but the man never failed to give me hugs when I needed them. It was just one of the things I loved about him.

'You knew about this,' I accused him when I let him go after two tight and cuddly minutes. 'You knew I was feeling bad about being left out from the bequests. And you had this letter all along and didn't tell me.'

He shrugged and kissed me soundly, dislodging my lipstick.

I didn't put up much of a fight.

'I begged your father to give it to you that night. It was why I came back last week and argued with him. Remember?'

I remembered his cryptic comment. *There are things you know nothing about, LJ, so you shouldn't assume you know everything.*

'Your grandmother wrote exactly one letter and it was to you. She loved you a lot, Lasya.' Ben's words were soft.

I sniffed some more. 'I can't cry. My makeup will be ruined. I can't have raccoon eyes around you again.'

'I don't mind the raccoon eyes,' he said gently.

'Damn you. Don't you dare be amazing when I am trying to stay mad at you.'

I sat down on the divan, feeling overwhelmed and very weepy. He sat down next to me and held my hand, threading our fingers together over and over again until I controlled the sobs.

In a lot of ways, he was like my dad. He didn't really talk much. But, God, he knew what I needed and gave it to me.

Finally, I smoothed the envelope and tore it open carefully. Out fell a small key, nondescript and ancient, judging by the patina on it. I examined it for a minute, but there were no markings on it to give a clue as to what it opened.

I focused on the letter, two sheets of printed paper and signed in Paati's shaky hand in Tamil.

'She wanted to write it herself, but the pressure of holding the pen was too much for her.'

'So you typed it for her.'

He didn't have to nod assent. I knew him. Knew his kindness and generosity. Knew he was one in a million and that I was lucky to have him. And, I was suddenly struck by the feeling that, somehow, Paati had known how right he'd be for me. That she'd somehow arranged for me to meet him and fall so hopelessly for him. That Ben was my real gift from Chandralekha Chakrapani.

It would be just like her to arrange my life from her heavenly abode.

It was a pleasing idea, so I tucked it away in a cherished corner of my heart. The heart that had finally expanded to include all of me and my family, with all of our flaws.

# Epilogue

*Dearest Lasya,*

*Did you know your mother named you after me? Lasya was my first name until your grandfather decided it was too modern and changed it. Your mother always loved it and I was so touched when she named you after me. It makes me feel like I will still live on, the best and most alive parts of me, in you.*

*My bright Lasya. My brave girl.*

*I am writing this letter in the hope that it will end this silly feud you have going on with your father, my son. I expect he will have to talk to you to give you this letter and it will be enough for the two of you to find your way back to each other.*

*I also hope you know that I didn't select any of my jewellery to pass onto you because you never wanted any. You weren't one for gold and diamonds but for the stars. And that's what I want to give you.*

*Enclosed with this letter is the key to a safety deposit box in Munnar's local bank. Your Thatha and I were there for the opening of the bank and I was the first customer to have a safety deposit box in this town, so it has a lot of history and memories attached to it.*

*Lasya, the safety deposit box and all the contents inside are yours. Yours to do with as you wish.*

*My lawyer, a terribly smart, good-looking young man named*
*Ben, will help you with everything you need to access it. I*
*hope you enjoy the gift I've given you.*
*I hope you live the life I always wished for you. One full of*
*joy and happiness and incredible success. I hope you find*
*some place for this family I have created and nurtured, in*
*your heart.*
*You see, they don't know this, but they need you too.*
*To tell their stories. The good ones and the ugly ones. To*
*remember them. To remember me. For all our lives and*
*beyond.*
*I won't be here when you read this letter but I hope you*
*know this, I love you so much. I always did. You were my*
*namesake—mine.*
*And I hope I remain yours.*

*Your loving paati,*
*Lasya Chandralekha Chakrapani*

Tears ran unchecked down my face by the time I finished reading it, the words blurring in places. Ben gently plucked the letter from my shaking hand and gathered me close, while I cried my heart out. I clutched him close, uncaring of smearing my makeup on his coat or that he was destroying my hairstyle, and I sobbed.

'She loved me so much,' I whispered.

He nodded, giving me a tremulous smile. 'Yeah. She could not stop talking about you. Every time I came down here to discuss the terms of her will, it was always "LJ this, LJ that". If I didn't know better, I would have thought she wanted us to hook up.'

I smiled a secret little smile, because I hadn't been wrong about that. Paati did want me to meet Ben. Me, not Ahalya. And it was selfish of me, but I so needed to know that.

'Paati had excellent taste,' I commented, kissing him on the nose, while he wiped my tears.

'She did,' he agreed. 'She picked you to carry on her name and legacy.'

I sniffed as more tears welled up. And I thought to myself, *I could marry this man. I could spend the rest of my life kissing his nose.* The words welled up in my heart, swelling my chest, making it as big as a balloon.

After all, I had thought he was going to propose to me. Why couldn't I propose to him?

I took a deep shuddering breath and said, 'Ben, will you—'

Right then, Jo barrelled into the room, the dupatta dragging on the floor behind her like a cape, and ran up to the both of us. 'Thatha has ordered me to bring you both out, right now, LJ atha. Kiki chitti[50] said to tell you to not do this with Ben uncle.' She scrunched her nose and puckered her lips in an approximation of a kiss.

I laughed and swung her onto my hip as I stood up. Ben held my hand on the other side and I could see us reflected in Paati's almirah.

A terribly smart, handsome man, a weepy-looking woman with shining eyes and a single dimple, and a child who was the very best of all of us.

I saw the future.

And I wanted it. A lot.

'Yeah,' I told Jo's reflection. 'Let's go. Our family is waiting for us.'

And we walked out hand-in-hand, the letter and key safe in Ben's jacket pocket, to face whatever waited for us outside the rooms of the bravest, most incredible woman I had ever known. My grandmother. The doyenne of the Chakrapani clan.

Lasya Chandralekha Chakrapani.

---

[50]Aunt

## Author's Note

The devasam and other Hindu rituals and colloquial terms as described in *The Worst Daughter Ever* are accurate to the best extent of my knowledge. Any fallacies therein can be taken as part of my creative licence.

# Acknowledgements

Writing this book was an exercise in pleasure, entirely and only made possible by the following list of people.

I'd like to extend a big thank you to the real Chakrapani clan—cousins, uncles, aunts, grand-uncles and grand-aunts—for being a source of strength and support for each other, through good times and bad.

My amazeballs grandparents, Susila and Subramania Viswanathan, who made my childhood so spectacularly special. The debt of gratitude, unconditional love and affection I owe them would fill an entire book much bigger than this one.

C.V. Raman, my grandpa, whose family owned Chakrapani Street in my hometown, without whom I'd have scrambled for naming Chakrapani Illam.

Charlie Puth's 'We Don't Talk Anymore' and *The Greatest Showman*'s soundtrack. This book came alive because of y'all. So, thanks!

Adam Driver: the man with the saddest eyes. Seriously. Saddest eyes. I wrote Ben Dewar mostly because I wanted to write about him.

My agent, Suhail Mathur of The Book Bakers literary agency, hustler extraordinaire who promised me that he'd make it all happen for me, one step at a time, and who hasn't let me down so far. Here's to climbing the damn mountain together, Suhail.

S, FK, Sue, Annabelle, Nikita, Ankita PB and Reshmy. A stronger tribe of women I couldn't ask for. There's no better rock on which I stand.

Debdatta, the world's best assistant. Period.

Raakhee Suryaprakash and Shilpa Suraj, my very first beta readers, without whom this book would have been a scathing treatise on the hypocrisy and prejudices of Savarna Brahminism in the Iyer community. They were nothing but supportive as they firmly said no to the treatise and turned this into a story about family, about friendship and love and a happily-ever-after.

My dear Sudesna Ghosh and Falguni Kothari for providing constant support, encouragement and special insights that refined this book so much.

Marv, E, and my own Batman. The nice guys. The best guys. The guys whom we all wish we could end up with.

Saswati Bora, who has been a keen and enthusiastic advocate of LJ's story since day one. I could not have asked for a more sensitive and receptive editor.

Debangana Banerjee, a very conscientious copy editor who helped my book shine.

Mehak Devgun, for designing the cutest, most accurate cover depicting LJ's sloth-like lifestyle, creating a cute and quirky family tree, and bringing the *Worst Daughter Ever* to colourful, vibrant life.

Thank you to Mom, my Own True North, for always believing in me and for having the prettiest name ever, so I just had to use it for LJ's mom.

And, lastly, The Big Guy In The Sky.